FAIRY

Godmothers INC.

Copyright © 2013 by Jenniffer Wardell

First Hardcover Edition: April 2013
First Trade Paperback Edition: April 2013

For information on subsidiary rights, please contact the publisher at rights@ jollyfishpress.com. For a complete list of our wholesalers and distributors, please visit our website at www.jollyfishpress.com.

For information write Jolly Fish Press, PO Box 1773, Provo, UT 84603-1773. Printed in the United States of America

THIS TITLE IS ALSO AVAILABLE AS AN EBOOK.

Library of Congress Control Number: 2013936245
ISBN 0988649152
ISBN 978-0-9886491-5-6

10 9 8 7 6 5 4 3 2 1

To Mom, who always knew.

FAIRY
Godmothers INC.

a novel

JENNIFFER WARDELL

JOLLY**FISH**PRESS
Provo, Utah

ONE

❦

Some Enchanted Dragon

Fairy Godmother Rule Number One: Never argue with a client. As long as someone's willing to pay for them, dancing elephants, solid-gold princes, and fifty-foot-high stacks of down-filled mattresses are perfectly fine requests. And never, under any circumstances, point out when a client is being an idiot.

"I'm sorry, but I'm afraid there's been some confusion." Shifting forward to find a slightly less uncomfortable position for her wings, Kate tried to keep her voice polite as she thought terribly insulting things about the woman sitting across from her. "Finding a nobleman who's been enchanted into a dragon isn't really going to be an option for your granddaughter. There's an unspoken rule among evil witches and sorcerers not to use a curse to transform someone into a member of an already sentient species—it's seen as an insult to be considered a 'curse' in the same light as a frog or a cow. The species rights groups get upset and lawyers show up.

The last case that went to court ended up dragging on for years."

"Don't be absurd." The Dowager Queen Beatrice of Nearby waved one of her delicately veined hands. "Any nobleman truly up to snuff would *insist* on a dragon form—nothing else is suitably dignified."

She and Kate were sitting in the queen's Lesser Purple Receiving Room designated for the queen's meetings with tradesmen and poor relations. The hard-as-rock chairs made Kate think longingly of the ergonomic desk chair with special wing cutaway back at her cubicle.

"Not that I intend to settle for just any nobleman, Katie. It has to be royalty of some sort—a king, a prince, or however those foreigners refer to their royalty." The queen pursed her lips a moment, considering. "Though I would have to personally meet any foreigners you suggested. None of this multiple wife nonsense for my little muffin, no matter how many genies he might have working for him."

Not bothering to correct what had to be the fifteenth "Katie" in the last twenty minutes, Kate waited for the old woman to finish, and rephrased, "I assure you that multiple wives won't be an issue, Queen Beatrice. We check on that during the interview process for all cursed nobles in our database, and those who meet your conditions end up in an optional category that's not a part of the particular wish-fulfillment package you selected. Unfortunately, the closest thing to a cursed dragon that Fairy Godmothers, Inc. is even aware of is a large lizard we eliminated from the database a few years ago. He was . . ." What had the phrase on the memo been? ". . . 'freer with his tongue than he should have been,' and we kept getting complaints."

The queen stared at her blankly, apparently deciding she hadn't heard anything that required a response. Kate sighed, green eyes closing for a few seconds as her wing muscles knotted just a little bit tighter. "Also, your granddaughter isn't insured for kissing dragons," she said tiredly, adapting the excuse the company had given them to keep any enchanted swords off the list. "There's too much of a risk that she'd be bitten, and the company refuses to be liable for the lifetime illusion spell the girl would have to wear to hide the resulting scar."

"Scar!" Horror at the thought did wonders for focusing Beatrice's attention. "I can't let my dear girl be subjected to *that*. What would she do with herself?"

"Of course, you can't," Kate said soothingly. "Luckily, the company has several other enchanted nobles to choose from." She forced a salesman's smile back onto her face as she turned to her enchanted mirror and quickly accessed the company's Enchanted Nobility Database (patent pending). After six years at Fairy Godmothers, Inc., she'd accepted the fact that sometimes flattering an idiot into agreeing with you was the only way to keep from killing yourself out of frustration. "Okay then, let's start from the top . . ."

Two—maybe twelve—hours later, Kate officially gave up.

"This is Eduardo de Esteban San Castillo the third, only heir to the Duke of Castillo. He enjoys fencing, riding, long walks on the beach, and generally being dashing. He is currently enjoying life as a pig, due to undisclosed activities involving the youngest niece of a mystical old woman." A company survey had shown that young female relatives of mystical old women were the number one reason royals ended up in the database, but Kate had learned long ago to keep little factoids like that to herself.

Beatrice wrinkled her nose in distaste. "I told you to show me something *dignified*, young woman, a creature worthy of becoming part of my family. I can't have my daughter marry a mere *pig*. I refuse to comprehend how any nobleman could allow himself to be turned into such a thing."

Any kind of smile having been abandoned long ago, Kate took a few slow, deep breaths and tried to convince herself that screaming would be a bad idea. "I'm pretty sure that certain sections of the animal kingdom started using a democratic system a few years ago." The sarcasm was wrong, she knew—one of the memos handed out at the last staff meeting had told her so—but she couldn't stop herself. "Maybe mayors are more open-minded about what they get turned into."

The queen's forehead wrinkled in confusion. "What does democracy have to do with anything?" she snapped. "And why would any self-respecting witch or sorceress want to curse a mere mayor? We should be looking at more dignified animals—a hunting dog, perhaps."

"I would be more than happy to show you another hunting dog, Queen Beatrice, but I'm afraid there were only four of them. The last one was Prince Tihold, whose fur you thought would clash with your son's carpet." Reminding herself that she didn't know enough about killing people to avoid getting caught—it took at least four years of graduate school to really make it as an evil sorceress—Kate pasted a smile back on her face and prepared to lie her wings off again. "You know, a select group of our *truly* fashionable clients have been requesting enchanted swans to sweep their loved ones off their feet. They feel that land-based animals have been overdone by this point in the season."

She felt no compunction about sacrificing some random swan-prince to this woman's clutches. Fairy Godmothers, Inc. had received database requests from at least thirty cursed swans, all of them nearly impossible to get disenchanted after Odette's little misadventure had hit the news a few years before. A tragic death in your lover's arms might sound romantic, but it tended to discourage clients whose goal was more along the lines of grandchildren.

Beatrice paused, briefly intrigued by the idea of having insider information. "But what about that one girl everyone was talking about—" And here came Odette. "I can't recall her name, but she got herself involved with that sorcerer . . ."

"*Her* family didn't hire a Fairy Godmother." Kate leaned forward slightly, a conspiratorial tone to her voice. Being a Fairy Godmother had also, Kate thought ruefully, turned her into a much better liar. "We at Fairy Godmothers, Inc. can be trusted to end our assignments with weddings, not funerals—"

She was cut off as the butler hurried in, announcing to the dowager queen that someone with infinitely more money and social connections required her attention in the Greater Pink Receiving Room. Beatrice swept off without a backward glance, leaving Kate torn between frustration at her easy dismissal and relief that she had temporarily escaped what was rapidly becoming her own private version of eternal torment.

If she stayed, it would be all too easy to get sucked back in. With a quick glance out the window and a few sketched lines in the air with her wand, Kate soon stood in the middle of the ornamental gardens out back.

Once the glow had cleared, Kate stuffed the wand in the waistband of her embarrassingly fluffy blue tulle skirt, a company uniform with an unfortunate amount of glitter designed for someone about four inches shorter. She reached up for a long, bone-popping stretch, groaning in a way she would've been embarrassed to be heard in public, then tucked an errant lock of messy, mud-blonde hair back into her ponytail and looked for a decent place to hide for a few minutes.

It was days like this that made her wonder whether she should have tried harder to fit in with the back-to-nature fairy group that her aunt had wanted her to join. Of course, thinking like that meant remembering she hadn't been cryptic enough to hold on to the Mysterious Old Woman internship her mother had set up, hadn't been sweet enough to win the interview for the Good Fairy job her father had wanted her to have so badly, and had even lost her teenage summer job at Fairy Toadstools Theme Park for being rude to a particularly hateful six-year-old.

Becoming a Fairy Godmother was the one thing no one had particularly wanted her to do, and most of the time she felt she didn't do too badly at it. As long as she managed to survive client meetings like this, she could accept that she had probably ended up where she should have.

Kate glanced back up at the receiving room window. Even if she sometimes fantasized about turning annoying, obsessively picky queens into lawn furniture.

A flash interrupted the rest of the thought, followed by the tinkling, highly copyrighted Fairy Godmothers, Inc. entrance music. Kate closed her eyes long enough to mutter something deeply insulting to the universe as a whole, then opened them fast enough to avoid getting hit by the short, sandy-haired intern who hadn't quite gotten the transport gates spell down yet.

As soon as the purple smoke cleared, she helped the young man up, at which point he practically launched himself at her in a state of almost total panic. "You didn't leave your beeper on!" he accused, a terrified squeak in his voice. "You know that creepy thing Bubbles does with her eyes when someone doesn't leave her beeper on, and it's always me she does it at, because I'm the only one left in the office! And I still really, really hate to teleport!"

Kate placed a hand on each of his shoulders, ignoring the not-undeserved yelling and making sure to look him in the eyes. "Ned, breathe," she commanded, waiting until he had done so before pulling out the star that served as the wand's beeper attachment. With a sigh, she stuck it in position on the tip—Bubbles would comment about it either way, but if she didn't see it, there would also be veiled threats about departmental guidelines. "I need to know—did her tone just make you want to hide under a desk, or did it also make you want to whimper like you'd been kicked?"

Ned stood and seriously considered this for a moment, calmer now that he'd been allowed to vent. "Just hide under the desk." He winced slightly as if remembering a less-than-soothing detail he'd missed. "But she was pacing a lot."

Kate sighed as she rubbed a hand along the back of her knotted neck muscles, wondering if this meant she'd have to start the meeting with Beatrice all over again. "So, I'll probably survive." She inclined her head toward the palace. "Did she mention what excuse I'm supposed to give for skipping out on a client meeting, or did you get stuck being the bearer of bad news?"

Ned's sigh was even louder than Kate's. "At least the spell for the excuse message is easy, or I'd probably still be setting myself on fire." The flames had actually come from Ned's one attempt at a ball gown spell. Thankfully, the "We apologize for any inconvenience, and will be contacting you shortly" twinkly lit message was significantly more Ned's speed at the moment. "Bubbles said she isn't an official client until she makes the rest of her payments."

Kate shook her head, more than happy never to see Beatrice

again. "At least you don't have to go up and listen to the clients yell at you anymore." She patted his shoulder in genuine sympathy, then squared hers and reached for her wand. "Good luck."

Ned tried to look encouraging as he held up his own wand, a faint scorch mark visible near the tip. "You, too."

"I'VE BEEN LOOKING at what you consider to be reports, Kate Harris. You should be grateful that I edit all departmental paperwork before sending it upstairs." Bubbles peered through her small wire-rimmed glasses at the files spread out before her. Her sleek, carefully-shaped gray bob, which took on a slightly pink hue from her own equally fluffy uniform, barely shifted as she moved. "Did you really have the future Count and Countess of DuBoir meet by dumping a large bowl of cream custard on the young woman's head? Even if you were running low on True Love, the usual dose should have been sufficient to complete the job with the class expected of a Fairy Godmother."

"Is this an early performance review?" Kate asked calmly, clinging to the stiffly pleasant expression she'd mastered during her previous sessions with Bubbles. A part of her wanted to explain that the Count and his future Countess were both terminally shy but had been eyeing each other for hours, and the custard had been the perfect excuse for the Count to rush right over and never leave her side for the rest of the night. Of course, the part of Kate that actually had self-preservation was ready with the muzzle before any damage could be done—management didn't approve of doing things the less efficient, old-fashioned way. "Because if so, my True Love use levels have been duly recorded." After, of course, the amount Kate had been expected to use that month was safely disposed of. She'd rather just dump it down the sink, but the ethics of contaminating an entire water supply with extremely strong love potion was something she didn't want to deal with. She had enough trouble dealing with the fact that it was considered part of the standard operating procedure, and silently fought against it with every bowl of custard or awkwardly sweet meeting in the garden that she could manage. Making a fuss never changed anything, but she took an immense amount of comfort in the fact that there were a handful of couples out there who were better off with Kate as their Fairy Godmother than anyone else.

"No, this isn't your performance review." Pursing her lips, Bubbles tapped a fingernail against the folder sitting in the center of her desk. "I just want to make sure you won't embarrass me if I assign you a special project."

Kate's jaw tightened. She knew it was going to be something like this, but she'd hoped it was just her pessimism talking. Apparently, her pessimism was psychic. "If you don't think I'm ready for a special project, I'll understand completely if you assign it to someone else. I wouldn't want to damage the company's reputation."

Bubbles narrowed her eyes. "When I get handed a last-minute assignment on top of double the case load I should be dealing with, I'm going to assign it to whatever Fairy Godmother I see fit." She twisted the folder around so that it faced the opposite direction, then slid it across the desk until it was in front of Kate. "At the moment, that Fairy Godmother is you."

Sensing that was her cue, Kate picked up the folder and opened it as carefully as if it contained something that might bite. On one side of the folder was a five-by-seven photograph of a young woman with golden blonde hair, huge violet eyes, and far more dirt than the usual "princess in hiding." Beneath that was the stack of nearly blank forms required for the Fairy Godmothers, Inc. standard wish-fulfillment package. The only writing on the front form was the approval signature along the bottom, a very illegible and important-looking name Kate didn't recognize.

Bubbles made a disgusted noise at Kate's continued look of incomprehension, loud enough for Kate to look up from the folder. "It's a special request from a member of the company's board of directors, who is personally funding the package," Bubbles explained coldly. "Not that *I* listen to office gossip, but I thought it prudent to let you know exactly who will be paying attention to this particular assignment of yours."

The statement shot a quick spurt of panic through Kate's chest, as Bubbles no doubt intended it to. Kate fought it down as she paged through the mostly empty forms, hoping to find something even vaguely useful about her new client. "None of the client's specifications have been filled out, nothing about the dress, the dance, anything. I don't even know the girl's—" The sentence remained unfinished as she found the name, scrawled across the top of page two in only slightly more legible writing than the signature. For her sake, Kate hoped briefly that "Cinderella" was merely a terrible childhood nickname used only by the occasional relative. "I don't even know who I'm supposed to be matching the girl up with. Is this sponsor paying for a prince, or will some sort of count or duke do?"

Bubbles slid a single sheet of printout across the table, the now familiar signature across the bottom and a sticky note attached to the front. "The girl gets the heir to the throne of Somewhere." She tapped a finger against the note containing the information too specific to be safely included in the official legalese of the contract. After all, if a jealous witch turned a prince into a statue before the wedding, it was easier and more cost effective to find a replacement than disenchant him. "At the moment, that person is Rupert Devlin Golden Montclaire Charming: square-jawed, golden-haired, and a reputation for being what PR departments commonly refer to as a 'rake.'"

That remark was a pointed suggestion to get the job done as quickly as possible. Princes who were "rakes" tended to make a job easier for the first fifteen to twenty minutes after he and the girl met, at least until the prince got drunk or was caught staring down another woman's dress and the girl lost interest entirely. Once warned, most Fairy Godmothers dumped on True Love as soon as the halves of the intended couple were close enough for the physical contact needed to make the potion work.

Kate's muscles were so tight her head was starting to hurt, a traditional side effect of these special little meetings with Bubbles. "When do you want me to get started?"

"As soon as possible." Bubbles swung her chair around to her office-sized enchanted mirror, clearly ready to dismiss Kate. "Another Fairy Godmother will be taking over your current case, and I'll be expecting your report of the completed contract in two days."

Kate's eyes widened at this last-minute shove off the cliff of certain failure. "I can't do this in two days! It usually takes a whole day just to do the initial consultation, and then we have to get the dress together, wait for the next scheduled ball since we haven't already made arrangements with the local royalty—"

"Fine." Bubbles waved her away with a hand. "A week then. But if you try and argue for more time, you'll be talking to the board of directors."

Knowing that a week was as good as she was going to get at

the moment, Kate nodded and escaped. Clearly, this was not going to be one of the more pleasant happily-ever-afters she'd had to pull off.

TWO

ᙍᙍᙍ

Attack of the Ball Gowns

The ball was in full swing, which meant a few guests had grown bored enough to actually start dancing. Prince Jonathan Alistair Crispin Lorimer Charming was busy hiding, though not even he could escape Lawton when his friend had been fortified by five glasses of sherry.

"You do realize, of course, that you kissed the young Countess Hanslen's hand a half centimeter too far to the right?" Lawton shook his head, tousled chestnut hair brushing the edge of his perfectly styled collar. "Bad show, Jon—your poor mother would be scandalized beyond repair."

Jon's gray eyes narrowed at him over the edge of a supposedly edible canapé, choosing not to dignify the comment with a response. Jon was, to his horror, actually a little jealous of the glass in his friend's hand. He could have been downing his own dose of sherry, or at least fortifying himself with a sip or two of that unfortunately pink champagne his mother loved so much, if he hadn't foolishly realized years ago that it all pretty much tasted like jewelry cleaner. "With the way her perfume was making my eyes water, it was lucky I managed to make contact with her hand at all," he muttered, glaring at the swirling, chattering crowds. "Rupert should be here."

"Do my ears deceive me, or did you just actually wish your older brother's company upon us?" Lawton stared at him hard for a moment, then his eyes widened in horror. "When you say things like that, it makes me fear for your sanity."

"I'm serious." Deciding that the canapé had been left too long under the heat spell, he checked to make sure no one was watching before shoving it deep inside a nearby flower arrangement. Almost immediately, the roses started to wilt. "With Rupert here, all I would have to do is keep an eye on his champagne intake and be ready to drag him away before he managed to crawl all the way down the front of some woman's dress. Without Rupert, I need to wear an outfit with enough gold braiding to hang someone, remember the names of at least forty-two pet poodles, terriers, and miniature dragons, and dance with women who can barely remember my name and keep referring to me as 'Prince Jeremiah.'"

Lawton merely watched him with an amused expression on his face. "Even after all these years, it still astonishes me how you can sit through six hours of border negotiation meetings without a whimper of complaint, but consider dressing up and dancing with rich, supposedly attractive people to be a torture worse than listening to your mother's singing." He paused, as if contemplating something. "If I let you drone on about the intricacies of trade regulations for a few moments, will that soothe you?"

Jon's eyes narrowed even further, pondering briefly whether

anyone would notice if he grabbed the glass of sherry and dumped it over the other man's head. "At least regulations and meetings eventually *do* something, Lawton. There, intelligence is considered *important*, and lying and remembering pointless details yield far more useful results than having some woman bat her eyes at you."

"And yet somehow, no one ever seems to question that you and Rupert are genetically related." Lawton's smirk was tinged with affection. "Are you absolutely certain you're not secretly a fairy changeling and no one's thought to inform you of that fact?"

"Wouldn't that be a lovely thought." Jon let out a long, tired sigh as he ran a hand through his hair. "Has anyone found Rupert yet, by the way?"

"According to my spy network, no." Lawton took another drink. "Both they and your mother's footmen have checked all the haunts your elder sibling might find himself at this time of night, including nearby taverns, inns, bedrooms, conveniently located piles of hay, and certain alleyways. The next step is ditches, though that seems unlikely." His expression brightened slightly. "Perhaps some cutpurse or jealous husband finally sent him off, and I should begin planning your eventual coronation party."

"I hope not." Jon shuddered as he stepped away from the corner, squaring his shoulders as he once again prepared to face the crowds. "Think of how much gold braid I would have to wear then." Fixing his best politician's smile back onto his face, he let the preening, bejeweled masses draw him inside for the next round.

"Duke Marin, welcome. Has your gryphon recovered from that illness yet? No? Do wish Snookums the best for me;" "Yes, yes, it's an excellent vintage. A small vineyard in the southern provinces—we're looking to increase its productivity;" "Baroness Stroud, you're looking absolutely exquisite this evening. What, that enchanting creature beside you is your niece? I thought she was your sister;" "Rupert seems to have been unavoidably detained, but I have been assured that he shall be along shortly. Believe me, I keenly feel his absence as well;" "Have you tried the canapés? I've heard they're delicious."

Repeat, ad nauseam (except for a nicely distracting couple of minutes when he needed to assist the Fifth Earl of Lockney out of an ornamental fishbowl, an incident which somehow managed to make him annoyed at Rupert all over again). Knowing he could only expect the same for the rest of the night, Jon soldiered onward until the press of people backed him into nine feet or so of overly embroidered, ruby-studded gold skirt—it was, at one point, more than eighteen feet across, but Jon had ordered someone to sedate the queen and quietly lead the dressmaker away before any major damage could be done.

Knowing he would pay for it later if he didn't, Jon turned around and looked down at the petite, white-haired, exaggeratedly-adorned woman. "Hello, Mother." He could tell immediately that she was seriously worked up about something, her enormous up-sweep tilting above her crown and her makeup showing the strains of too much emotion. He tensed, hoping desperately to hear that she'd worked herself into a fit over something as simple as the terrible-smelling canapés, or the discovery that rubies were suddenly out of fashion. "You're looking as lovely as ever."

"Jon." Yes, that was definitely desperation filling her eyes. She took his arm, Jon's brief wince of pain the only sign of her death grip. "Something terrible has happened!"

Jon swore silently, ratcheting the crisis up to a staff strike, or worse. Ordering himself not to have a headache until whatever was going on had been dealt with, he led his mother to an area of the ballroom more conducive to private conversation. Her smile fell almost as soon as they were out of visual range. Jon took a deep, steadying breath. "Now, tell me what happened," he said.

"It's your brother." The queen sniffed and dabbed her eyes with the handkerchief Jon handed her, though thankfully, a full bout of tears didn't seem to be in the immediate future. "They've . . . they've found him. They found my boy."

Jon froze, then mentally indulged in a string of curses that would have horrified his mother's sense of propriety had she been able to hear them. "Where?" His mind raced to account for a situation that would sufficiently worry his mother, who had previously dismissed one particular incident involving Rupert, an entire vat of stolen gravy, three serving girls, and an extremely friendly troll woman as "boys will be boys." Did he need the palace lawyers? The fire brigade?

Not to mention that he was now definitely on his own for the rest of tonight's ball, and possibly even longer.

"In the . . . oh, I can't quite bear to say it . . . library," she continued, glancing around, in case anyone had overheard, then lowered her voice ever further, "by the *books*. Can you imagine?" Her face tensed in remembered worry, though not quite far enough to crease and risk wrinkles. "I don't know what could have happened to him. He's resting now, poor dear. He looked so peculiar . . ."

Jon's eyes snapped into focus as a few key words dropped their calling cards into his brain in an entirely unexpected order. "Reading?" he asked slowly, unwilling to keep the incredulousness out of his voice. She should be cheering that her oldest son had expressed some sort of interest in words that had nothing to do with a wine list or an invitation to the next party. Admittedly, the book had probably something to do with hunting, or women. Still, any attraction to written words lined up sequentially could be seen as a hopeful sign for the future. "You want me to save him from *reading?*"

His mother nodded emphatically, missing the emotional subtext of her son's statement entirely. "Of course. It's far too unsettling for my darling boy." She released his arm, relaxing as if all had once again been settled with the universe. "You need to talk to him, delicately of course, and find out what led my poor angel to such a state."

"Not without dragging him down here and tying him to one of the ornamental railings," Jon snapped, the anger rising a little faster than he was prepared to handle at the moment.

His mother blinked, face slowly filling with horror at the suggestion. "Don't you dare! Rupert's much too sensitive . . ."

Jon opened his mouth, then snapped it shut before he could say anything he would regret later. He took a quick step back, along with a deep breath that wasn't quite as steadying as he might have hoped. "Naturally." It would disturb the nearby guests, he was sure, if he shook his mother until her crown fell off. "Far too much so to be subjected to me in my current mood."

"Well, of course, but—"

He backed away. "I'm going to take a walk, Mother. Don't wait up."

Her eyes widened, sparking with anger at the possibility of being dismissed. "But Jon, you need to be—"

"It's for the sake of your hair, I assure you. Goodnight, Mother."

MOONLIT WALKS WERE best reserved for a city's shopping

district—not quite as much privacy, but less chance of attracting farmers with shotguns or embarrassing questions from the local constables. Few people in the kingdom got close enough to the royal family to know what any of them looked like, and the average homeowner didn't consider gold braid a sufficient excuse for a strange man to wander around his property in the dead of night.

Not that Jon had even the braid as an excuse anymore, having abandoned it for basic, comfortable black before he'd left the palace. Grinning once more in relief, he tilted his head back, soaking in a sudden breeze that, at this corner of the city, smelled faintly of cheese and horse carriages. His city, he'd always secretly considered it—though he doubted the store owner closing up across the street would have been suitably impressed by the claim.

He should be heading back in the direction of the palace, he knew. He was calm enough now that he was ready to soothe his mother, make sure the band had been paid, and find out exactly what was happening with Rupert. He'd fantasized through the years about what would happen to life at the palace without him there to keep it running smoothly, but his imagination kept pointing out possibilities like roving bands of creditors and his father permanently going into hiding, which always caused him to lose the taste for fantasizing rather quickly.

Jon's grandmother, who hadn't visited the kingdom since he was about twelve, remained horrified that Jon refused to do his duty as a proper younger son and start questing. After all, hadn't Cousin Horace already won a bride and one-sixteenth of a kingdom by defeating an ogre that could only be smitten with an enchanted safety pin on alternating Tuesdays? And Rupert was two years older, and the product of the son she actually liked.

He had tried pointing out to her that he technically had an *entire* kingdom, since he did most of the actual running of it, but she had scoffed and said that any sensible king would have advisors to take care of that part of ruling. She was perfectly aware those advisors inevitably ended up evil and tried to take over the kingdom, but that was the sort of thing that made life more exciting.

Jon sighed, turning back home as the final handful of shop lights flickered out to embrace the darkness. If he hurried, he might even have a chance of sneaking in a few hours of actual sleep.

He stopped as a sudden flash of light caught the corner of his eye, then turned to investigate the sound of tinkling bells that followed. Before he could, however, something bumped against the back of his calf, and almost immediately Jon hit the pavement stones as a falling weight shoved him forward and off his feet.

A hand landed on the pavement near his eye, wreathed by a lingering curl of purple smoke. A second later the weight was gone and a cloud of blue tulle was sitting beside him. "Sir, I am so, so sorry." The woman sounded deeply embarrassed, hand touching his shoulder as if she was trying to decide whether or not he'd let her help him up. "I know it's no excuse, but I was helping a friend of mine get some practice at work. The aim seemed good enough, and I was tired and wasn't really looking where I was going. I am so, so sorry . . ."

Bemused, Jon pushed himself to a sitting position and discovered that all that blue tulle was attached to a head of soft-looking dark blonde hair, extremely guilty-looking green eyes, and a pair of almost translucent wings fluttering nervously at her back. When she realized he was upright, the apology trailed off. She moved toward him. "I hurt you."

Confused, Jon reached up and touched his forehead, making contact with a slight bump that almost immediately started to hurt.

Then her fingers were there, batting his away, examining the rest of his scalp with a surprisingly gentle touch. "Now, I know I'm not a nurse, but you'd be surprised how many girls end up doing a face plant the first time they try to walk around in glass slippers." She leaned back enough to look into his eyes, no doubt checking for their ability to focus. "I don't think you have a concussion," she continued matter-of-factly, her earlier embarrassment disappeared. "But if you start feeling dizzy you need to see a doctor straight away."

"Yes, ma'am." He grinned up at her. After a moment, her own mouth started to curve upward in a tentative smile. Then, a clock started in the tower of a nearby bank, the chimes seeming even louder than usual on the nearly silent street. The woman tensed and pulled away from him.

"If you're okay, I . . . I need to go." She scrambled to her feet, hands brushing at her skirt as she took a step back. "Work, you know."

Jon stood as well, cursing whoever decided that enormous clocks were city assets, and himself for not thinking to stand up early and help her to her feet.

"It was nice meeting you." She smiled at him again, a little regretfully, and gave him a half wave. "I really am very, very sorry about falling on you like that."

"Wait." Not the most creative line, especially when she hadn't technically gone anywhere yet—though her eyes widened. At least there wasn't any more backward movement. "I . . . It's . . ." Nothing. For pity's sake, he was *royalty*. He was supposed to be able to do this sort of thing in his sleep. "Where are you going?"

Oh, smooth, Jon.

But instead of looking horrified, the woman seemed almost

relieved as she pulled a file out of the waistband of her skirt and flipped through a few printouts. "1612 Candlewick Lane," she read off. He noticed she was nearly as tall as he was, a fact he found more intriguing than alarming. "Apparently, I should turn right at Broadway, then take a left at Pumpkin Drive." She looked up. "Is that right?"

She was handing his excuse to him on a serving tray. Of course, he admitted to himself, he would have lied if he had to. "They built a wicked witch rehabilitation center right in the middle of Pumpkin Drive late last year. To get to the other side you need to double around to Sparkle Street, then take a left past the Cursed Items Pawn Shop and go down . . ." He shook his head with mock solemnity. "You know what? It would be easier for me to just lead you there. You can keep an eye on me and make sure I don't succumb to that concussion you were worried about."

She started in surprise, then that smile crept back up on her face. He grinned back, deciding instantly that his family could survive without him for a few more minutes. And if by some miraculous chance they ended up having to survive without him for a few hours, so much the better.

"I'm Jon, by the way," he offered. Not more than that, not yet, especially when previous experience seemed to suggest it would either send her into an irretrievable state of nervousness or start a fawning session that would utterly disappoint him. "This, in case I'm being too subtle, is your cue."

She hesitated, then held out a hand. "Kate." Her hand was a little warmer than his, and it was only when she pulled away that Jon realized he'd probably held on a little longer than was socially appropriate. She glanced down at her skirt, wincing slightly. "I don't suppose I need to tell you what I do for a living." She hesitated again, and he wondered what he'd done to spook her in the last few seconds. "On second thought, maybe you'd better just tell me those directions again."

Okay, job issues he could handle. His grandmother didn't really believe in using Fairy Godmothers, Inc., but had still nearly resorted to getting Jon's father one before he'd finally met and married Jon's mother. The company was at the top of more upper-class address books than a dressmaker who knew how to take off twenty pounds. "Does your job require you to do something illegal?"

Something flashed briefly across her face, then vanished. "No."

"Does it involve people with large swords?" Carefully, he took a step closer.

"Not for years, and even then they usually like what I'm doing." She paused, looking like she was about to say something, but decided against it. "Definitely not for years."

"Is it fattening?"

"That's a new one. But to answer it, no." She paused again. "Not usually."

"Then I insist on providing you with a directional escort," he said gallantly, grinning at her again. "And let me be the first to say, welcome to Somewhere."

She stared at him for a long moment, then her smile slowly eased back. "Okay, then, good sir. Lead the way."

THREE

Godmother-Client Privilege

The universe, Kate decided, had a cruel sense of humor.

Every Fairy Godmother who had been at the job more than a week knew that no one ever really tripped over an attractive, fairly charming guy who was good at making you smile and apparently liked you enough to follow you wherever you were going. Things like that only happened when a Fairy Godmother was behind the scenes choreographing everything. The more cynical ones believed such an encounter took choreography *and* a dose of True Love, which meant the guy would also be in the mood to fall in love with a desk chair if it were in the right place.

So, there was no way she was supposed to be walking with her hand tucked around Jon's warm, strong arm, listening to his surprisingly detailed commentary about the local stores and neighborhood landmarks. Things like this barely happened to princesses, let alone Fairy Godmothers, and she might think he was up to something if his clothes weren't *clearly* tailored while hers were usually bought on sale. That left a prank, which her co-workers didn't hate her enough to try, or True Love, which would have left her feeling too dizzily romantic to be thinking such depressing thoughts.

Jon turned to look at her, apparently noticing her pensive expression. "Are you okay?"

She blinked, hoping he wasn't about to quiz her. "I'm fine."

He hesitated for a second, looking worried. "I'm sorry for the more-than-you-ever-wanted-to-know tour guide. Feel free to just muzzle me when I get too boring."

"You're not boring!" Kate insisted, wondering for a surreal moment if he'd been having his own silent self-esteem meltdown while she'd been distracted with hers. The thought was completely ludicrous, but it jerked her thoughts back into the moment better than anything else could. "I'm just going over what little I know about the client."

"Ah, work." He nodded. "I sympathize."

"Do you work around here?" She kept her voice bright, trying very hard not to be distracted by the way his hair curled at the back of his neck. "Or did I knock you down on your way home?"

Jon tensed at the question, subtly enough that it was really only perceptible in the sudden twitch of his fingers. Kate froze, knowing she'd somehow said something wrong, and she loosened her hold as she waited for him to yank his arm away.

Instead, he let out a breath. "I work . . . at the palace, as sort of a diplomatic secretary," he said after a minute, his voice almost apologetic. He looked over at Kate. "I'm expected back, actually. I just . . . needed to get away for a little while."

Kate nodded, fighting a sudden and absolutely ridiculous surge of relief. Sure, she couldn't let herself talk to him again, but that was probably safest for everyone.

They walked together in silence for a moment, Jon glancing over every few steps. "Can you tell me a little about your current assignment?" he finally asked. "I don't know how tight the confidentiality restrictions are for Fairy Godmothers."

Kate tensed a little as she looked at him. A lot of people thought being a Fairy Godmother sounded fascinating, right up until the point when she started telling them all the details. The fact that she actually enjoyed the details just made her feel stupid. "It's . . . not very exciting," she said eventually. "You don't really get the interesting stories until you've been working with the client for a little while."

He smiled. "Isn't it sad that the really interesting stories have to start out as miserable days at work?"

Kate couldn't help the emerging return smile, shifting her gaze to the nearby townhouses before she did something embarrassing like lean her head against his shoulder. "Believe me, if Fairy Godmother assignments weren't naturally short I would have beaned someone in the head long before now."

Jon chuckled. "I actually knew a girl whose aunt hired a Fairy Godmother to secure her engagement to the eldest son of a local duke. Of course, the duke's wife was less than thrilled with the match, and hired a witch to make the problem daughter-in-law go away."

Kate nodded. "I heard about that one. They had to send in a whole team of re-beautification specialists, who then came back to the office and immediately dished out all the juicy details to anyone within earshot." She grinned. "Apparently, she was picking warts out of her hair for weeks."

"Believe me, she deserved it. A few years before the witch thing, she tried to make her cook redo an entire fifteen-layer cake because the icing clashed with her ball gown." He winced at the memory. "Threw such a fit about it she actually made the entire serving staff burst into tears."

Kate raised an eyebrow. "A fifteen-layer cake is nothing compared to a flying elephant. She was the beloved pet of a client who was paying us millions, and the client insisted her Snookums absolutely *had* to be gowned to match her mistress." *Not* one of her favorite cases. "That large an animal in lemon yellow puffed sleeves is not a pretty sight."

"I can imagine." Jon looked impressed, and Kate felt something inside her lift in a way she didn't dare look at too closely. "But I'll see your elephant and raise you a man convinced his dead wife had come back to him as his extremely loud and vulgar pet parrot, and refused to make any political decisions without consulting with her first."

The stories went back and forth, reality mixing liberally with exaggeration as each did their best to top the other. Jon turned out to have a very, very nice laugh, and managed in turn to make Kate laugh at more than one of his descriptions.

She didn't even feel self-conscious when she caught him very carefully not looking at her wings. "They come from my father's side of the family," she explained, giving them a sample flutter. Freed from social constraint, Jon's eyes focused on them. "My dad didn't have any, but apparently they show up on girls more often than they do boys. I don't mind them as much as I used to, but they do limit the places you can buy a shirt."

"You look good in them," he said offhandedly, seeming not to notice as Kate's cheeks went pink. "Forgive me if this is too personal a question, but . . . can you fly?"

Kate shook her head. "Sadly, no. Their strongest power was making me knock over anything within about a two-foot radius until I was about sixteen."

"How efficient." Jon grinned. "I used to have to run into everything."

All too soon, Jon slowed to a stop at the top of a street that appeared at first glance to be exactly like all the others they'd passed. He pointed to a shorter, shabbier townhouse than the ones surrounding it. "1612 Candlewick," he said quietly.

"Ah." She stood there a moment, arm muscles refusing to listen to her brain's sensible order to let go of Jon now. "I . . . should probably get going."

"Probably," Jon said, and Kate forced her arm to pull away. He hesitated for a second, then shoved both of his hands into his pockets. "I could maybe . . ."

She shook her head, trying to ignore her suddenly cold fingers. "I don't know how long I'll be." Her arm lifted a fraction, but she pulled it back when she realized that touching his hand again was probably an extremely bad idea. "It's . . ." She took a deep breath. "It's been very nice meeting you, Jon."

It was about the dumbest thing she could have said to him, but that didn't really matter, because this was undoubtedly the last time she'd ever see the man again. Which was a good thing, really, and she should be relieved they were saying goodbye before anything terrible happened.

Which she was. Really.

Jon stood there for a moment, not saying anything, then nodded. "You too, Kate." He turned and walked back up the street.

Quickly, Kate turned the opposite direction and headed toward the yard behind 1612.

KATE HID BEHIND a decorative wall before transporting herself into the townhouse, deciding that bright lights and purple smoke might bring a little more attention from the neighborhood insomniacs than she'd like. Once she was inside, she padded through the dark kitchen over to a small, appropriately shabby room that always held the poor yet attractive young relative. Pushing back the dingy curtain and wiping her hand on her skirt, she gave a resigned sigh and pulled *it* out of her pocket.

By *it*, she meant the Official Fairy Godmother's Incorporated Grand Entrance Accessories Package, Royal Class B Model (testing not yet completed). A few explosions had already been reported, but management refused to go back to the far more reliable earlier model. "Can't do without the background accompaniment," they said. "We're certain our dedicated field agents are good enough to work out any minor bugs for themselves. After all, we thought you were worth hiring, didn't we?"

As always, Kate didn't touch anything without consulting the instruction manual first. (Apparently, things needed to be done in proper order to keep swans from going crazy—poor Missy was a harsh enough lesson for even the most stubborn Fairy Godmother.) Pushing buttons A, B, and E at the same time started the spotlight, while pushing C and then E started the mist. Since nothing had gone wrong yet, Kate went on to add the background music, rose petals, and miniature spinning disco balls. Skipping the sections on swans and trained doves—after all, there wasn't anyone around to tell on her—she went through the steps on confetti and fireworks a bit faster than she should.

Tulle, it seemed, caught on fire only slightly more slowly than confetti.

"Um, could you use some help with that?"

Of course, the client would have woken up by now. "No," Kate snapped, pretending she still had some dignity left. "I think I have it under control."

Once she was sure the fire on her skirt was safely out, Kate looked up to see Cinderella staring at her with avid interest. "I think one of your swans flew out the window," the girl offered, pushing her impossibly golden hair out of the way of her soft violet eyes. "I can wait here, if you need to go get it."

Kate decided to pretend she hadn't heard that part. That way, she wouldn't have to feel guilty about it. "Don't worry about it." Kicking the last disco ball out of the way, she straightened herself out the best that she could and resumed a decent approximation of the official greeting pose. "Hello, Cinderella. I'm your Fairy Godmother." After a long pause, Kate shot the girl a stern look. "If we could avoid mentioning the fire from this point out, I'd appreciate it."

As it turned out, however, Kate needn't have worried. "Oh, that wasn't fire, that was just smoke," Cinderella said dismissively. "I can do that just by cooking." Her forehead furrowed in thought. "I'm not supposed to feed you, am I? Because dinner sort of turned green and bubbly, and I threw it out because not even Belzie would eat it. She eats *everything*, which might be bad for the people at the party thing they decided to go to." She looked up at Kate. "Have you ever had food turn green and bubbly?"

"Ah . . . no." Valiantly, Kate tried to yank the conversation back to its original purpose. "Actually, I'm—"

"You can call me Rellie, by the way." Rellie pushed down her covers a bit more, revealing arms covered in appropriately ragged nightgown sleeves and a couple of small, incredibly out of place pink bows. "I'm sorry I don't have my tragic heroine dirt on—I usually put it on in the mornings."

"That's *okay*," Kate said firmly. "It's not going to matter in a few minutes, because I'm here to give you something." The phrasing from the official script loomed in her head, and Kate closed her eyes a moment in annoyance before giving in. "Something like 'the one secret wish of your pure, gentle, and cruelly abused young heart,' to be more precise."

Rellie's forehead wrinkled in confusion. "But what if I don't know the secret wish of my pure . . . whatever the rest of that was? Do you have a test or something to help me find out?"

Kate paused, a little surprised by the question and how rarely it came up. Most of the clients she talked to felt that finding a husband and moving up in the world fit in nicely with what they wanted for themselves. She was tempted to like the girl. "I'm sorry, but no. The company just assumes that your heart's desire is going to be wearing a fancy dress to a royal ball, riding in a nice carriage, eating too much cake, and somehow or other making the prince fall madly in love with you."

"Oh." Rellie's brow furrowed even further. "But that's kind of stupid, isn't it, just assuming what somebody's heart's desire is going to turn out to be? I mean, not that dancing and cake and princes aren't nice and all, but what if what I've always really wanted to be was a rhinoceros—"

"A rhinoceros?" Kate repeated in astonishment, stalling for a chance to think. Please, don't let the girl mention elephants. "I suppose I could turn you into a goat if you really wanted, but a rhino's a little out of my league. Besides, this isn't exactly the best climate for that sort of animal. Think of the transportation costs."

"Oh, I wasn't saying that I wanted to be a rhinoceros. From what I've heard, they're kind of smelly, and only the baby ones are cute." Rellie's face gave no sign that she'd considered Kate's response anything but totally serious. "I'm just saying that it's a perfectly good thing to want, and that somebody somewhere probably does. It's the kind of thing you should be prepared for, just in case it ever comes up." Her eyes went distant. "A bunny rabbit, on the other hand . . ."

Deciding that she would be here all night if she let this continue, Kate snapped her fingers to get the girl's attention. "I'll be sure to list several possible animals when I mention it to my superiors," she said as calmly as possible. "But right now all we have is the cake, the dancing, and the handsome prince." At Rellie's less-than-enthusiastic look, Kate took a step closer. "Really, feel free to ignore the whole 'secret wish of the heart' thing—someone in PR came up with that, and I don't think any of them have ever actually met a client. Think of it more as a sort of . . . prepackaged adventure."

When Rellie started looking confused again, Kate sighed. "I can probably make the dress furry if you want."

This perked her up. "Will it make me look like a bunny rabbit?"

Feeling the sudden urge for sarcasm about to overwhelm her, Kate took a deep breath and silently schooled herself into patience. "It's a little warm for fur, but I'm certain that something more like a swan or a big wedding cake would be more than doable." Now, if she could keep Rellie from asking questions for just a couple of minutes . . .

Rellie opened her mouth, like she was about to say something, then seemed to think better of it and shrugged. "I'd prefer a big pink birthday cake instead of a wedding cake, if you don't mind. The frosting on wedding cakes never seems soft enough. Ice cream, though . . ."

Kate sighed again. "Ice cream?"

"Oh, yes—" She flinched, one porcelain hand coming up to cover her eyes as if she realized a problem with something she'd said. "But don't tell everyone else that I even know about things like ice cream and wedding cakes, okay, let alone eat them? Maleeva, Lucinda, and Belzie get so upset when I say things like that, and then there's all this squawking and running around . . ."

"I promise I won't say anything," Kate interjected quickly, not wanting to get her started again. "And Maleeva and company are your wicked stepfamily, I suppose?" Which, naturally, was one of the many things no one had bothered to mention in the file. With her luck, there was probably even a ferocious guard dog around her somewhere, just waiting for a Fairy Godmother-flavored snack.

Rellie blinked. "My stepmother and stepsisters. They practice every day to be very, very wicked, and strive to do their part to make sure I have the appropriate upbringing for an abused innocent." The last bit was said with all the inflection of a dutifully memorized line.

"I'm sure they have. Now, though, we have other things to worry about." Kate held up a wand, hoping to distract Rellie from any more potential segues. "Like getting started on your wonderful, possibly furry dress?"

"Okay, as long as you think it's fine without the extra dirt. Maleeva always gets so annoyed with me when I forget in the morning."

At least she wasn't asking for a dozen pink doves to follow

her around everywhere, Kate reminded herself as she held up her wand. "Okay. They don't like us to mention this part, but I need some actual fabric for the spell to turn into your fantasy dress. Do you want me to just use the nightgown you have on, or is there something—"

The rest of the question was cut off by the sound of maniacal barking. Kate jumped and whipped around to face the door. She deserved it, she guessed, for being stupid enough to even *think* about something like a psychotic guard dog.

She turned back to find a perfectly calm Rellie, fingers over her ears. "Please tell me that thing belongs to the neighbor," said Kate.

Rellie squinted at her. "What did you say? I can't hear you with my fingers in my ears."

Taking a deep breath, Kate walked over and pulled Rellie's fingers out of her ears. Then, she leaned close and raised her voice to be heard over the sound of the dog, not wanting to ask a third time. "Is that your stepmother's dog?"

Rellie nodded. "She calls him Demon Beast." She shrugged at Kate's disbelieving expression. "He can get a little crabby sometimes, particularly when someone interrupts his beauty sleep. Not that it helps much."

"Is there a way to get him to stop?"

Rellie thought about it. "Well, getting rid of whoever's interrupted his beauty sleep usually helps."

Making an exasperated noise, Kate left Rellie's room and went to the nearest kitchen window to see if she could figure out who she was going to have to try and save. When she caught sight of the dark silhouette standing on top of the decorative wall, dangerously close to where the barking was coming from, her treacherous brain recognized the shape. "Jon?" she breathed, then realized that wasn't going to get her anywhere. Quickly, she swung open the window and called, "Jon!"

The dark head turned. "Be with you in a second." His voice sounded far too cool and collected for someone that close to potentially losing a limb. The barking intensified, and his gaze immediately snapped down to the source of the noise. "Just as soon as I figure out how to do it in one piece."

Rellie moved to stand beside Kate at the window. "Oh, poor guy. Do you know him?"

Kate opened her mouth, fully intending to provide some sort of intelligent explanation that was a complete lie. Nothing quite came out because, well, that was *Jon* just outside the window. "He's a . . . friend of mine," she said, far too entranced for her own good. Thankfully, reflex threw in a last-second addition. "My assistant."

"Then you're probably going to want to get him in here, then." Rellie shook her head with a sigh. "Really, have you thought about getting a knight of some sort instead? With all that smiting they do, they'd be *so* much more useful in this sort of situation."

FOUR

A Few Extra Flourishes

Surprisingly, Jon felt less like an idiot trying not to be killed by the dog than he had walking away from Kate.

He'd once spent three days talking to a diplomat who hated him on general philosophical principles, and eventually Jon managed to earn both the other man's grudging respect and several acres of highly lucrative magical beanstalks. Persistence, not to mention selective deafness, was the key to any good negotiation.

Fueled by the fires of determination, Jon had turned around and headed straight back to 1612. If the route Kate used to get in wasn't obvious, he could hopefully catch the glow from the nearest window and knock. If he looked needy enough, she'd *have* to let him in.

Then, the townhouse's resident attack dog and his pearly white teeth of death made an appearance, abruptly altering Jon's future plans to include a relatively safe perch at the top of a nearby wall.

Rabid barking was not a confidence builder, and he had a sudden vision of being discovered by the neighbors the next morning and having to explain things to the constables. After which, of course, he'd still have to sneak back into the palace.

He heard Kate call his name, and a few moments later she saved him with some truly awful classical music that somehow caused the dog to fall asleep. Not a dignified way to get out of the situation, no, but at least Kate wasn't looking at him like he'd lost his mind.

"You're the only person I'm ever going to admit this to, but I'm suddenly more appreciative of that stupid entrance package," Kate said as she helped him through the window, traces of worry still in her voice. "Rellie told me the dog was lulled to sleep by terrible music, so all I had to do was turn it back on."

"She didn't even light her skirt on fire this time," the blond girl—Rellie, Jon guessed—added helpfully.

"I have no idea what she's talking about," Kate said, eyes still on Jon. Even after he was safely standing, her hand lingered a moment before letting go of his arm, a small gesture that did embarrassingly useful things for his confidence. "Are you all right?"

Jon smiled in what he hoped was a reassuring manner, even as a little glow of pleasure flared to life in his chest. "I'm fine." He held his arms out for her inspection, amused when she actually gave him a quick once-over. "No blood was drawn."

The blond girl who'd been a spectator all this while eyed him critically. "You really don't look much like a Fairy Godmother, not even as an assistant." She pointed at Kate as a convenient example. "They're all supposed to have *wings*, for one thing."

Kate winced. "He . . ." The sentence died when she failed to find a believable excuse. Jon, however, lied on command on an almost daily basis, and since this had technically been his idea to begin with, he stepped forward into the breach.

"You're right—I don't have any wings." Rule one in trying to lie your way out of a confrontation: The first thing to do is agree with the other person; not only was it an excellent delay tactic, it usually had the added bonus of seriously confusing them.

Her brow furrowed. "Well . . ."

"Unfortunately for me, only A-level Fairy Godmothers are is-sued that particular set of equipment." He leaned forward conspir-atorially, gratified when he saw the corner of Kate's mouth quirk up. "Personally, I think I'm somewhere in the Qs at the moment."

The girl, presumably Kate's client, didn't look convinced. Jon could practically hear Lawton laughing at him all the way from the palace. "Then why aren't you dressed like her?" the girl asked. "She's all sparkly and looks like you guys are supposed to in the stories, except for the whole no gray hair or wrinkles thing. You, though . . ." She waved a dismissive hand at Jon's far less glittery outfit. "You need *lots* of help."

Encouraged by the amusement in Kate's eyes, he widened his own. "You really think I'd look good in a dress? I keep trying to talk them into letting me have a blue one to match Kate's."

The girl paused a moment, as if seriously considering it, then wrinkled her nose at whatever mental picture she'd conjured. "Okay, you have a point. Since it looks like you probably aren't sure what's going on yet, I'm Cinderella, but you can call me Rellie. You guys are gonna give me a dress and prince and stuff, which is supposed to be my heart's desire, but isn't really." She smiled. "But that's okay. Your boss said it could be pink."

Jon raised an eyebrow at Kate, who just shook her head. "Remember what you said about interesting stories?" she reminded him. Then, fixing a cheerful expression on her face, she focused her attention back on Rellie. "So let's get started, shall we? What do you want to do first?"

Rellie furrowed her brow, giving the matter some serious thought. "Wait—don't you have to do the dress first? I mean, it's not like you can start the ball now or drag the prince guy over here."

"True." Kate sighed, her long, graceful fingers tucking a loose strand of hair behind her ear. It hit Jon that as an unanticipated side benefit of this, he was going to be able to see Kate in action.

"Remember, though," Kate said. "I said I needed some base clothing to start out from. Not that it has any effect on the final product, but after a couple of lawsuits based on loss of rags, you have to pay attention to this sort of thing."

"Oh, what I'm wearing will be fine." Rellie looked down at her ragged nightgown, petting one of the bows like it was a small kitten. "Maybe some of the bows will even stay . . ."

"I'll do my best." A brief, almost affectionate smile appeared on Kate's face before her expression slid back into what he suspected was "professional" mode. "Now, let's see what accessory options you have to choose from for your dress." Kate pulled out the folder and started to open it before Jon plucked it out of her hand with a grin.

"Assistant, remember?" He opened the folder and scanned down the brief notes on the case, flipping through the mostly blank pages on the off chance he had missed something. When he got to the page that listed who Rellie was going to be matched up with, he went perfectly still to mask his sudden kick of panic. "She's going to end up with . . ." He looked up just in time to see Kate making shushing motions with her hands, and immediately cut off the thought. Apparently, they hadn't gotten around to discussing that part yet.

Rellie's interest was momentarily piqued. "Does it say anything about the other stuff I'm going to get? Like furry pink boots?"

"I haven't gotten that far." He returned his attention to the file, making himself relax. There were far worse options out there for a future sister-in-law—if anything, *she* was getting the worst of the deal—and the files clearly weren't going to give him away. The paperwork didn't even mention Rupert had a brother, let alone his name.

He could definitely work with this. Braced with the reminders, he refocused on the facts in front of him. Behind the specific information on the current client was an entire set of printouts, complete with tabs that appeared to be some sort of company manual. He flipped through the different sections—social introduction, shoes (that was a big one), dress—before scanning the list of options. "Let's see—'The client may determine color, sleeve shape, material, and assorted decorations, so long as it meets appropriate standards to sufficiently dazzle the highest of royalty.'"

Rellie looked at Kate. "Do Fairy Godmothers *ever* use words that make sense? What does any of that even mean?"

"It doesn't mean anything," Jon cut in, remembering what his mother put the kingdom's dressmakers through on a regular basis. "All being of high rank means you can wear absolutely anything you want, and most of the time you'd want to wear the most insane thing you can get a hold of. Last season it was serving spoons . . ."

His voice trailed off as he realized that both Kate and Rellie were staring at him. Kate, he noticed, seemed to be fighting off a smile. "Never mind." Jon cleared his throat awkwardly. "Leftover work-related trauma. Nothing to worry about."

Kate didn't say anything, but the smile won out for a moment before she turned back to Rellie. "So, let's get back to the dress, shall we? I'm guessing you're going to want it to be pink, but what about the sleeves? Something with ruffles, maybe?"

Rellie thought for a moment. "Can they be long and billowy, like birds' wings?"

Kate's brow lowered a moment as she thought. "Since customer complaints got rid of the feather option last year I'm not sure how wing-like they'll really be, but I'll see what I can do." Straightening her shoulders, Kate muttered something under her breath as she stepped back and waved her wand in a precise set of swirling motions. A cloud of fairy dust and a few sneezes later, Rellie was decked out in a silky pink ball gown with a huge, full skirt, long gauzy bell sleeves, and a wide edge of lace at all convenient edges (pink, naturally).

Jon vowed never to mention this particular talent of Kate's to his mother.

Rellie looked down, carefully examining every inch of gauze and lace, then gave a tragic little sigh. "Well, that's a nice start, but . . ." Her voice trailed off hopefully.

"Bunnies. Yes, I know." Covering her eyes with one hand, Kate used a different flourish to change the whole ensemble into pink fur. After a moment, she risked a peek between her fingers. "Somehow, it's even worse than I thought it would be," she muttered, low enough for only Jon to hear.

She was right—bows were *not* supposed to be furry. Still . . . "Not that I don't agree with you completely, but I feel obligated to mention that Rupert might actually like it. He has a thing for hunt—" He noticed Rellie was suddenly close enough that she could hear what they were saying, and Jon's gaze met hers with the brightest and most cheerful expression he could manage. "Bunnies. He has a thing for bunnies."

Rellie eyed him with suspicion, then shrugged and made a few twitchy tugs at her collar. "The neck itches." She made a face, and then that dreamy look came back into her eyes again. "Are you sure I can't have feathers?"

Kate shook her head in what Jon suspected was mock solemnity. "Even if I could talk them into bringing the feather option back, I'm afraid it itches even worse than rabbit fur."

The girl looked doubtfully at her, before sliding her attention back over to Jon. "Really?"

"Oh, definitely. Sometimes there's even a rash." Grateful, Kate flashed him another one of those "us against the world" looks. Jon grinned at her, finding himself rather enamored of the idea that, for once, there was someone else on his side.

Rellie looked back and forth between them, then sighed dramatically. "Oh, all right. No sense in asking for trouble like that. Would really, really sparkly be any easier? Like a whole bunch of stars all mushed together?"

Kate gave the wand another flourish.

"No, more than that." Rellie held the skirt out to get a better look at it. "Lots more."

Kate turned to look at Jon. "Cover your eyes." When he raised a disbelieving eyebrow, she narrowed her eyes and pointed her wand at him. "I am *not* going to be responsible for making you go blind. Seriously, cover your eyes."

Jon obligingly covered his eyes, leaving just enough room to watch Kate do another flourish.

Rellie made a disappointed noise. "I said lots more."

Another flourish.

"I don't really think you're taking me seriously."

Kate glared, then did two quick flourishes in a row.

"Ahhh! I can't see! The glare's blinding me!"

"Exactly." Kate paused, and Jon risked peeking again in time to see about half of the sparkles vanishing from the dress. As Rellie blinked the dancing white spots out of her eyes, Kate folded her arms across her chest. "I'd say this would be a good time for you to stop having so much input, Rellie."

"No, no, wait! I can do this, really." She rubbed her porcelain white chin. "It's just so hard. I mean, there's so many choices, and it's not like I've ever had to think about this sort of thing before . . ." Suddenly, Jon heard the sound of a door opening and shutting at the front of the house, followed by muffled arguing. Hearing it, Rellie's expression cleared. "I know, I'll go ask my stepmother! She spends so much time telling me all about this sort of thing, she must know *everything* about it. It'll be perfect!"

"Stepmother?" Jon's eyes widened at the possible implications. "As in 'obligatory wicked stepmother,' whose entire purpose in life is to spread discomfort and misery wherever she goes?"

"Pretty much." Kate looked even more alarmed than Jon felt. Of course, she was the one who knew exactly how bad these things could get. "Listen, Rellie," she started, already heading toward the girl. "I don't think this is such a good idea . . ."

Rellie, however, was already bouncing out the door. "Don't worry," she smiled, disappearing past the rag curtain before they could even blink. "I'll be right back." Kate and Jon looked at each other, then chased after her.

"So, this is the girl that's going to marry Prince Rupert?"

"Yeah." Kate looked back at him. "Have I scared you yet?"

Jon sighed. "Only because they're perfect for each other."

THANKFULLY, THEY CAUGHT up with her before she made it even halfway to the room where the voices were coming from. Together they yanked her flat against an appropriately shadowed wall, and Kate covered Rellie's mouth with her hand as an extra precaution. Then, slowly, they started the long, careful process of edging back toward the kitchen without being discovered.

That is, until one of the voices became loud enough to make out individual words. Jon found himself freezing in place when the name "Prince Charming" floated across his ear.

"We didn't even get to *see* him, Mother!" The voice was whiny, almost sharp—the sound of someone who still thought she was six years old, despite the addition of breasts and several feet in height. "We didn't get to see *anybody* who was worth *anything* at that stupid ball!" The volume and shrillness seemed to increase with every word. "And do you know why? Because we were too busy getting chased off by the palace guards!"

The sound of a slap made Rellie's eyes widen, and Jon added his hand to Kate's to further silence any potential commentary. Inwardly, though, he groaned in frustration.

He *remembered* these three.

"You will *never* speak to me that way." Even furious as it was, this second voice was everything a person expected out of a wicked stepmother—low, cultured, and almost offhandedly snide. Jon imagined she spent quite a bit of time practicing. "And it certainly isn't *my* choice that we never make it into a ball. If I had clever, attractive daughters instead of you useless lumps, the guards wouldn't be a problem."

"You always say that, but I didn't see you do any better with the guards." The third voice grated like a knife across exposed nerve endings, the only one of the three he'd never thrown out in person.

Luckily, though, they persisted in thinking of him as some sort of captain of the guard. "In fact, it looked as though you nauseated one of them."

Jon winced in sympathy for the guard as he heard Kate smother a snicker.

There was another slap, but the other sister—Lucinda, he recalled—was right there to pick up the refrain. "You said Cinderella was going to take care of this! Having a poor, tragic stepsister we abuse was supposed to get us *invited* to things!"

The second sister gave a nasty chuckle. "What she didn't mention is the stepmother of that poor, tragic girl usually ends up being forced to dance to death in red-hot iron shoes . . ."

There were two more slaps, both at once, then another set of two that seemed to come from the opposite direction. At that point, the slapping noises became so frequent that Jon lost count, and with a look at Kate they began the long process back to the kitchen.

Once they'd made it back to the relative safety of Rellie's corner, Kate practically sagged in relief. Rellie sat back down on the bed, eyes still wide enough that there could be a real risk they'd be permanently stuck that way.

Jon ran a tired hand through his hair. "I know they're technically going to end up being in-laws, but would you mind if Rupert permanently bans those three from the palace? We tend to torture people with canapés instead of anything fatal, but there's no need to make the royal family suffer."

Kate straightened, smoothing a hand over her hair as she pulled herself together. "I usually suggest it—it never works to reform them, no matter how often the client insists on trying." She glanced over at Rellie, then leaned in closer to Jon and lowered her voice again. "What's Rupert like, by the way? I know he's a rake, which I'm pretty sure Rellie won't even notice if he buys her some pets, but if he's not at least nicer than her stepfamily then I'm going to have to come up with something."

"He's fairly nice even when compared to normal people," Jon assured her. "He's not exactly the sharpest sword in the armory, but he'll buy her an entire zoo just for being less trouble than his mother is."

Any further observation was cut off when Rellie blinked and shook her head before focusing back on Kate. "This is really interesting and all, but can we get back to my dress? If I can't ask Maleeva, I'm going to have to keep trying and trying things until I find out what I like . . ."

"No." Kate said firmly, then shot a worried glance in the stepfamily's direction. Lowering her voice to a whisper, she held a warning finger up in Rellie's direction. "The one you have right now is just fine."

At Rellie's pout, Kate sighed. "Okay, fine. You can give me some suggestions. But Jon has actually spent time in the palace— he goes first." She turned toward him. "Anything else you think Prince Rupert might be looking for in a woman?"

Now it was Jon's turn to sigh. "Cleavage."

Kate chuckled. "At least you're honest." Turning to Rellie, she said, "Okay, your turn. Any changes you want made that won't injure the people around you?"

Rellie twirled a lock of golden hair, thinking a moment. "These sleeves are too floppy. Can you make them shorter and poufier? And add some more sparkles." Her eyes widened as she remembered. "But only a little bit more. Not like the later stuff."

"And *whose* idea was the 'later stuff?'" Kate muttered. Still, the wand came up and around in a different pattern, the magic dust came out again, and when it was gone Rellie's dress was only little more sparkly than it had previously been. The girl jumped up and down and clapped her hands. Kate nodded in satisfaction. "Perfect. Now we just have to get you to that ball, nudge that Prince in your direction, and all of us can get a decent night's sleep."

A clock chimed in the distance, enough to trigger an unfortunately relevant memory in Jon's brain. Briefly, he considered trying to take care of the problem without warning her about it, but one lie of omission was more than enough for a potential relationship to deal with. "You'll never know how much I hate to say this, but there might be more to it than that."

Both women's heads whipped around to look at him, and he could already see the dread settling in Kate's face. Sharing some of the same feeling, Jon took a deep breath and continued, "This morning starts the beginning of fancy banquet season at the palace. There's not another fancy dress ball scheduled for at least the next three months. Were you planning on having to wait that long?"

FIVE

Technical Difficulties

Kate glared down at the folder in her hand, wondering if turning it into a snail would make her feel any better. "Not a single detail about the ball she's supposed to be going to, just a vague assumption that one would magically show up when we needed it." She squeezed her eyes shut for a few seconds. "How long has this fancy banquet season been in effect?"

"Ever since the current king and queen took the throne." Jon was sitting beside her now, the worry audible in his voice as his hand rubbed gentle circles along her back. She wished more than anything that she was in any condition to suitably appreciate it. "It's the only time of year the queen's willing to wear the same dress more than once."

"She sounds like one of our clients." Kate took a deep breath, reminding herself to be calm. The only way this was going to get solved was if *she* came up with the solution, and that wasn't going to happen if she was busy wishing terrible things on management. "Is there any way someone else in town is rich enough to be holding a ball in the next few days?"

When Jon shook his head, Rellie bounced off the bed and moved toward them. "How does he know that sort of thing and you don't?" She peered hard at Kate as if waiting for an answer, then went on before anyone had time to come up with a good enough lie. "And seriously, aren't you supposed to have the ball ready before you even come see me?"

"Usually, it's at least a month between when a job gets booked and when a Fairy Godmother is sent out, mostly so that someone in Research can make sure there's a fancy dress ball going on when we need one." Kate scowled, cursing herself for not thinking of this when Bubbles handed her the assignment. Not that it would have changed anything, but . . . "I should have *known* Bubbles wouldn't think about a little thing like prep time when she had a chance of making one of the directors happy. She claims she is capable of walking on water when she is out in the field, so she expects us to do the same."

Rellie moved closer, fascinated. "There's actually a real person named Bubbles? Does she wear pink and giggle a lot?"

Kate squeezed her eyes shut at the visual conjured by Rellie's questions. "Only when she's had too much to . . . *oooh*." The sensation of Jon's fingers gently attempting to work out the dozens of kinks in her neck chased away any remaining words. "Don't . . ." An embarrassingly pleased noise cut off the rest of the sentence, and she found herself tilting her head back in a completely involuntary gesture. This . . . this . . . was probably not a good idea. "Don't . . . do that, really."

Jon instantly moved his hand away, unfortunately, doing exactly what she'd told him to. After a second, he rubbed a hand across the back of his own neck. "Sympathetic muscle aches," he muttered, not looking at her. "Just trying to get them at their source."

Worried suddenly that she'd embarrassed him when he was undoubtedly just trying to be nice—and *more* worried that she kept caring so much about what he might be feeling—Kate touched his arm. When he turned to look at her, a little reluctantly, she offered him a sheepish smile. "Thank you. It was . . ." She took a deep breath. "It was really good. It just . . . makes it a little hard to think."

Jon grinned, looking more than a little relieved. "I know what you mean," he said softly, and Kate realized suddenly how little distance there was between them at the moment.

"You know, Jon," Rellie cut in, down on her knees now and watching them with enraptured interest. "If you managed to magically come up with one of those fancy dress balls Kate's been talking about, she *really* looks like she'd be willing to kiss you right now."

"*Rellie,*" Kate growled, pushing herself forward to properly lunge at the girl and cut off any more useful observations she might be interested in making.

Then Jon's voice cut in, suddenly thoughtful. "Actually . . ."

Surprised, Kate looked back at him. "You can find me a fancy dress ball?"

"Possibly, though that depends on how much emphasis you're placing on the 'you.'" Jon hesitated. "I might have some vague chance in getting the queen to ask for one, but with this little lead time I'm not even sure she'd be enough to persuade Madame Stewart to marshal her forces and get everything pulled together. For something like this you'd have to go straight to the Madame herself, the queen's personal entertainment organizer, and she won't even give me the time of day after that unfortunate incident with the ice archer.

"I doubt I'll be able to convince the woman of anything on my own. But she loves Rupert, both because he's pretty enough he matches the statuary, and he actually enjoys eating those disgusting canapés she makes. If I can convince him to persuade her that we need a last-minute ball, we should be fine. And if I mention there's more alcohol at a fancy dress ball, and that fewer people will accidentally try and carry on an intelligent conversation with him, I won't have any trouble getting him to agree with me."

Rellie perked up at this. "Do you think I could learn to get him to agree to stuff that easily?" she asked.

Kate blinked, surprised. If Rellie's advisors could keep her away from bunnies long enough, there was a chance the palace wouldn't know what hit it. "Well, that's certainly something to look forward to, isn't it?" She pushed herself to her feet, forcing a brightly pleasant tone to her voice. "So, now that Jon's saved our lives as far as the ball is concerned, do you think we can finish up quietly enough to not blind me or catch your stepfamily's attention?"

There was another pause, just long enough to draw attention to itself, before Jon stood. "I need to go," he said, voice as equally bright and pleasant as Kate's. "It tends to unnerve the palace guards when anyone but Rupert wanders in after two o'clock in the morning."

Kate's stomach sank. She had barely known him for an hour, and now she was never going to see him again. Why was the second goodbye so much harder than the first? "So when are you coming back?" asked Rellie. She busied herself by smoothing her big pink skirt out around her into what she probably considered a more pleasing shape. "Because I've got a lot of toiling and scrubbing I have to do during the day tomorrow, but I should be free after everyone else goes to bed." As if realizing something, she turned to Kate. "How long is this going to take, by the way? I mean, I'd love to have you guys come over again, but I'm sure there's more to this Fairy Godmother stuff than just hanging out with the clients."

Kate sighed, brushing her hair behind her ear as she gave Jon time to exit gracefully. It would be better if she didn't have the opportunity to watch him go. "I'm not sure yet when the ball will be, but I'm definitely going to get everything else done as soon as I can, within a week. We've got the dress taken care of, but we're going to need shoes, a carriage . . ."

"Dancing lessons," Jon added. He lifted his chin as Kate turned to look at him, confused. "For some reason, Rupert decided to actually pay attention during all of those dancing lessons the queen made him take. If Rellie doesn't have at least some idea of where her feet go, her big moment is going to be ruined when she trips over her skirt."

Kate hesitated, not quite certain where this was going. "She'll just have to move slowly and trust me to make sure the song ends early."

"Or I could teach her." Jon raised an eyebrow, a hint of challenge in his voice. "And you, too, for that matter. It's not nearly as painful and complicated a process as etiquette teachers make it out to be." The corner of his mouth curled up into a half-smile. "Who knows, you might even like it."

So, that was what people meant when they talked about a person's heart skipping a beat. "But—"

She felt a tug on her skirt from Rellie. "I'm not sure about this whole dancing thing, but if I trip I might tear the skirt of the really neat dress you made me." The girl made her eyes go big and plaintive as she batted her lashes up at Kate. "Do you really want to have to go through all the yelling it took to make it all over again?"

"She's right," Jon teased. "Think of the poor dress."

Kate stared hard at Jon for a long moment. "Thursday night, then? Ten o'clock?" she asked finally, still waiting for him to say no. It was absolutely ludicrous to expect someone to have their schedule open with only two nights advance notice. "Just across the street?"

Grinning, Jon nodded. "Thursday night it is." Looking very satisfied with himself, he rubbed his hands together. "Now, does anyone know how I'm going to get past that dog and Rellie's step-family with all of my body parts intact?"

AFTER JON HAD made a relatively dignified exit through the window, Rellie practically bounced to her feet. "That was fun to watch, but it's probably time to get back to me now. Didn't that contract you mentioned say something about you having to make me pretty shoes?"

Kate forced her still-jumping insides to settle and refocus on the business at hand. "Yes, I'm going to make you some pretty shoes." She took a quick look around the barren room, searching for the client folder she had tossed. Unfortunately, a quick look didn't do it, and Kate had to get down on her hands and knees to peer into the herd of dust bunnies that had colonized the area under the bed. "You know, I thought tragically abused stepdaughters were supposed to be good at this whole cleaning thing."

Rellie made a face. "Do you know how *gross* dirty things can be?" Leaning over the foot of the bed, she reached into the mass of dust bunnies and magically pulled out the folder. "Besides, I'm getting better at finding stuff. I even figured out your guys' secret."

Kate's head shot up at that last snippet of insight. "Oh, really?"

"Yeah—it was easy." Distracted momentarily by a hot pink sticky note peeking out from the file's edge, Rellie sat back on the bed and began thumbing through the pages for it. "I mean, come on, how could a Fairy Godmother's assistant be a guy . . ." She looked up for a moment. "He could be a Fairy Godfather's assistant if there was one. But that would say he was assisting a Fairy Godfather, which you are not. You may not be old, but you're still totally a girl." She paused. "You guys really need to sort this out."

Kate sat down, taking a few seconds to work her way back through Rellie's tangent. Thankfully, none of it seemed like anything that would come back and bite her later, so she relaxed. "It may sound silly, but we're all supposed to be called Fairy Godmothers, no matter our gender. It's the name of the company, and the employees are representatives of the registered trademark, that sort of thing."

"Oh, okay," Rellie replied, the whole thing clearly already beyond her comprehension or caring. "But since the other guy's clearly just somebody from the palace and not really a fairy anything, I can just call him Mr. Assistant Guy, right?" Finding the sticky note somewhere in between disclaimers and a list of house entrance protocols, she triumphantly peeled it off and stuck it on the wall. "Or your lover bunny, if you'd like that better. I wish I could give you more options, but lover opossum and lover chicken just sound silly."

It took Kate a second to realize that her mouth was hanging open. "Lover . . . chicken . . . we aren't—didn't . . . I . . . ah . . ." She decided to stop talking before she came off looking like an even bigger idiot than she already did. "He has a name, you know—Jon."

"But that's just so boring. Mr. Assistant Guy is more fun to say." Rellie leaned forward and handed Kate the folder. "Now, let's get back to my cute little shoes. I think it'd be the very best if they were—"

"Pink. Yes, I know." Grateful that the topic had moved to much safer ground, Kate turned the file around and started flipping through it. "But they recently redid the minimum requirements for the shoe portion of the package you'll be receiving, and if I don't take that into account now I'll probably end up having to redo the shoes entirely. Ah, here we are."

"Oh, let me read it. Please, please let me read it," Rellie chimed in, doing a miniature version of her usual bounce. "It's not like I'm going to get the chance to do this sort of thing again, and I don't want to get to be a wrinkly old woman and suddenly think I missed out on something."

Kate just looked at her. "If you think reading files is exciting, you *really* need to get out more."

"Probably." She shrugged, completely unconcerned. "But isn't that what this whole thing's about? Me getting a little action?"

"Action? Do you even know what that—" Kate stopped, deliberately shutting her eyes for a moment. "Never mind. You've got the nasty habit of answering questions like that honestly, and I've suddenly realized that I don't want to know." She held the folder out. "Start in the middle of the second page, under 'footwear specifications.'"

"Sure." Plucking the folder from Kate's hand, Rellie dropped it on her lap and furrowed her forehead in what was no doubt an adorable manner. "Such tiny writing—no cute curlicues or anything. Let's see, 'The shoes must of course be the pin . . . pinnacle of the girl's look, like delicate little jewels pointing the way to the young prince's heart.'" She wrinkled her nose. "That's dumb. Why would a guy care about what shoes I was wearing?"

"Let's just say the guy who wrote the manual was a very interesting person." Kate shook her head. "Just keep going, okay? I'll explain later."

"Okay. 'As such, the shoes should not in any way be dictated by the dress—its style is, to a certain extent, dictated by the client, and our tastes are far more trustworthy than hers will no doubt prove to be.'"

Kate looked down at her poufy blue skirt, wincing a little at the irony.

"The shoes should, as described earlier, have all the qualities of the jewels which they will em . . . emulate. As such, they should be clear like the facets of a diamond, sparkling with each step the girl should take. Though the Fairy Godmother may tint the shoes to match the client's dress, the shoes should be made out of glass—"

"Glass?" Kate interrupted. "You've got to be kidding me." Reaching over, she snatched the file out of Rellie's hand and started scanning, hoping the girl had somehow misread something. "No, you're not kidding me, are you? Geez, do these people have any contact with reality?" Groaning, she rubbed her eyes. "Okay, okay. I'm sure there's a way I can work around this. Plastic, maybe, though the sparkle would be harder and I don't know how much fun that would be for you. Maybe they would consider a shimmer close enough to a sparkle—"

"Wait, they actually want me to walk around in glass shoes?" Kate didn't even get the chance to respond before the girl's eyes widened in horror. "What if I want to start jumping up and down or something? The shoes would get smashed and make my feet all cut up and bloody and disgusting!"

"Which is why I will figure out how to take care of this," Kate said, trying her best to sound soothing. "I just . . . need a little while to work out the details." Stretch details out to mean "a plan of any kind," and she could actually claim the last statement had been honest.

"I'm sure Mr. Assistant Guy could help. He looks kind of like that cute guy who shows up on the coins sometimes—it'd probably be more fun with him, too." Distracted from her sudden fear of dangerous footwear, Rellie stopped playing with one of her new bows and glanced up at Kate. "You sure do blush an awful lot, you know that?"

"It's been a recent development," Kate muttered, closing the client folder and stuffing it back in her waistband. Then, more loudly, "I'll be back tomorrow, and you'd better hope I can change management's mind about glass footwear by then." She waved her wand for what would hopefully be her last transportation spell of the night. "Because if I can't, there's going to be a four-foot stack of liability forms in your future."

Rellie gave Kate a little wave as the glow kicked in. "Why?"

Kate turned to step into the spell. "Do you know how much you could sue us for if the prince ends up stepping on your toes?"

SIX

Family Dynamics

Lawton pressed a hand to his friend's forehead as if checking for fever. "Seriously, Jon, you're beginning to frighten me. And I am far too sober to be forced to deal with genuine emotion right now."

Jon inclined his head toward the glass Lawton had set down. "Should I come back in fifteen minutes?" When it became clear the other man wasn't about to be distracted by a mere joke, Jon rolled his eyes and stepped away from his friend's hand. "It's not like I want to entrust Rupert with all my worldly possessions, Lawton. I just need to ask him something."

"And if that was how you had introduced the situation, I would have simply responded with a bit of witty repartee and happily moved on to a far more interesting topic of conversation." Lawton shook his head and took a quick, bracing drink of his abandoned brandy. "But what you actually said was that you needed Rupert's *assistance* with something, implying that you have slid so far into derangement that you feel your daily activities would actually be improved by the involvement of your idiotic elder brother."

Jon sighed, forced to acknowledge that Lawton actually had the shadow of a point. "I need us to squeeze in one more fancy dress ball before the start of banquet season," he explained. "But last time I tried to talk to Madame Stewart, she chased me around the kitchens with a serving fork. I thought Rupert would probably have better luck."

For a long moment, all Lawton could do was stare at him. "Are you actually planning on attending this ball, and thereby volunteering for what you consider to be an evening of unspeakable torture?" he asked finally. "Or, as I am profoundly hoping, is this part of some sort of complex psychological torture you plan to inflict on the unsuspecting? Be warned—if you do not answer properly I will feel it my duty to force the attentions of the nearest medical professional on you."

Jon raised an eyebrow, a little surprised at the genuine worry he heard in Lawton's voice. "I'd probably be there for at least part of it, just to make sure everything starts smoothly," he conceded, working out the details in his mind. "After everyone is sufficiently distracted, however, I plan to slip out and enjoy the rest of my evening far away from the palace." And, ideally, convince Kate to spend the evening with him. They could find a nice little restaurant somewhere on the far edge of town, take some time to just enjoy one another's company.

Lawton once again picked up his brandy, seeming somewhat soothed by the calculation hinted in Jon's explanation. Plotting, he understood. "You know, if you had used the word 'scheming' from the beginning you could have saved us both a terrible headache."

Taking a drink, his eyebrows drew together speculatively as he studied Jon over the top edge of his glass. "Though the question of why still remains. Have you become a masochist while I wasn't looking? Because if you have, at least have the good sense to practice it in a more amusing field of interest. I know some women who can do marvelous things with velvet whips and chains."

Jon's eyebrows lifted as his brain attempted to fit Lawton, whips, and chains into the same picture. "I am quite certain that wasn't something I wanted to know about you."

Lawton shrugged before moving on. "Did you lose a bet of some sort?"

Jon narrowed his eyes. "You were kind enough to cure me of that, remember?"

Lawton's face burst into a smile at the happy memory. "Ah, yes. It was a pleasure watching you wear those animated trousers for an entire week. The speculative look returned to his face. "What is it, then? Other gambling debts, perhaps? Some form of ludicrously elaborate repayment?"

Jon sighed. Apparently, this was going to be a full interrogation. "When was the last time you saw me anywhere near a gambling table? Rupert does that enough for both of us."

"True." Lawton nodded in acknowledgement. "A duke's wife you're suddenly desperate to see again?"

Jon raised an eyebrow. "Which one—the black widow who's on husband number nine, the woman who's convinced she's an elfin princess, or the former frog who still croaks when she thinks no one is looking?"

Lawton brushed aside Jon's impatience with a dismissive gesture. "There are only three reasons for a sensible man to do anything at all—money, power, and women. You have more than enough of the first already, along with a distinct unwillingness to be a decent human being and spend it on the same trash as the rest of us. If this was one of those dull, political plays you do so well you would have confessed before we even started simply to get me off your back, and I've heard no sign of—" He cut off abruptly as his gaze snapped to Jon's, one eyebrow shooting upward. "If I remember correctly, you were out almost obscenely late last night."

"Which means that I'm tired." Jon took a deep breath, fighting for patience. "And the idea of decking you is sounding better by the second. Do I have *any* chance of finding out whether or not you've seen Rupert lately?"

"Don't interrupt me while I'm having a brilliant insight. If it helps, you're perfectly free to deck someone else once I've left the room." Even as he spoke, a supremely self-satisfied smile made its way onto Lawton's face. "For the moment, though, I am far too intrigued to go anywhere."

No. No, no, no. He trusted Lawton with nearly everything, but there were still far too many parts of this that could go wrong to let *anyone* else get involved. "I was walking," Jon explained, voice calm. "And thinking. We brooding, younger son types have been known to do that on occasion, you know."

"So I've been told." Lawton took a ruminative sip in order to extend the moment. "The question that springs to mind, however, is whom were you walking and thinking with?"

Jon hesitated for a fraction of an instant before responding. "A large, balding man named Richard, if you must know. I'm holding interviews for a new best friend."

Lawton's smile remained in place. "I've always admired your ability to lie with a straight face." Setting down his nearly empty glass, Lawton slung a companionable, confining arm around Jon's shoulders as they walked. "So, am I familiar with this fetching creature?"

Jon sighed, giving in. "No, and you won't be until I'm absolutely certain she won't run away screaming."

Lawton's smile slid into a delighted grin. "Which suggests, happily, that you have found a woman you actually consider worth holding on to. And, given the fact that music and dancing appear to be involved in the lady's wooing, my guess is that you have discovered her someplace livelier than one of your dusty political meetings."

"Actually, she needs it for work."

That stopped Lawton in place, both eyebrows shooting up. "Really?" He digested this. "Tell me you're not trying to free one of Madame Stewart's scuttling assistants. Not only would you be forced to face her wrath, but your mother would have an absolute fit—"

The sound of someone crying started in the distance.

Both men stood listening, then Jon squeezed his eyes shut as if fighting off an impending headache. "That doesn't sound like my mother, does it?" When there was no response, Jon opened his eyes. "Please tell me that doesn't sound like my mother."

"Actually, I don't believe it does." Lawton cocked his head thoughtfully. "The queen tends to have a more fluttery edge to her sobbing, and if she were the culprit it would have likely evolved into a wail by this point." He shook his head. "I can't recognize it."

Jon sighed, moving away from Lawton toward the sound. "If it's not her, then she probably still caused it somehow." Which was worse, in a way—the maids' big tearful eyes always ended up making him feel guilty they'd had to deal with his mother in the first place. He paid the queen's personal staff ludicrously high wages—hazard pay—but at times it still didn't seem like enough. "For pity's sake, I told Mother she can't have one of her nervous breakdowns in front of anyone who hasn't been cleared for hazard pay."

Lawton hurried to catch up. "You do realize, don't you, that if Rupert is anywhere within earshot he is undoubtedly running *away* from the sound of sobbing."

"Yes, but if I don't—" Jon stopped. "Wait. You're coming with me?"

"It would seem that way, yes."

"I thought copious weeping gives you a headache."

"True." Lawton smiled slightly. "But if I let you too far out of my sight, you'll escape my clutches and I'll lose my opportunity to pry more information about your new lady love out of you." He squared his shoulders. "For gossip of that quality, I'm willing to accept the risk."

Jon shook his head as the crying stopped for a few seconds before starting up again. "Remind yourself of that once she starts sobbing into your shirt."

The crying remained fairly steady as they spent several frustrating minutes attempting to locate the source. Excepting a family curse that needed fulfilling, a secret treasure that needed hiding, or an annoying relative who needed getting rid of, the sheer number of various nooks and crannies found in the average royal castle were extremely annoying.

"I was wrong," Lawton finally admitted somewhere in the depths of the fifth floor alternate study. "No gossip could possibly be worth this much exercise. I'm going back to drinking myself to death."

"That might be . . . wait." Jon stopped. "There it is, under the desk. I can still hear the occasional sniffle." Waving Lawton into silence, Jon placed his hands on the top of the desk and leaned over, almost but not quite able to see the space beneath. "May I ask who's hiding under there?"

"A lost soul," came the response in a decidedly male voice. A decidedly *familiar* male voice. "Wandering without direction, goals, or the power of positive . . ." There was a pause. "I don't quite remember that bit, but it's something I definitely don't have. Now please go away."

After a long moment of silence, broken only by the sound of fresh sniffling from under the desk, Jon slowly turned to look at Lawton. "Please tell me that didn't sound like my brother."

Lawton's eyes were wide. "If you feel a comforting lie is really what you need right now, then of course."

Jon closed his eyes briefly. "That's what I thought." Straightening, Jon walked around the desk and reached a hand into the shadowy area beneath. Grabbing the closest convenient bit of what felt like Rupert, he pulled without being too concerned about the possible side effects.

"I say, Jon, what are you—" Rupert's head accidentally slammed against the underside of the desk, and any more protests were cut off in a moan of pain as he was dragged out and into the light. Disheveled and completely filthy, Rupert gingerly rubbed the top of his head as Jon stepped back with a glare. "Ow, ow, ow. And just in case you didn't hear me the first time, ow."

"You'll live," Jon snapped, folding his arms across his chest. "I know I'm going to regret asking this, but what in the *world* is going on here?"

Rupert sniffled again, peering up at his brother. "You could have just *asked* me to come out, you know. It would have been a *goal*

I could have set on the way to enli . . . inli . . . the light thing that philosophers get so excited about."

Jon counted slowly to ten before letting himself speak again. "Rupert, I'm serious."

"So am I," Rupert said sadly, pulling a handkerchief from the wreckage of what had been his second-best hunting outfit. "I'm searching for my inner child. It wasn't in the gardens or the old toy room, and I've forgotten where that seamstress's room was." He blew his nose, then glanced up at Jon again. "Have you seen it anywhere? My inner child, I mean—I think the seamstress quit years ago. I'm not sure what all the fuss is about, but apparently finding it is very important."

Jon just looked at him, completely confused. "Have you been drinking the gardener's special onion liqueur again? I keep telling you, I've seen half a cup of the stuff make giants get tipsy."

"I *know* that." Rupert rolled his eyes, looking disgusted. "Besides, I've decided to give up drinking entirely. It was a . . . a . . . ." He hesitated again, looking up at Jon. "It's that word that means holding back too hard. People use it to talk about underwear sometimes."

"Repressive?" Lawton chimed in helpfully, clearly fighting hard not to laugh. Unfortunately, Jon had absolutely no time at the moment to think up a suitable retribution.

"That's it! A repressive tool used to trap me into an unhealthy situation. There was something else in there about this thing called an id, too." Rupert's brow furrowed. "I really didn't understand that bit."

Keeping a death grip on his patience, Jon crouched down in front of Rupert and took a hold of Rupert's shoulders. "If you do not start making sense this *instant*," he told his older brother very solemnly, "I will tell Father you've heard the call and want to devote the rest of your life to becoming a priest." A pause. "A desperately impoverished priest, who has to spend all his time wearing scratchy robes, doing heavy lifting, and giving food away to poor, dirty people."

Rupert considered this for a few moments. "The book really didn't mention anything about scratchy robes or poor, dirty people, but it would give me time to think about when it was I made the wrong turn on my life track." He sighed, resigning himself to his fate. "Is there someplace where I could be a priest without the scratchy robes or the heavy lifting? I'm not sure what else a priest does, but I might be willing to try it."

Okay, now Jon was starting to get nervous. "Rupert," he said carefully, getting to his feet just long enough to drop into a nearby desk chair. "Please explain to me, slowly and clearly, what started all this. Don't leave anything out."

"Well, there was this really great tavern, and about a week ago some of the lords and I were drinking and talking the barmaids into sitting on our laps." Rupert's eyes got distant as he went back into the memory. "The next morning I woke up in the alleyway behind the bar with my trousers in the shape of an unusual hat."

Lawton snorted in amusement, but Jon couldn't help a quick stab of retroactive panic. He'd have to start sending guardsmen with his brother everywhere, just to be able to sleep at night.

Rupert, seemingly unaware of either reaction, moved on with the story. "And it was that moment, as I tried to remember what day it was and where I could find a servant to help me readjust my pants, that I realized there was something missing in my life. The drinking and wenching and throwing money at people just . . . just wasn't as fun as it used to be."

"What happened next?" Jon asked.

Rupert blinked, returning to the current reality. "I found a book."

Jon's eyes narrowed in disbelief. "You've never cared about books before. What made you . . ." His voice trailed off as memory slammed him between the eyes. "A book?"

They've found him in the library . . . by the books . . . I don't know what could have happened to him . . .

Foreshadowing would be considerably more useful, Jon thought, if people could learn to recognize it before the foreshadowed problem actually became an issue.

"It was gigantic, chock-full of these immensely long and pointless words that I couldn't even begin to understand. I thought at first that I'd just ignore it like usual, or find you and ask you to make sense of them for me, but after a while they just started— I don't know—speaking to me." Rupert looked up at Jon, very serious. "Not really, of course, but I liked it. Do you think there's another book somewhere that has a step-by-step guide about how to actually do all of it?"

Jon dropped his head back to stare up at the ceiling, drained of all the energy necessary to keep it upright. Just when he thought he knew how to anticipate anything that could possibly go wrong. "Seriously, Rupert, I couldn't tell you." He rubbed a hand across his eyes. "You'll have to find someone else to ask."

Tomorrow night was definitely too far away.

At the sound of the door creaking open Jon dragged himself upright, just in time to see a thin, graying head with a casual-wear crown perched rather haphazardly on top. The man tensed when he saw how occupied the room was.

"Welcome, Your Majesty," Lawton said casually, moving aside

a little in case he had to make room for the king. "Apparently, we're throwing a party."

The king surveyed the three of them with weary resignation, then eyed his elder son as if afraid the prince was going to suddenly leap up and bite somebody. Instead, Rupert merely lifted his chin and scooted around so he faced as far away from his father as he could possibly get, the exact same way he'd pouted when he was eight and the cook had refused to allow him to recreate a jousting match in the kitchen.

The king looked like he wanted to bolt. When he turned to look at his youngest son, the question clear in his eyes, Jon sighed. "Don't worry. I won't make you try to sort any of it out." When the king sagged a little, relieved, Jon pointed behind him. "If I remember correctly, Father, your current study is downstairs. Three wings over and two doors to the right."

The king nodded, clearly ready to slip out much more quietly than he'd slipped in. Before he could completely escape, however, Jon lifted a hand to show he wasn't quite finished. "And I promise not to give Mother the same set of directions . . ."

The king froze.

". . . if you convince Madame Stewart to throw one more fancy dress ball within the next two weeks." Jon recognized he was being cruel—there had been plenty of times when *he'd* been tempted to spend the day hiding from his mother—but it was clear Rupert wasn't going to be much help.

The king hesitated a moment, horrified, then gave a single resigned sigh. A second later, he nodded.

Jon pushed himself to his feet. "You should probably change studies again, though, within the next week or so. I think she's started bribing the maids."

The king nodded again, mouthing a silent "thank you" to Jon. Then, after a long hesitation, he glanced back down at Rupert. "He hasn't said anything about a 'happy place' yet, has he?"

Jon shook his head. "Not yet."

"Good." Then he was gone.

After the king left, Rupert scooted back around to face Jon. "We're really not very good at opening the lines of communication in this family, are we?"

Lawton, showing unusual sensitivity to Jon's needs, walked over and smacked Rupert upside the head.

SEVEN

Impossibilities

"Of all the ridiculous . . ." Making a frustrated noise at the transparent, squishy sock-thing that now covered her foot, Kate waved her wand and turned it back into the sensible slip-on she'd worn into work this morning. Turning back to her magic mirror, she double-checked that, yes, she had followed the spell as it was written. Either the original Fairy Godmother had mistyped when she'd added it to the system, or Research and Development was thinking of extremely strange things to do with their days off.

Moving on to the next spell, Kate glared, as if she could intimidate it into doing what she wanted. Then, preparing herself for the worst, she carefully rotated the wand three times counterclockwise before bouncing it twice. The magic swirled, starting the transformation.

"Hey, wha—"

Kate flipped the mirror facedown as she shoved both wand and transforming shoe under the conference table. She looked up, however, only to see Ned's sheepish expression as he held up his brown lunch bag.

"Sorry," he said, adjusting the very large Fairy Godmothers, Inc. manual he'd tucked under his other arm. There was no need for the apology, as she'd been the one to tell him about the room in the first place, but over the last several months she'd realized that it was his default reaction. "It's the only place I can eat where Bubbles never seems to find me."

Kate sighed, pulling her wand out from under the table and setting it beside the mirror. "Why do you think I'm here?" Turning the mirror upright again, she gestured for Ned to sit down. "Office rumor has it that one of the managers before Bubbles used to meet the secretaries back here, and hired someone to put a spell on the room so his wife wouldn't catch them. About half the staff know the secret by now, but we all have a vested interest in making sure none of the current management team find out."

Ned's eyes circled the room, a dreamy expression on his face. "Now *that's* some magic I'd like to get my hands on," he said, dropping into a chair and setting both his sack and book on the table in front of him. He gestured toward the laptop as he pulled out a sandwich. "Doing some research for an assignment?"

"Yeah, I—" Jerking upright as she realized she'd never checked on her latest attempt at an artificial glass slipper, Kate stuck her head under the table. Confirming that the spell had, indeed, gone wrong once again, she straightened with a muttered insult about systems administrators. Ned, thankfully, never minded when she said things she shouldn't. "Wouldn't know a glass slipper if they fell down a set of stairs in one . . ."

Eyes wide, Ned stared at Kate and then ducked his head under the table to look at Kate's shoe. When he lifted his head again, there was a confused expression on his face. "When did the company get a spell for furry slippers? Are they a new part of the Sleeping Beauty Special or something?"

"No—they're stuck in the middle of the glass slipper section of the spell database." She shook her head. "Though how someone could get fur and glass confused is completely beyond me."

"You have to work with glass slippers on this one? Ouch." Ned took a bite of his sandwich, discreetly elbowing the manual a little further out of the way from himself. "The rest of it's got to be going better, though. Right?"

Kate rubbed a hand across her eyes, attention fleeing a million miles away. Jon . . . there was no way he was going to be there tomorrow night. He'd forget, or he'd get too busy, which meant there was absolutely no reason for her to be suddenly thinking about his smile. Or his deep, steady gray eyes. Or working out what she might possibly say on the off chance that he *was* standing there.

"Kate?"

Yanking her brain back to reality, she looked up and shot Ned a tired smile. "Sorry—I was up kind of late last night. As for the rest of the case . . ." She smiled a little more at the sympathetic expression on Ned's face. "Let's just say it's been interesting."

He nodded in understanding. "Interesting as in 'steam would come out of Bubbles' ears if she ever found out about it'?"

That was as good a way as any to describe it. "Oh, once I got past the man-eating dog it was really more strange than bad. As long as I keep Rellie away from the sparkles and don't try to follow her logic too closely, she's actually an okay person to be around."

Kate paused as a thought hit her. "Actually, she'd probably really like it if she could wear furry slippers to the ball."

Ned's eyebrows raised a little in interest. "Really?"

"Really." Kate eyed the younger man's sandwich, realizing absently that she hadn't eaten lunch herself yet. Hopefully, the vending machines were slightly less scary than they had been last week. "Very fond of rabbits, that girl."

Ned thought about it for a moment. "I like rabbits."

Hearing something dangerous in the younger man's voice, Kate turned her attention back to Ned. "Ned," she said carefully. "It's really not a good idea to go there."

Ned looked up quickly, appearing defensive enough for Kate to know she hadn't totally missed the target. She knew he sometimes snuck a peek at her files, and Rellie's had been sitting out on her desk this morning. "I didn't say anything!"

"I know," Kate said kindly. "I'm just reminding you that there's still a Prince Charming in her immediate future."

"I know, I know," Ned muttered, slouching a little in his chair as he took another bite of his sandwich. "It's not like I can dance, anyway."

Dancing was another thing Kate was having a hard time not thinking about. There was the chance, of course, that Jon could miraculously produce the palace ball that she so desperately needed, but it seemed far more likely that she and Rellie would end up having to crash one of those fancy dress dinners. Maybe Rellie could make her entrance about the same time as the flaming dessert.

Kate shook her head, cutting the picture off. She'd come up with something, then rewrite it into a much more approved version when it came time to put the report together. After this long as a Fairy Godmother, she'd gotten pretty good at it.

Still, it was probably a good idea to move on to a safer topic. "So," she said deliberately, waiting until Ned looked up again. "How has your morning been?"

Ned sighed, but at least the moroseness had left his face. "The employee complaints folder is crammed full *again*, mostly with stuff about company uniforms, but the black hole Bubbles usually dumps them into has broken down for the second time this week. Which means, of course, that she made me sort through them while I was waiting for the repairman." He made a face. "Then, after it was fixed, she just dumped them into the black hole anyway."

Kate was sympathetic. She remembered her own early days at the company and wished she could do more to help him out. As it was, a sympathetic ear and a few tricks like the secret conference room were all she had to offer. "It'll be easier when things aren't quite so busy. Then I, or one of the other Fairy Godmothers, will have enough time to let you actually come out and shadow us like you're supposed to, and you'll be far enough away from Bubbles she won't be able to give you quite so much busy work."

"That would be nice." Still, Ned sighed again. "At least she hasn't hunted down some talking mice for me to babys—"

Before he could finish the sentence the conference room door swung open, making them both jump and Kate grab for her mirror. When the Fairy Godmother on the other side turned out to be Chloe rather than Bubbles, both Kate and Ned relaxed a little.

Until, of course, they heard what she had to say. "They've finally brought Thea in," she whispered, looking slightly nauseated. "She's . . . It's . . ." She stopped, shaking her head. "I can't say it. You just have to come see." Then she ducked out of the room.

Ned's eyes widened as he and Kate quickly gathered their things and stood. "What happened to Thea?"

Kate tried to deny the dread that was already working its way down to the pit of her stomach. "Word is that she had her client's final ball scheduled for last night, but she didn't show up to work this morning," she said quietly. "Her client called the office to complain about an hour ago."

Ned hesitated, eyes absolutely huge by this point. "What's going to happen to her?"

Kate's brow lowered. "I have no idea." She started to lead the way out, when Ned stopped her with a hand on her arm.

"Uh, Kate?"

She glanced back at him, half an ear listening for anything she could hear from the main office. "What?"

He pointed down, a mildly apologetic expression on his face. "Your shoe."

"My . . . Oh, no." Muttering insults at herself for not taking care of it earlier, Kate stepped back and let Ned go ahead of her before pointing her wand at the offending fur slipper. The right wave started its transformation back to her own, much more familiar shoe, and she stayed behind a few seconds to let it finish before pushing the door open and stepping into the hallway.

Of course, inappropriate footwear was clearly going to be the least of her worries over the next few minutes.

When Kate caught sight of the crowd forming around the tightly closed doorway to Bubbles' office, her mind immediately started coming up with worst-case scenarios. Everyone was utterly silent; the crowd's attention focused on one of the Fairy Godmother desks. Thea was short enough that several rows of heads blocked whatever she was doing, but Kate could hear her singing softly to herself.

After a moment, Kate realized she was hearing a love song.

Horrified, she tapped Glenda on the shoulder. One of the most experienced Fairy Godmothers in the office, Glenda had taken Kate under her wing when she was first starting out. "What happened to her?" Kate whispered, terribly afraid she already knew. They all made macabre jokes about the variety of disasters that could happen if something went wrong with the True Love, and Kate knew that one or two of the other Fairy Godmothers disliked it enough to lie about it on their reports the same way she did. But this . . .

When Glenda turned to look at Kate, the shock and pity were evident in her eyes. "The poor girl," she whispered, helplessly shaking her head. "The poor, poor girl."

Kate's heart sank. "Oh, no."

Glenda nodded. "Her client insisted that her skirt be even wider than the princess's, then promptly proceeded to knock over the prince and practically everyone else at the ball with it. At one point Thea didn't get out of the way fast enough, and when she fell against the chair her True Love vial must have cracked and spilled onto the seat. She didn't notice, and when she set her hand down in the same spot while trying to get up . . ."

Before the sentence was finished Kate started pushing her way through the crowd, needing to see the full extent of the damage for herself. True Love was supposed to be used only in the tiniest amounts, small enough that the bottles came equipped with spray nozzles to minimize the dosage. The moment the victims' hands touched and their eyes got soft and dreamy, the lid went back on and the potion wasn't used again.

Here, though . . .

Thea was huddled on the edge of one of the desks, tears streaming down her cheeks and arms wrapped tightly around an elaborately coiled metal chair. The song, thankfully, had faded into humming, wavering and weak like someone trying desperately to comfort herself. Her wings, which were office-issued since she hadn't been born with a set of her own, tilted awkwardly as if she'd slept in them the night before.

In her eyes, total panic glinted just beneath the swamp of romantic fog.

Kate closed her eyes, feeling the anger she usually tried so hard to hold back rise up in her throat. The True Love hanging on the company-issued chain around her neck burned like a tiny brand—employees always had to have theirs on, in case a manager noticed—and for a moment she hated herself and everyone around her for being helpless . She moved forward again, determined to do what little she could and at least get the girl someplace more private.

The sudden sound of a door slamming open cut through the crowd, and heads turned to see Bubbles grimly stalking out of her office. As she stormed by, Kate caught sight of a fabric star pinched between two of her fingers. Bubbles peeled off the paper backing and jammed the star onto the end of her wand, all the while continuing to walk through the crush of people as if none of them were there. Obligingly, they stepped aside to let her through, and within moments Bubbles was standing in front of the huddled Thea. She grabbed the girl by the chin, jerking her head up and over so the side of her neck was exposed. With her other hand, Bubbles shook the wand until a fine pink mist formed around the star, then slapped it against the bare skin on the side of Thea's neck.

For a small eternity, nothing happened.

Then, finally, the clarity returned to Thea's eyes. She flung the chair as far away from her as she could, smashing it into a desk and sending several folders and a stack of paperwork flying. She proceeded to drop to her knees on the floor and burst into tears. One or two of the other Fairy Godmothers tensed, warily eyeing Bubbles as they tried to decide whether or not to rush to Thea's side to offer comfort.

Bubbles, for her part, simply looked down at Thea with a stony expression. "You're fired," she said flatly, then lifted her head to lock gazes, one by one, with each and every Fairy Godmother she could see. "If you people aren't competent enough to do the job that the company has put so much time and money into training you to do, leave now. I will *not* tolerate any more embarrassment."

She turned on her heel and stalked back to her office, yanking the star off her wand and crumpling it into a ball on the way. Only when the door slammed shut did everyone finally start to move, heading either toward the still-crying Thea or far enough away to discuss the episode in peace.

Before Kate could go anywhere, she felt a hand grab her arm. She turned around to find Ned's panicked eyes staring back into hers, his grip tightening just a little more than was comfortable. "Kate?" he asked hesitantly, a single word that Kate knew contained several remarkably hard-to-answer questions.

She gently put her other hand on top of his, searching for something comforting to say that wouldn't sound like a complete lie. Nothing came, however, and all she could do was wish there was a big enough difference in their ages to make it safe for her to hug him. "Try not to think about it," she told Ned quietly, giving his hand a quick squeeze. "Most of the time people are so cheerfully dazed they don't even notice that something made them that way."

"*I would notice.*" Desperation gave Ned's words a surprising amount of volume, and Kate looked around to make sure they hadn't caught anyone's attention before pulling him into a relatively private corner.

"Take a deep breath," Kate ordered, waiting until he had done so before continuing. "I didn't bring it up before now because you haven't even been assigned any cases yet, but you can do your job as a Fairy Godmother without ever having to use it." Her voice was low enough no one else could overhear, and she kept a steadying grip on the hand that was holding her arm. "All you have to do is doctor your reports and make sure you get rid of the True Love you're supposed to have used, and neither Bubbles nor anyone else will ever know that you're not continuing on exactly like you were trained to do."

"But I'll still have to carry it around, and what about if I'm out with another Fairy Godmother and they're using it?"

She kept her voice as calm and even as possible, knowing any tension or anger he saw in her would only make him more upset. "There are other Fairy Godmothers who don't use it. If you're assigned to shadow one who does, stay far away from them while they're giving the client the dose. And when you finally have to start wearing your own vial, I'm sure we can find some way of wrapping padding around the outside so there's no chance of it breaking like Thea's did."

Practicality might not have been quite as good as comfort, but at the moment it was all she had. Still, the words were enough to help Ned relax a little. His grip on her arm eased to the point that Kate could carefully pry his fingers off without injuring either of them, but the fear continued to linger in his eyes. "I really think I'm going to worry anyway," he said, glancing back to where Thea had been. "Accidents happen all the time, Kate, especially to people like me."

"At least Bubbles seems to have an antidote." One that she seemed very familiar with using, which somehow made the whole thing that much worse. No one was ever that prepared for something unless it kept happening.

Ned seemed relieved by the reminder. "How many of those star patches do you think she has?"

Kate rubbed a hand across her stomach, wishing she had the magic needed to settle it. She suspected it was going to take her a long time to forget this, no matter how much she wanted to. "Hopefully, more than enough for everyone."

EIGHT

Moving Along

Thursday, naturally, took a small eternity to get through. Had the ambassador's rambling stretch the meeting out for yet another five minutes, Jon was ready to hit the man over the head with a piece of statuary and bury him behind the palace.

As it was, Jon was still a full twenty-five minutes later than he should have been. He finally arrived outside Rellie's house, breathing harder than was dignified, barely biting back frustration at himself and the universe in general. Kate was no longer at the meeting place they'd decided on, but there was a faint, reassuring glow coming from one of the back windows suggesting she hadn't yet wrapped up her work for the evening.

Steeling himself to deliver whatever apologies Kate felt were necessary before she'd forgive him, Jon climbed to the top of the decorative wall in the backyard. Opening the bag he'd brought with him, he carefully dropped down to the other side and took a few steps toward the house. When he heard the expected warning growl, he dumped the leftover chicken he'd brought on the ground and headed quickly toward the backdoor in the desperate hope that they'd remember to leave it unlocked for him.

The dog wouldn't eat forever, after all, and Jon didn't think he could handle Kate having to rescue him twice.

Thankfully, the door *was* unlocked and he made it inside with no further rescuing required. Jon began working out his introductory apology as he crept through the darkened kitchen toward the voices coming from behind the cloth-covered door. If he started out too dramatically she wouldn't believe a word he said, but if he were too nonchalant she'd think being here on time hadn't mattered to him.

As he knocked into a broom and sent it crashing to the floor, it became painfully clear that sneaking through the dark was not the best place for deep thought.

Jon went perfectly still as a pale hand reached out to yank the rag curtain aside, revealing Rellie fully decked out in her ball gown. At the sight of him, her huge violet eyes widened in satisfaction. "Mr. Assistant Guy is here!" she announced, loudly enough Jon winced. She turned to look back into her room, since Kate had apparently decided Jon's belated arrival wasn't worth getting up. Dammit, he knew he should have brought flowers.

At least he had something else to offer. "Yes, Mr. Assistant Guy is here," he announced. "And as promised, plans are being made for a fancy dress ball even as we speak. I'll make sure you get the details as soon as I have them." When there was no response from Kate, it took effort to keep his voice cheerful. "Now, I seem to remember someone saying something about dance lessons?"

"Me!" Rellie raised her hand. "I *told* Kate you were going to show up. Can we start now, so I can see how the skirt gets all swirly when we spin around?"

Only silence followed the question, too complete not to be intentional. Jon shoved his hands in his pockets, fighting off the threads of panic that were starting to worm their way through his stomach. She couldn't be *that* angry, could she? Being late was a regular risk of juggling a day full of meetings and reports, and he'd thought that of all people she would be the one to understand that. If she couldn't—

Kate appeared in the doorway, staring at him over the top of Rellie's head with something close to shock in her eyes. She opened her mouth, looking like she was about to say something, but after another moment of silence snapped it shut and went right back to staring at him.

Confused, Jon mentally reviewed the last ten minutes for anything he'd done that could have possibly put that expression on her face. "I didn't think the outfit was that bad." He kept his voice as light as possible, hoping to at least lessen some of the awkwardness. "If you'd like, I can go home and change before coming back."

Rellie turned back to him. "That's just being silly. If you went home, you'd be even *later* than you already are, and then we wouldn't have any time to do any dancing at all!"

Jon's attention stayed on Kate. She had blinked at the sound of his voice; the stunned look finally starting to fade out of her eyes as she took a deep breath. "You look . . . you look just fine," she said. As she relaxed, the corners of her mouth curled upward into a small smile. Jon felt something in his own chest ease at the sight as he smiled back. "Are you sure you're up for dancing lessons, though?"

Jon's grin widened as he swept both women the courtliest bow Lawton had ever shown him. "Madame and milady, nothing would please me more than to lead two such fetching creatures around the nearest impromptu dance floor." When he glanced up, Rellie had her arms folded across her chest, staring at him like he was nuts. Behind her, Kate was miming applause and looking like she was trying not to laugh.

Jon's mood shot up another few notches.

Straightening, he followed Rellie into her sleeping area, gently touching Kate's arm as soon as he was close enough. "I'm sorry I'm so late," he murmured. "The ambassador wanted to cram in one more meeting before he left tomorrow morning, then decided that I had to hear the entire history of not only his country but also *every* person he's ever met."

Kate shook her head. "It's okay," she said quickly, wincing at something. She hesitated, then laid a hand against his upper arm. "Are you sure you have time to do this? I mean, I'm at least getting paid to be here, but it sounds like right now is your first chance to take a break after a day full of meetings."

Jon studied her expression, doing his best to gauge exactly what Kate was trying to say. When he saw her face start to close off, he lifted her hand off his arm and brought it to his lips for a kiss. "I am taking a break," he said, watching her eyes widen a little at the touch. "Though I will admit to fantasizing about having you keep me company through a few of those meetings."

A second later the smile he'd been looking for was back on her face. "If you can teach Rellie how to dance without getting yourself killed, I'll sit with you through however many meetings you want." When he raised an eyebrow in question, her smile widened. "Rellie was showing me a few of her dance moves before you—"

Kate abandoned the rest of her sentence to grab his hand and yank him forward, moving him quickly enough only his ear was grazed by the wildly swinging arm that came twirling by. Faintly alarmed, Jon turned to see Rellie spinning madly around the tiny room, head thrown back and arms outstretched in total disregard of anything that might be in the way.

"Rellie." When that seemed to have no effect, Kate increased her volume. "Rellie!"

Finally registering that someone was calling her name, Rellie stopped, dropping her arms to her sides as she looked at Jon and Kate with a brightly expectant expression. When she noticed Kate looking at her sternly, she scowled right back in frustration. "You guys were taking *forever*," she insisted, lowering her voice only when Kate jabbed a finger upward where Rellie's stepfamily presumably slept. Apparently, they'd had this conversation already. "I had to get started without you."

Jon squeezed Kate's hand once before stepping away from her. He had to get through this before he had a chance to talk Kate into a few lessons. "Well, now we're *all* ready to get started." He rubbed his hands together, taking a quick survey of the room he had to work with. Kate moved to sit on the bed and free up as much floor space as possible. "I thought we should begin with a basic version of the waltz," he told Rellie. "It's one of the easier dances, and if you alter the timing a little it'll work with pretty much anything the palace musicians know how to play."

"Okay." The girl shrugged, then held her arms out to Jon. "Teach me."

Grateful he'd never been responsible for giving Rupert any

complicated lessons, Jon moved until they were at the appropriate dancing distance (close enough to get into position, but far enough Jon wasn't at risk of being knocked over by Rellie's skirt). Rellie still didn't move, apparently confident that someone else would continue to know what needed to be done, so Jon was left to place Rellie's left hand on his shoulder, taking her right hand in his. "This is the proper dance position," he explained, deliberately making eye contact with Rellie in the hopes of getting her a little more involved in the proceedings. "Pretty much any time you step out onto a dance floor, this is the way you and your partner are going to be starting out."

Rellie wrinkled her forehead. "But what if I don't want to hold the guy's hand?"

"You only have to worry about holding Prince Rupert's hand," Kate contributed from her perch on the bed. After a moment of consideration, she turned to Jon. "Is there anything particularly wrong with Prince Rupert's hands? Sweatiness? Too strong a grip?"

"Well, having never actually held Rupert's hand, I can't really say for certain how pleasant the experience is." Jon raised an eyebrow at Kate, who simply grinned in response. "But I have seen him dance with several women, and none of them seemed to have minded."

Rellie nodded, satisfied with the answer. "Works for me. So, what do we do next?"

"Next," Jon explained patiently, "you take a step back with your left foot."

Rellie started to take a step back, then stopped. "Wait a minute." She looked up at Jon. "Which one is my left foot?"

Jon took a deep breath, then shook their joined hands. "The one on this side." Apparently, he'd have to wrap up this particular portion of the evening earlier than he'd expected if he wanted any time with Kate.

Rellie took the step back, still looking down as if she could see through her layers of skirt. "Like that?"

"Yes." Jon took the corresponding step forward. "Now use your other foot to take one step back and to the right."

Rellie looked back at him with skepticism. "If I step back *and* to the right, that's two steps."

"Not if you do it like this." Jon demonstrated the step and waited while Rellie paced back in the same general direction. He followed through with his portion of the steps, then told Rellie to move her feet together.

Rellie raised her eyebrow. "This sounds a lot more like just walking around the floor than it does dancing." There was a pause. "Are you sure you're doing this right?"

Jon considered this for a moment before making an executive decision. It was a wise man who knew when to cut his losses, and it wasn't like anyone else was going to even notice. "You're barefoot, right?" When she nodded, he moved them both back to the dance's first position. "Step on my feet."

Rellie looked at him like he'd lost his mind. "I thought that was something you *weren't* supposed to do when you were dancing with somebody."

"It's okay as long as you do it carefully and they give you permission." Though the response didn't seem to comfort her at all, she climbed onto his feet and Jon tightened his grip around her waist to keep her from falling. "Now, hold on."

Slowly, he started to dance.

Even at a nice sedate speed, the first turn made Rellie shriek a little and cling to him as if he were dangling her over a cliff. After a few minutes, panic transformed into wide-eyed delight. "Look, Kate!" Rellie called out as Jon swept past, turning her head around as far as it would go to get a better look at her Fairy Godmother. "I'm dancing!" Kate smiled at her, clearly pleased for the girl. "And you're doing a wonderful job at it."

"Unfortunately, it does end up being a little harder than this," Jon interjected, already wondering if he could talk Rupert into simply letting Rellie stand on his feet like this at the actual ball. "But we can worry about that another night. I just wanted you to get a feel of what dancing can be like after a little practice."

Rellie grinned up at him as they started into another time around. "Okay, so maybe you do know how to do this whole dancing thing." Then, without warning, she leapt backward off Jon's feet and began moving around the floor on her own. Even though Jon couldn't see her feet, it was clear Rellie's moves still had miles to go before it could be called a waltz. Thankfully, it was also considerably closer to actual dancing than the earlier wild spinning.

Jon watched her a moment, surprised to find himself a little proud of her. When his eyes met Kate's, they grinned at each other, sharing the moment. As soon as Rellie was sufficiently distracted, he held a hand out to Kate. "Your turn, milady." He was careful not to let the words become a question, which would have been more gentlemanly. It would also have given her the chance to say no.

She froze, caught completely off guard despite Jon's definite memory of having discussed this previously. "You . . . I thought . . ." She stopped, eyes sliding away from his. "You know what? Let's not worry about that." Her voice was artificially light. "There's not a lot of call for dancing Fairy Godmothers. We should be focusing on Rellie."

At this, Rellie halted mid-twirl, staring at Kate with a deeply affronted expression. "You can't say no to dancing lessons! You get to spin around and make your skirt all swishy, and Mr. Assistant Guy is just starting to get good at his part."

Jon wisely restrained any response and merely attempted to look dignified. If Rellie felt the need to help him with his case, he wasn't about to argue.

"You should be saying thank you to Jon for being here to give *you* dancing lessons," Kate chided Rellie, deliberately keeping her eyes on her rather than Jon. "He's a very busy man, and I'm certainly not capable of helping you with that part of the evening."

"Which is why," Jon interjected smoothly, watching Kate go still, "you should come over here and let me give you your first dance lesson."

Slowly, she turned to look at him, their eyes locking for a few seconds. Then, she pushed herself to her feet and walked over to him. Taking the hand he held out, she hesitated briefly before putting her other hand on his shoulder. "I'm not standing on your feet," she said quickly, a hint of warning in her voice. "I'd be staring over the top of your head as we danced."

It occurred to Jon that he'd be receiving an excellent view either way, but restrained himself to a grin as he tightened his arm around Kate's waist and pulled her considerably closer than he had Rellie. "Whatever you feel comfortable with." He flattened his hand against the curve of her lower back, keeping her in place.

Kate tightened her grip on Jon's shoulder. "So." The word had a definite breathy edge to it. "Back with my left foot, then back and to the right with my other foot?"

"Exactly." Together they followed through with the first two steps, then along the rest of the basic box step. When their feet moved together for the last time, he smiled at her. "Keep doing that until the song's over, and you pretty much have a waltz."

Kate's brow lowered. "But . . ."

"But nothing. We're simply moving on to the next phase of the lesson." He rubbed her back in small circles, trying to ease some of the tension out of her body. "Which is for you to relax."

She opened her mouth, then closed it and narrowed her eyes at him. "I need to pay attention to the steps so I can make sure I'm doing them correctly. I don't want to end up crushing your toes."

"You've already shown that you know the steps beautifully, and the only way you could possibly crush my toes is by driving a carriage over them." He stared into her silvery-green eyes, wishing he could read the emotions swirling just below the surface. He wanted her to smile at him again, wanted to see that sparkle of light come back. "And I would be more than happy to have them stepped on by such a beautiful, intelligent woman."

She blushed slightly, eyes darting away from his again. "Let's see if you still feel that way after you've had them flattened for the fifth time in as many minutes."

"Kate." Jon attempted to keep his voice even, but the surprise in her eyes suggested he hadn't quite managed it. He exhaled slowly, voice gentle as he tightened his fingers around hers. "Trust me." She squeezed his hand back, making his chest tighten. "Trust yourself, and trust me."

Kate stared at him for a long moment, tension slowly seeping out of her. "That doesn't sound like a traditional part of a waltz lesson," she said softly, the corners of her mouth curving upward.

"I'll admit, I have added a few flourishes."

Before Kate could respond, Rellie slapped a hand on both of their arms, shocking them back into reality. "You guys aren't going to get any dancing done just standing there!" She gave them a stern look before twirling off again in example. "Move, you two! Move!"

Grinning at each other, Jon and Kate obliged.

NINE

Family Bonding

The secretary barely looked up when Kate teleported into the executive office the following morning, waiting a few minutes before finally acknowledging her presence with a bored expression. "Do you have an appointment?"

Holding both hands and the folder behind her back, Kate reminded herself one more time that the only way to get through this was stubborn patience. It had taken fifteen minutes of not-quite-arguing with Bubbles to even get here, since only supervisors' wands could connect to any of the executive or director offices. Despite her earlier threat, it seemed Bubbles was only interested in Kate talking to upper management when she could use it as a punishment. "I'm the Fairy Godmother assigned to the case Director Carlson requested. I need to get his approval on a small change that's been made to the original package."

After a brief, appraising look, the secretary made a dismissive gesture in the general direction of the waiting area. "Director Carlson has an extremely busy schedule." Without even glancing at the phone, she returned her attention to the magazine she'd been reading. "I'll see if he's available."

Kate didn't bother to respond, having no doubt this was where the secretary was prepared to end it. Clearly, she was going to have to find her own way in. She scanned the room to see how likely she was to get past the front desk, and whether or not there were any hulking security guards who might frown on her trying to sneak into the back offices. When she caught sight of a bit of waxed paper sticking out from the edge of the secretary's garbage can, she stopped and looked at it more closely. A faint streak of something like white icing lined one edge.

Encouraged, Kate turned back to the secretary. "How do you feel about bribes?" she asked brightly, the better to pretend she was joking should the woman not go for it. "Theoretically, of course."

The secretary's head lifted with a speed that would have surprised anyone who had been watching her the last few minutes. "What, theoretically speaking, did you have in mind?"

Making sure the smirk didn't show up on her face, Kate held up a single finger. "One bakery item from Sprat's, your choice, paid for and delivered to your desk sometime tomorrow."

"I do love their Poisoned Apple Tarts." The secretary pondered for a moment, fingernails tapping out a drum roll against her desk. "But how do I know you'll deliver?"

Kate shrugged, trying to look as honest as someone offering a bribe could manage. "I'm too smart to cheat the person who has access to my pay records."

"You have a point." Decision seemingly made, the secretary stood and led Kate toward one of the offices. "Carlson's been in for more than an hour. From the crashes I've been hearing, it sounds like he's working on his putting game." Stopping at a door with a brass plaque slightly bigger than all the others, she pushed it open. "Mr. Carlson, your ten o'clock appointment is here."

The pale blond, slightly pudgy man who had been staring at the shattered remnants of a framed picture turned around with a confused expression. As he moved, his putter swung out to knock over an empty garbage can. "I don't remember you saying anything about a ten o'clock appointment."

"I try not to worry you in advance, sir," the secretary replied, quickly slipping out of the room before any further explanation had to be provided.

In the absence of his normal source of information, the man's attention moved over to Kate, who felt a little shock of surprise when she noticed the man's violet eyes—they were only a shade or two paler than Rellie's. And there was something about the shape of his mouth . . . "You don't happen to know anything about golf, do you?" he asked, already moving back to his abandoned golf ball. "I bought a ball enchanted for super distance, but when I tried a practice hit it buried itself a couple of inches into the wall."

Kate took a deep breath, giving herself a quick mental jolt. Now was *not* the time to get involved in Rellie's secret family history, especially with as little time as she had to pull this off. "Unfortunately, I don't. What I actually needed to speak to you about is the Fairy Godmothers, Inc. package you purchased." The man stopped, confused again, and Kate couldn't keep her voice from sharpening a little. "For Cinderella? The girl who lives with her stepmother and two stepsisters on Candlewick Lane?"

A flash of guilt crossed the man's face. "You don't have to get snippy about it—I've had a very busy week." He leaned down to pick up the ball, then looked back at Kate. "Nothing's gone wrong with that, has it?"

She watched him carefully for a moment before taking another deep breath. "The assignment is going fine. But there's been a slight scheduling delay with the fancy dress ball, and I need you to approve another week to finish putting together the package."

Jon had sounded so cheerful when he'd first told her about the ball, only to turn immediately apologetic when he'd gotten the mirror call later that night telling him about the delay. He'd seemed so upset that he hadn't made the *miracle* happen more quickly, which was totally delusional of him and surprisingly sweet at the same time. She'd had the insane urge to kiss him for it before good sense prevailed and pushed the thought away as soon as possible.

So far, she hadn't been able to stop a small, disobedient part of her brain from counting down the hours—five, plus thirty-two minutes—until she saw him again.

Carlson paused. "Everything's still according to plan, right? The first step was getting her an appropriately wicked stepfamily, and now she's got to get married off before she's too old. Once the wedding happens, I won't be responsible for her anymore." He smiled. "Then I can think about golfing full time."

Kate nodded, biting back a sharp comment he wouldn't understand or would get her kicked out of the office. "Everything is still going according to plan."

Carlson breathed a sigh of relief, setting the ball down on a gold-colored tee that looked like a permanent part of the floor. "Then do whatever you need to do. Just let me know when they have the wedding ceremony." He swung the club back, dramatically enough that Kate had to back up to avoid getting hit. He froze mid-swing and looked over with worry. "Do I have to sign anything?"

Pulling the appropriate sheet out of the folder, Kate kept one eye on the golf club as she moved close enough to hand Carlson the paper. "Along the bottom." After he signed and handed it back to her, she hesitated before shutting the paper back in the folder. "Director Carlson?" Though the golf ball had reclaimed his attention almost immediately after he'd set down the pen, Carlson did glance back up at the sound of his name. "Is there another paper I need to sign?"

Kate opened her mouth, a thousand completely unhelpful questions swirling around in her mind. She shook her head. More information would not make the truth sound any better. "No." She turned, heading for the door. "Good luck with your golf game."

The next crash came before the door closed behind her.

LATER THAT NIGHT found Kate in Rellie's room reading one more time over the coordinates Jon had given her. The spare room they were shooting for was five floors up on the southwest corner of the palace, and even if Jon wasn't there when they arrived he swore he'd only be a few minutes.

Beside her, Rellie was starting to look impatient. "This is to make sure you don't transport us into a wall or something, right?" The tone of her voice suggested the possibility of ending up in a wall struck her as far more interesting than standing there reading coordinates.

"There are safety precautions built into the transport spell to keep that from happening." Refolding the piece of paper and putting it back in her pocket, Kate lifted her free hand to move the wand in the sequence that would activate the transport spell. "Now, don't let go of my hand, or . . ." She paused, hunting for a threat the girl would find suitably persuasive.

Rellie looked up at her. "Or you'll poke me with your wand?"

Kate sighed as the magic began swirling around the wand. "Close enough." Then, murmuring the incantation, she sketched the outline of a doorway in the air. The wand left a glowing pathway, and once she connected the final corner light flooded the entire rectangle. If she squinted, Kate could just barely make out the room on the other side.

Rellie grabbed her hand. "No more double-checking. Let's do this."

A moment later they stepped through the glow and into a gently lit room. Kate hoped this was what the back rooms of palaces looked like and she hadn't just teleported into some duke's den by mistake. Rellie tightened her grip on Kate's hand, uncharacteristically silent in the face of a new experience.

As soon as her feet touched the ground, another hand shot out to steady her. As the magical light faded Kate found herself staring into Jon's relieved gray eyes. She couldn't stop herself from grinning at him, heart bobbing in her chest like a balloon, and he grinned back as Rellie let go with her usual wide-eyed, delighted expression. "That. Was. So. Cool!" The girl jumped to punctuate the last word, throwing her arms up in clear preparation for a victory dance. "Can we do that every—"

Careful to move in such a way that wouldn't dislodge Jon's arm at all, Kate put a finger to her lips and gestured for Rellie to dial her enthusiasm down several notches. "I know it is exciting, but we still have to be quiet. Jon is letting us use this room of the palace because there's more room here than at your stepfamily's house, but that doesn't mean we can bother the rest of the people who are here."

For a second Rellie looked like she was going to pout. "Wait a minute. If Jon's just a Fairy Godmother's assistant, how did he get us into the palace at all? And if you're in charge of him, why didn't you just do it?"

Out of the corner of her eye Kate saw Jon shoot her a glance, silently asking if she wanted him to once again handle the lying duties for the evening. Kate gave him a tiny shake of her head while keeping most of her attention on Rellie. Kate had come up with the lie in the first place; the least she could do was help keep it moving occasionally. "Jon has a relative who works in the palace. He's the one who arranged for us to use the room."

She tensed as Jon's face went perfectly still. Rellie, at least, looked cheerful again. "So can we get started dancing now?" The words were spoken in a whisper as audible as most people's speaking voices, but at least it was a start.

Jon retrieved a jacket from the back of a chair and returned to where Kate and Rellie were standing. "Hold your hands out in the proper dance position." When Rellie did, he draped one sleeve of the jacket over her right shoulder and put the end of the other in her outstretched left hand. "Tonight, you get to dance on your own." He moved her other hand to press against the back of the jacket until it held the garment against her stomach. "This is one of Rupert's favorite jackets, and tonight it's going to serve as your practice partner." Rellie looked skeptically at Jon for a second, then experimentally petted the deep purple velvet of the jacket. "This is really his favorite jacket?"

Jon nodded.

Rellie considered this. "It's a pretty jacket," she decided, then thought of something that made her expression go dreamy again. "I wonder what this Rupert guy would think about sparkles . . ." Without waiting for a response, she spun off in what was probably the closest to a waltz she would ever get.

Watching her, Kate couldn't quite stop smiling. If Rellie and Director Carlson were related, like she suspected, he was an idiot for not being here to see things like this. "Do you really think she and Rupert will do all right together? I know she doesn't seem like she's looking for a lot, but she deserves to be happy," she murmured to Jon as he moved toward her.

"There's always a chance," he said quietly, face softening as he watched Kate watch Rellie. "You know, you sounded like I always imagine a mother to sound."

She turned, shifting so they were that much closer. "Is that a good thing?" Faintly, Kate heard her good sense telling her it was a terrible idea to let herself get this emotionally involved with Jon, but when he looked at her like that it was almost impossible to hear it at all.

"I certainly appreciated it," he said, moving his hand just enough so his fingers wrapped around hers.

Heart threatening to burst out of her chest, Kate turned back to look at Rellie before she did something ridiculous like declare her undying love for him. "When I told Rellie you had a relative who worked in the palace, your face changed." She turned back to him. "Did I say something wrong?"

Jon hesitated, then shook his head. "No, it's just . . . you surprised me a little." His expression became rueful. "I really do have a relative who works in the palace."

"Ah." She hesitated. Given the use of the word "relative" she doubted the person was a member of Jon's immediate family, and there was something about the careful way he said it that suggested it was a less than easy relationship. "Do you . . . get along okay?" she asked, knowing the question was stupid but not sure of a better way to phrase it.

"I . . ." Jon took a deep breath, a strange smile flickering onto his face. "You know, I'm honestly not sure how to answer that question. We end up having to spend a lot of time together." He shook his head and squeezed Kate's hand. "What about your family?"

Kate shrugged. "We don't spend much time together at all," she said matter-of-factly, not quite looking him in the eye. "I'm an only child, and my parents separated after I moved out. My mother and I make dutiful phone calls about once a week, but beyond that we pretty much leave each other alone."

"There are moments I would kill to have that kind of arrangement," Jon admitted, reaching over with his other hand to tuck a stray lock of hair behind Kate's ear. "Your father, however," he continued softly, "sounds like a man who clearly has no idea what he's missing."

A lump caught in her throat as she smiled at him; she coughed, hoping her voice didn't betray her. "Right now, what I'm missing is a very necessary dance practice with a smooth-talking man standing next to me."

Jon grinned again. "Far be it from me to let such a travesty continue." He lifted his arm as they moved into position. "May I have this dance?"

And they were off. At first Kate focused on each step she took, trying to assure herself she was getting better. She'd practiced the steps in the privacy of her own apartment, hoping to speed up the learning process as best she could. No matter what Jon had said, flattening his feet was still a possibility she was in no mood to see.

When they were like this, though, with Jon pulling her closer than proper form probably allowed and saying things to make her laugh, it was easier to let herself enjoy the moment—let herself pretend they could do this forever.

As if on cue, Jon surprised her with a sudden dip. His grin widened at the way she clung to him. "So, I was wondering," he asked, feigning casualness as he lifted her up for another twirl. "How involved do you want to be in the preparations for the ball?"

Kate lifted an eyebrow. "Is that a trick question?"

He chuckled. "Okay, then, how willing would you be to keep me company tomorrow while I take care of a few things for the ball? It won't take long, and I'll even throw in a personalized tour of the city."

Her heart, who had apparently given up on good sense long before her head had, skipped a beat again. "Really?"

"If that's a forgivable but misplaced lack of self-esteem on your part, then yes, really." His voice was warm and a touch exasperated. "If it's a shock that I have the presumption to even ask something like this, then I throw myself at your feet and beg for mercy."

Kate didn't restrain the laugh that bubbled up. "Do I have to answer that?"

Jon's eyes sparkled like a little boy's. "Not if you say yes."

Kate grinned. For a second she felt like flying. "Then yes, I'd love—"

Rellie's shriek cut off the rest of what was about to say. Both Kate and Jon whipped their heads around to see Rellie clutching

Rupert's jacket to her chest, staring at the surprised man standing in the now-open doorway. The man, Kate noticed in horror, was wearing an unobtrusive, but very definite crown.

Oh, *no*.

"*Your Majesty*," Jon said quickly, giving the words nervous emphasis as he stepped forward. Kate tried to slip her hand out of his so she could get out of his way, but at the first pull Jon's grip tightened to the point she had no choice but to follow. "You don't usually spend time in this area of the castle." The nerves were starting to sound a lot more like annoyance, but since that would be a really bad way to talk to your boss, Kate hoped she was just reading him wrong.

The king looked carefully at Rellie for a moment, then at Kate for what felt like several days. Finally, he turned his attention back to Jon. "You were right about the maids." He paused. "It seemed wise to try someplace new."

Jon sighed, closing his eyes a moment. "Fantastic."

Rellie, having gotten over her initial shock, chose this point to decide silence was no longer the most interesting option available to her. "You're the king, aren't you?" she said, dropping Rupert's jacket to move toward the king with her hand outstretched. "I guess I'm going to be your new daughter-in-law."

Kate, whose hand was still firmly attached to Jon's, groaned when she realized there was no way she was going to be able to stop the girl in time.

To the king's credit, he barely flinched, but his attention swung back to Jon with a surprising amount of speed. "Daughter-in-law?" he asked.

"This is Rellie. She's got a Fairy Godmothers, Inc. contract to marry Prince Rupert," Jon responded, and Kate couldn't help but notice the look of sympathy the king shot in Rellie's direction.

Turning to Kate, the king said, "And your friend?"

"This is Kate," Jon said firmly, lifting their joined hands where the king couldn't help but notice. "She's Rellie's Fairy Godmother." Sensing her cue, Kate curtsied one-handed.

The king stood in silence, watching them, and Kate wondered if he thought Jon was lying somehow. Finally, he blinked, smiling a little as if something pleasant had occurred to him. "Ah," he said, giving a small, respectful bow in Kate's direction. "I am very pleased to meet you."

All Kate was capable of was a nod. "I'm pleased to meet you too, Your Majesty."

The king then turned his attention back to Jon. "If you'll excuse me, I need to speak to Lawton about a report." Before Jon could respond, the king stepped out and closed the door behind him.

Jon winced slightly at the sound of it shutting, causing Kate to turn to him with a worried expression. "How much trouble are you in?"

"As long as the queen doesn't hear about this, I should be able to deal with it," he muttered, glaring at the doorway for a few more seconds. "Though I may want to avoid Lawton for the next few days."

Kate wondered who Lawton was, but didn't want to stress Jon out more by asking. Rellie picked up Rupert's jacket. "He seemed like a nice guy," she said to the room in general. "I wonder if he liked my dancing?"

TEN

Errands

It was almost impossible to strike the right balance of speed and silence when sneaking away in a hurry. The faster he was, the more noise he inevitably made. The more careful and quiet he was, the more time there was for someone—

"Jonathan!"

Jon froze at the sound of his mother's voice behind him, a little shrill with desperation and suppressed emotion. Briefly, he fantasized about getting his hands on a disappearing spell, then gave in to the inevitable, and dragged a stoic smile onto his face before turning around to face the rapidly approaching queen.

"Hello, Mother." He caught hold of the book before she was about to slap it against his chest, wondering why in the world he'd thought *Lawton* was the person he needed to avoid this morning. "I take it you're upset about something?"

"I thought you were going to take care of this!" Attempting

and failing to yank the book back out of Jon's hands, she blinked back a sudden rush of tears as she jostled the wide velvet circle of her skirts. Presumably, a foot was stamping somewhere underneath the flounces. "Your brother is *suffering* through something that I . . . I can't even begin to understand, and you're just . . . just . . ." She finally let go of the book, hands flying to her chest as she gave her son a teary, affronted glare. "What *are* you doing?"

"Walking down the hallway," he replied blandly, keeping his temper in check as he narrowed his eyes at the title of the book in his hands. *Defeating the Dragon Within.* Where in the world was Rupert getting these books from? Jon knew for certain the castle library hadn't had anything new added to it since his great-grandfather had developed a thing for really terrible elfish poetry, which his grandmother had quarantined for the sake of the nearby volumes. "And, since you've taken the terrible, dangerous book out of his hands, it appears as if you've already handled the situation."

"I didn't take it out of Rupert's hands," the queen corrected sharply, missing the sarcasm. "I couldn't *find* his hands, let alone any other part of his poor, fragile body. And I looked *everywhere.*" She sniffed, eyes filling with dramatic tears. "He normally stops by for a few minutes to let me complain about your father, but I haven't seen him all *day.*"

Given his mother's stellar parenting skills and general level of distractibility, that didn't necessarily mean anything. Still, it wasn't as if Rupert was the quietest person in the castle. Flipping the book open, the first edge of uneasiness hit him as he thumbed through several of the book's illustration-free pages. The margins were filled with what appeared to be extremely confused notes, connected by little arrows and circles to certain parts of the text.

There were also several question marks, one of which had been written large enough to cover almost one entire page. All of it was in Rupert's manly, nearly illegible handwriting.

Maybe he should sit down when all of this was over and have a long, serious talk with Rupert. After, of course, he found every single one of these books and locked them up somewhere.

Still, there was no way he was going to encourage his mother by admitting any of this. Shutting the book with a decisive slap, Jon tucked it under his arm before giving his mother a curt bow. "When I do see Rupert, I assure you I'll share your worry and displeasure with him in suitably vivid execution," he said, scanning the hallway behind her for the best exit route. There it was, just past the suit of armor and through the double doors. "Now, however, I'm afraid I have an appointment I'm running late for."

Before his mother had time to do more than gasp in protest, Jon sidestepped her and hurried toward the aforementioned doors at a pace barely short of running. Once safe inside one of the palace's many workrooms (medium to medium-large wood-based repairs with an in-house specialist on singing wardrobes and enchanted doorways), Jon handed the book to a passing page and requested that it be taken up to his office. With a friendly nod to the busy craftsmen, he wound his way through the noise and wood shavings to the outside door and freedom. All he had to do was push it open, and then—

"I suggest you give up now. It will make things infinitely easier on both of us."

Great. Despite the brief, impractical appeal of slamming the door in Lawton's face and bolting in the opposite direction, Jon sighed and stepped outside completely before shutting the door behind him. "Lawton, I'm really not in the mood for this right now," he said, doing his best to hide how very much he wanted to be somewhere else. He knew that avoiding this entirely was going to be impossible, but if he could just postpone it for a couple of hours . . . "I'm meeting with several suppliers in town, and if I'm late for the first appointment it's going to throw the entire day into chaos."

Lawton glared at Jon as if he hadn't spoken. "Your father asked me for more information about your Fairy Godmother, Jon, very reasonably assuming that your *best friend* would know more about the apparent love of your life than a man who spends most of his life figuring out the most effective places to hide." Lawton's voice, for once, didn't contain even a trace of humor. "That very reasonable assumption did not actually turn out to be *true*."

"It wasn't as if I planned it that way, Lawton. I hadn't wanted *any* of you to meet her yet."

Lawton raised an eyebrow. "Oh, *that's* a comforting response."

Jon's eyes narrowed into a glare. "If it mattered that much, why didn't you just send one of your spies to figure out who I was meeting? As this morning has proven beyond a shadow of a doubt, I'm *clearly* no good at sneaking around without people noticing."

Lawton shot Jon a long, piercingly silent look, expression free of even the barest flicker of emotion. "Did that help?" he said finally, voice tight.

Jon stared at Lawton for a moment, then sighed. "Not really." He rubbed a hand across his eyes, knowing the truth would be more effective than any apology he tried to offer. "It's just . . ." He hated feeling guilty. "I haven't exactly told Kate what I do for a living."

Both Lawton's eyebrows lifted. "And when, precisely, were you planning on breaking the news to your beloved? Your wedding?

Your third anniversary? The first time someone tries to drop a crown on her head, perhaps?"

"I'll *tell* her." Jon nearly growled in frustration. It would *not* be a good idea, he knew, to meet Kate in this mood. "As soon as I've got the Rupert and Rellie situation handled—"

"Your father mentioned that particular detail as well," Lawton cut in, his normal, dryly amused expression back in place. "Please extend my deepest sympathies to the girl."

It took a considerable amount of restraint for Jon not to actually growl this time. "As soon as I have the Rupert and Rellie situation handled," he repeated firmly, "I will take Kate to a nice, quiet little restaurant where neither of us has to even *think* the word work. I will then buy her a wildly expensive meal, and after she's started eating, explain to her that the real reason I work in the palace is because, technically, I'm a prince. If I do it right, hopefully she'll forgive me before they bring out the dessert."

Lawton studied Jon with a certain amount of fascination. "If you're that aware forgiveness will be required, then why sidestep the truth in the first place? Most people see someone with royal lineage as a rather considerable romantic coup."

Jon hesitated, then sighed. "She . . . she talks to me, Lawton. When I tell her things about work she not only doesn't roll her eyes, she actually seems to *understand*. She's spending her Saturday keeping me company while I run *errands*, and she let me give her dancing lessons I know she didn't want because they gave me a reason to keep hanging around while she was working." He lifted his hands helplessly. "Things like that never happen to Prince Jonathan."

No one spoke for a moment.

"I see," Lawton said finally, expression far more gentle. "Clearly, I must meet this woman, if for no other reason than to get a head start on the sparklingly witty toast I will be expected to deliver at your wedding."

Jon's eyes widened at the comment. "Actually, it's probably a good idea that you not mention the word 'wedding' yet." At Lawton's raised eyebrow, he continued, "I know, I know, but I haven't had nearly enough time to work on my lead in. After the ball . . ."

Though the too-knowing expression was still on his face, Lawton gestured his acquiescence. "We'll focus on today, then. Were you planning on taking a moment to purchase flowers of some sort as a peace offering for being late?"

Jolted by the reminder of the time, Jon looked down at his watch and swore softly. "I'd planned on the flowers, but as a peace offering," he muttered to himself, moving past Lawton to hurry down the pathway. As he had expected, Lawton followed him. "I cannot *believe* I keep doing this to her . . ."

"If we take my private carriage, we can hurry the process along somewhat," Lawton contributed. "We can walk the last few blocks, as is undoubtedly your normal practice during these interludes."

"Oh, really?" Even when Lawton was right, it was always a good idea not to let him get too comfortable about it. "How can you be so sure of that?"

"The same way I know you plan on forging the king's signature on any purchase forms to keep Katharine from connecting your name to the royal family." It was impossible not to hear the smile in Lawton's voice. "I've taught you well."

THREADING HIS WAY through Rapunzel Square's traditional crush of morning shoppers, Jon fought the urge to smooth his hair one more time as he searched through the swirling people for a glimpse of Kate. It helped that his hands were currently occupied protecting a recently purchased bouquet of spring flowers from being battered into a colorful but definitely unromantic smear.

From behind, Lawton gave him an impatient tap on the shoulder. "I'm aware that a man in love is rarely inclined to listen to reason, but wouldn't a quieter meeting place have been more conducive to encouraging a budding romance?"

"I wanted her to get a real taste of the city," Jon replied absently, a nicely casual response that revealed nothing of his irrational, little-boy hope for Kate to love it just as much as he did. "Besides," he added, still making his way through the crowd, "we're meeting in that little garden area on the south side of the ornamental tower, which is as close to quiet as you can get on a . . ."

The words trailed off as he finally found Kate, who seemed to be caught up in a rather animated discussion with a brown-haired young man Jon had never met before. Given his almost transparent wings, and that Kate looked like she was enjoying the discussion, it seemed more than likely she'd brought him along from the office.

Jon slowed to a stop, deeply annoyed with the universe as a whole as he narrowed his eyes at the man.

A moment later, Lawton stepped beside Jon in order to get a better look at the situation. "She looks promising," he decided after a moment. "Clearly able to hold her own in a conversation, and pleasant enough to the eye not to intrude upon her other attributes." When Jon didn't respond, Lawton turned to look at him. "I feel inspired to gently point out that she's not the only person who brought a guest along to this little gathering. And, though I am rarely a betting man, I would wager that she's planning on having her guest depart as quickly as you are yours."

Jon slowly exhaled, feeling stupid. "Well," he said briskly, starting forward again, "at least you're the only one who saw that."

"Not that I'm ever going to let you forget it."

There was no safe response to that, but Jon was thankfully saved from having to admit it when Kate caught sight of them. When her eyes met his and lit up, everything else was forgotten. She called his name, waving as if she didn't already have his full attention. She was out of uniform for once, with a clingy violet top and long, flowing gray skirt, and Jon was suddenly convinced that whoever had invented poufy dresses had no idea what men actually found beautiful.

Maybe there was a way to get ball gowns outlawed.

Finding himself grinning, Jon hurried forward until he was sufficiently close enough to reach out and take Kate's hand. "Should I start with a heroically dramatic and possibly believable explanation for why I'm late, or just get down on my knees and beg for your forgiveness?"

Kate laughed. "You weren't *that* late." She moved a little closer, squeezing his hand. "Besides, the worst that could happen is that I would have given in and bought something at that little bakery a few doors down."

Jon held out the flowers toward her. "Will these make up for the fact that you didn't? I didn't know what your favorites were, but . . ."

His heartbeat sped up as her eyes widened, then blinked in what appeared to be slightly awed delight. "You brought me flowers," she said softly, smiling at him as if he'd done something wonderful. Kate took the bouquet, hand lingering against his, then leaned over and pressed a quick kiss against cheek. "Thank you."

She looked slightly embarrassed as she pulled back, but didn't apologize or let go of his hand. Jon was possessed by a sudden, wild urge to run out and buy her an entire flower shop. Or perhaps an ornamental garden.

Before his imagination could get far enough to offer her the nearest enchanted forest, Lawton stepped forward. "Pardon the intrusion, but I've heard so much about you," he said smoothly, hand held out in a silent request for hers. "I'm Lawton, an old friend of Jonathan's. I must say, I am *extremely* pleased to meet you."

Kate began to give him her hand when she realized it still held the bouquet. She stared at it for a second, as if trying to decide something, then squeezed Jon's hand again as she turned to her friend with a sheepish expression. "Can you hold these for a second?" she asked, holding out the flowers.

Jon's chest tightened as Kate's friend grinned and held out a hand. She gratefully passed over the flowers before giving Lawton the free hand he'd asked for. "Sorry about that. I'm Kate, and it's nice to meet you. Don't give Jon too much trouble about letting us use the room for my client's dance lesson. He was really doing me a huge favor."

Looking highly amused by the entire exchange, Lawton dropped a precise courtly kiss on Kate's knuckles. "Believe me, my dear Katharine, I have plenty of other things to torment the man about. I must say, though, I had no idea Fairy Godmothers were allowed to be so much more exquisite than the average princess."

Eyebrow raised, Kate gave him a wry smile. "Do I dare ask what you mean by 'average,' or am I better off not knowing?"

The question was enough to startle a chuckle out of Lawton, who kissed her hand again. "You'll fit in beautifully, my dear."

Before Kate could ask what precisely it was that Lawton meant by his little statement, Jon held his free hand out toward Kate's associate. "I'm afraid we haven't quite finished the introductions. I'm Jon. I've been working with Kate on her current assignment."

The other man smiled. "I'm Ned, and I work with her the rest of the time." They shook hands. "I've been hoping I'd get the chance to meet you."

Jon's eyebrows quirked up in interest as Kate shot Ned a look that was both confused and faintly alarmed. Seeing it, Ned flushed slightly. "You finally let his name slip Wednesday when I got you talking about working with Rellie. And as excited as you've been to go to your appointments, I knew something had to be up."

Kate's cheeks reddened, and Jon carefully wiped the grin off his face before she had the chance to glance in his direction. "I'm always happy to meet a friend of Kate's," he said instead. "But I'm afraid she and I really need to be going."

At this, Lawton shot Ned a sly grin that was anything but comforting. "And while they're gone, you and I can retire to the nearest bottle of scotch and swap stories about our dear occupied friends."

Ned's eyes widened briefly in horrified fascination at the possibility, but thankfully, he shook his head. "Actually, I really need to be getting back to the office," he said, and Jon noticed a relieved expression on Kate's face that matched his own. "The more files I get organized now, the fewer I have to do when Bubbles is there looking over my shoulder." Ned turned to Kate. "I'll put those old research files back for you, too."

"Thanks." She paused. "Do you want me to start the door for

you?" When he nodded, she pulled her wand out from her waist-band and began sketching a complicated pattern in the air.

While this was happening, Jon turned to Lawton, who was watching Kate work with fascination. Normally, Jon would have been supportive, but right now he was very unwilling to encourage anything that kept him from getting some alone time with Kate. "It's time for *you* to really need to be getting back to the palace," he muttered, nudging Lawton in the shoulder and gesturing back in the direction they'd come.

Lawton raised an amused eyebrow, but didn't respond until the glow had faded and Kate turned back to the two men. "My dear lady, I'm afraid I must say farewell," he told her, sketching a quick bow before turning to leave. "Jon's possessive streak is beginning to show."

Jon's glare followed him through the crowd, but it faded when Kate squeezed his hand again. When he turned to look at her, she grinned. "They just wanted to make the idea of running errands seem relaxing," she said warmly, her thumb gently trailing back and forth along his knuckles—it did wonders for improving his mood. "So, where are we going first?" she asked.

Jon lifted their joined hands to kiss the back of hers. "Actually, I was thinking those errands could wait a little while. Let's get started on that tour of the city I promised you."

"Sounds good to me." Still smiling, Kate looked out at the swirling crowds. "I know I haven't seen much of it yet, but I think I could really get to like this place."

ELEVEN

※

Prep Time

A few days later found Kate standing in the backyard of Rellie's stepmother's house, wiping away the pumpkin seed clinging to her left eyebrow. "And that," she said, reminding herself she'd been the one who felt the need for an object lesson, "is why we're supposed to use only fresh pumpkin."

"Point taken," Rellie sighed, then grabbed a chunk of golden blond hair and tried to finger-comb out the orange vegetable guts splattered through it. They'd spent the last few hours out there, attempting to put the girl's carriage together while the stepfamily and Demon Beast slept off some sort of late night party inside. Thankfully, pumpkins explode rather quietly. "I suppose that now's not the time to tell you that Maleeva used up all the newer ones lobbing them at orphans, is it? They make Lucinda bloat right up, and Belzie gets really mad because she thinks Lucinda's secretly making fun of her."

Kate sighed, closing her eyes briefly. "The morning before the ball? No, not really." She'd never really been comfortable saving something this big for this close to the main event—too many things could go wrong—but it was either do it now or find a nearby giantess and rent a few days' worth of space in her hopefully carriage-sized refrigerator. There was nothing *less* romantic than a gigantic wheeled pumpkin that had been sitting in the sun for a week, especially when the client had an extremely sensitive gag reflex. "Do you have fresh squash of any kind? I'd rather not have to deal with a crookneck, but maybe I could make some sort of decorative finial out of it."

Rellie scooped a bit of pumpkin out from under the edge of her collar. "We did." The pause that followed said "but" louder than words could. "Then someone told Lucinda that bathing in pureed squash worked as an aphrodisiac. We're still not sure if it worked or not, but she had cows following her around for weeks after."

The corner of Kate's mouth twitched a little, but she forced it back into a relatively responsible expression. "Okay, that'll be a no on the squash. Do you have any horror stories about watermelons to share?"

Rellie brightened. "Sure! I love telling people about those. There was this one time that Belzie—"

Kate held up a hand, the smile sneaking up a little further this time before she managed to flatten it. "Let's save that for later. Right now, we need to focus on getting you a carriage for tonight's ball." Her eyes narrowed as she considered their rapidly shrinking range of options. "Do you have any smaller vegetables? Or fruit? Anything but cherries—you can't get those enchanted pits out of the backseat with a crowbar."

Rellie winced, as if she wished she could be more helpful. "Belzie doesn't really like fruits very much, unless they're covered in whipped cream."

"Of course, she doesn't," Kate said, leaning against the wall on which Jon had taken refuge that first night. "You know, if either of us had any sense we'd just ignore this part of the contract and have me just teleport you straight into the palace. It might make the grand entrance a little harder, but—"

"I'd sort of been wondering about that," Rellie piped in, looking surprisingly focused and thoughtful.

Kate's brow furrowed. "About whether the grand entrance was going to be a little harder if I made us a door?"

"No, silly," Rellie said exasperatedly, shaking her head. She sat down on the lawn, finding an area free of the pumpkin carnage. "The contract, I mean. Since I'm the one who got the Fairy Godmother, somebody had to have bought me the contract, right? I really can't imagine Maleeva doing it, but who else is there who would worry about whether or not I'm going to get married to somebody?"

Kate hesitated, trying to work out what would be the best answer to give Rellie. She didn't care at all about protecting Carlson, and though she was *almost* certain about the whole fatherhood thing, there was always a chance she could be wrong. And more importantly, could finding out someone like Carlson was your dad be considered *good* news? "How much do you know about your family?" she asked, thinking hard. "Not your stepmother and stepsisters, but the people you lived with before you came here."

Rellie considered the question. "I was at an orphanage for a while, with a whole bunch of other girls who were trying to get placed with the right kind of stepfamily. Before that," she shook her head, "I don't really remember much." Decision made, Kate took a deep breath. "It's probably better to think of this guy like the people in charge of the orphanage. Now that you've been with the stepfamily for a while, he thinks it's time for you to move on to something bigger and better."

Rellie raised an eyebrow at her. "A pumpkin carriage is something bigger and better?"

This time Kate didn't even bother fighting the chuckle that escaped. "If we can make this work, it's going to look better than you think. We change the color, put on fancy wheels, get a whole bunch of gold or silver accents—" She stopped, making a frustrated noise as she remembered the problem at hand. "Of course, before we can do any of that we have to find a fruit or vegetable that will work. Is there anything left in the larder that hasn't had something disturbing happen to it?"

Forehead wrinkling in thought, Rellie began ticking the list off on her fingers. "Well, there are some tomatoes, but that just seems like a really bad idea."

"That's putting it mildly. Anything else?"

"Onions?"

"I hope the look on my face is enough of an answer to that one."

"Bananas?"

Kate rolled her eyes. "I am *not* going to be responsible for the running gags that would follow from letting you drive to the ball inside an enormous banana."

Rellie's forehead wrinkled even further. "Bananas are funny?"

"Ah, well . . ." After deciding there was no safe way to answer the question Kate closed her mouth, not quite able to look Rellie in the eye for another second. "Just believe me when I say bananas aren't a good idea."

Rellie made a face, as if she knew she was missing something. "Do you think I could get Mr. Assistant Guy to tell me why bananas are funny?"

Kate grinned at the thought. "You could try," she said, fondly imagining the expression on Jon's face as Rellie broached the question. She'd apologize after, once Rupert and Rellie were staring deeply into each other's eyes, and she and Jon had snuck off to that little restaurant he'd told her about. They'd make each other laugh, and they'd enjoy each other's company so much the owner would have to kick them out eventually because they'd have forgotten what time it was.

Maybe they could even keep seeing each other, without having to pretend that it had anything to do with work.

"Thinking about him again, huh?"

Jerked back into the present, Kate blinked rapidly and tried to pretend she hadn't become transparent as a pane of glass. "I don't know who you're talking about."

"Mr. Assistant Guy." Rellie smiled at her, fingers playing absently with one of the bows on her rags outfit. "You had the same sort of sparkly, happy look on your face whenever you dance with him during the lessons." She sighed dreamily. "And other times, too, but I forgot exactly when."

Kate took a deep breath, slowly letting it out again. Then, giving in to the glow inside her, she smiled. "Really?"

"Really." Rellie looked thoughtful. "Hey, do you think I'll start looking like that every time Rupert's around?"

For just a second, Kate wished she were dealing with the

banana comment again. "I don't really know," she admitted, wishing she could give the girl a better answer. If she saw any kind of a spark she'd do anything she could to encourage it, but she didn't feel right making any kind of promises in advance. "I don't think there's any way you can know unless you meet him."

Rellie thought about this for a moment, then shrugged. "What about apples? I think there are a couple of them in the very back of the pantry."

Kate blinked, lost for a moment, but after a few seconds of mental hunting, managed to relocate the thread of the conversation. "For the carriage? No." She shook her head. "Different package entirely, and we'd have to get your stepmother way more involved than I'd like. Besides, do you know how hard it is to get seven dwarves together on such short notice? They have a union now."

"I suppose I could get a pomegranate from the neighbors."

"Not unless we want a lawsuit from the National Association for Retired but Still Mighty Gods and Goddesses (NARSMGG)." Kate winced a little at the memory. "Ever since their enforced retirement, they've become really obsessive about the copyrights they hold to major mythic elements. Persephone is their lawyer, and since it was a pomegranate that left her stuck married to Hades, she's especially sensitive about them."

Rellie just sat there, then looked at Kate with a worried expression. "Is it okay if I have no idea what you're talking about?"

A smile snuck back onto Kate's face. She'd never admit it, but Rellie was easily becoming one of her favorite clients. "Be grateful." After the silence stretched on long enough to make it clear that Rellie had no more suggestions, Kate sighed. "We're just going to have to go down to the market and find an acceptable piece of fruit. Even if I have to pay for it out of my own pocket, it's worlds better than having to use the spare carriage."

"Wait a minute." Rellie straightened. "If you already had a carriage ready and waiting somewhere, why did you make me do all that worrying?"

"Believe me, having the spare carriage doesn't mean that you're going to *stop* worrying." Kate grimaced. "I'd even take a non-magical carriage over it, and those are always dangerous, because we can't get insurance on them. Seriously, let's just go buy the fruit."

Rellie raised a disbelieving eyebrow. "I've seen Maleeva before she puts on her makeup in the morning. How bad can this extra carriage of yours really be?"

"Remember the pumpkin?"

Rellie waved a dismissive hand. "It was a little goopy, but it wasn't really that bad."

"Okay, but don't say I didn't warn you." Kate lifted her wand, deciding to conjure the spare carriage just long enough to prove her point. Even a few minutes would be recorded in the database, which meant she'd get teased for it, but it would be easier than arguing Rellie out of her curiosity. "Unless you want to have a wheel land on your head, now would be a really good time to take a step back."

As Rellie frantically scooted back, Kate moved the wand in a series of flourishes necessary to transport the spare carriage into their immediate vicinity. Then, folding her arms across her chest, she waited for the purple smoke to clear.

As always, it was the smell that hit first.

The carriage's dark green color wasn't so bad, so long as you ignored the warts and the fact that its shape had an unfortunate resemblance to a sausage. But the scent, bitter and vinegary and choking, erased these minor details as part of its full-frontal assault on the brain. It swept over, burning nostrils and stripping taste buds as it seeped into anything and everything unlucky enough to be around it.

All in all, it was something Fairy Godmothers, Inc. was very careful not to mention in their advertising.

"Eewww! That's just . . . eeewww!" Rellie coughed, the death clamp on her nose making her voice honk a little. "Is this why you said you can only use fresh stuff to make the carriages? Because if it is, you were totally, totally right, and I'm really sorry I ever argued."

"Office legend says it started out as a proper cucumber carriage. But parking at the ball was crazy, like it always is, and the Fairy Godmother who first created the thing took a chance and parked it on private property. Unfortunately, it turned out that a giant lived there, and the poor thing was part of his canning project before anyone noticed." With her wand, Kate pointed to the bite mark on the back end of the carriage. "The giant himself picked up on the problem and returned it to us eventually, but by then it was far too late."

Rellie glared at the thing for a moment, still holding tightly to her nose. "He should have kept it," she said, turning to Kate. "Can you please, please, please get rid of this so I can stop plugging my nose? We don't even have to make a carriage at all—the transport thing was fun, and it doesn't stink so badly my eyeballs start burning."

"Works for me." Kate didn't bother to hide the amusement in her voice. Her eyeballs were burning just as much as Rellie's, but it was always entertaining to see other people's reactions. "The only animals we've been able to get near the thing are enchanted goats, and they start trying to eat the wheels after about five minutes." She quickly lifted her wand and waved the carriage away, deliberately blocking out the faint scent of pickle still lingering in the air. "And I'm fine with just transporting you over there. It'll mean we have to start your grand entrance from the inside, but as long as we avoid people while we're getting ready I think we'll be all right."

Rellie's eyes widened. Slowly, her face grew nervous. "You mean like the sort of thing that made your dress all smoky that first night you showed up?"

"I thought we were going to avoid mentioning that again." But Rellie looked like she was actually beginning to panic, so Kate moved closer and sat down beside the girl. "I promise you, we're not going to set your dress on fire," she said soothingly, deciding to take a chance and put an arm around the girl's shoulders. "All we have to do is skip the part with the fireworks, and as long as we make sure to avoid any candles there won't be a source of flame around to get us into trouble."

At the mention of fireworks, Rellie looked at Kate in disbelief. "You guys set off fireworks inside a building? No *wonder* you accidentally get lit on fire sometimes."

Kate couldn't help the chuckle. "The fireworks actually aren't so bad—they're just illusions, so there's no chance of fire. It's the swans you have to worry about. They can get vicious."

Rellie looked at her for a second, confusion clear on her face, then shook her head. "I don't want to know."

"Smart girl." Kate went over the different aspects of the grand entrance package, picking through the ones she was certain wouldn't horribly backfire on her. "There will definitely be spot-lights and confetti hearts, though. And, if you want, we can even go a little extra on the rose petals."

Rellie perked up in interest. "Are they pink?" Kate smiled. "How could they be of any other color?"

Suitably distracted, Rellie took a moment to consider the mental picture of rose petals and little confetti hearts. "Pink is good," she said cheerfully, then her eyebrows lifted as an idea hit. "Is there any chance I could get some—"

"No." Kate shook her head, not needing to hear the rest of the request to know what it was. "Unless you want to be the one following them around with the bag and the scooper, no rabbits are going to be involved in the creation of your grand entrance."

Rellie wrinkled her nose again. "Good point. Let's just go with the roses and the confetti hearts. Do I get a grand exit, too?"

Kate shook her head. "Sadly, tradition insists that the girl make a quick exit out one of the backdoors before midnight. I'm sorry that I won't be there to help, but Jon said he was going to ask Lawton to guide you out. We were just going to have you leave in the carriage we made, but since you want me to just transport you I'll ask him if they have a spare carriage you can use."

Rellie held a hand up to interrupt. "Wait. Why do I have to sneak out at midnight? Not that I won't want to if the ball's boring, but what if I'm actually having fun?"

Kate shrugged apologetically. "Budget-cutting measures. All of the spells shut off at midnight except for the shoes, and they only stay because of a deal the company made with a wholesaler."

Rellie's eyes were big and pleading. "Is there *any* chance you could—" When Kate shook her head, Rellie allowed herself one dramatic sigh before bouncing back to her feet. "If it's going to go away at midnight, can I have my dress earlier than planned? I probably shouldn't wear it while I'm scrubbing the floor, but if I shake it off after, I can swish around in it while I do the dusting." She twirled a little. "If I mix enough gin into the pancake batter, Maleeva won't even notice."

Kate just stared at the girl for a moment, making a mental note to pass that bit of advice onto the next client before shaking her head and returning to the task at hand. "Though that may be arranged, one stain or spill and I'd be stuck spending the afternoon in the uniform maintenance department getting your dress dry-cleaned. We're going to wait for the dress and shoes until just before we do the teleporting."

"Am I still going to be stuck with those glass shoes you were talking about? Because I was thinking about what you said about Rupert stepping on my toes, and I don't think it would help the magic if I screamed because there was a broken piece of glass stuck in my foot. And I really don't want to get blood on this dress."

Kate smiled, secretly proud of herself for already having a plan for this part. "Actually, we're not going to have to worry about that," she said confidently, pulling out the set of old, nearly worn-out slip-ons she'd brought from home (Rellie never seemed to be wearing shoes, and Kate didn't want to get within fifty feet of any of the stepfamily's closets). "I have the perfect solution right here."

Rellie looked skeptically at the shoes. "I don't think they match my dress."

Reminding herself not to be annoyed, Kate pushed herself to her feet. "Just be grateful you didn't have to find them yourself." Mentally reviewing the order she'd cobbled together from two separate sets of shoe spells, Kate circled the wand counterclockwise three times around her open palm before spiraling it upward like an ice cream cone. Then, because just using flourishes would make the spell take about twenty minutes, she sprinkled in a couple of preprogrammed keywords random enough that normal conversation wouldn't accidentally trigger them.

Rellie's brow wrinkled. "Badgley Mischka?"

A swirl of fairy dust, and there they were. Kate held the newly transformed shoes out to Rellie with pride. "Voila. Your shoes."

Fascinated, Rellie gently poked the completely clear shoes, now far more ornate and festooned with tiny, equally clear bows. "Are those . . ." The clear shoes bent under Rellie's finger, making her yank her hand back in surprise. "Okay, those aren't glass."

"Think of it as a glass substitute." Kate held out the shoes, gesturing for Rellie to try them on. "Believe me, they'll be much more comfortable to dance in, and if you decide you want to leave one behind at the end of the evening you can just kick it off."

"Why would I want to leave one behind?" Rellie, who had dropped to the ground to put on the shoes, froze and looked up in confusion. "They're pretty, and I don't think Rupert's going to be very happy with me if I start throwing my shoes at him."

Kate fought back a smile, both amused at the image and pleased that the girl clearly liked the shoes. "Actually, the girls normally leave it just outside the front doors so the prince can find them after they mysteriously run off." She paused, thinking about some of the things Jon had said about Rupert. "With your prince, though, we should probably leave an actual note with your address on it."

Rellie finished putting on the sandals, then stretched her feet out in front of her and wiggled her toes in satisfaction. "That makes *way* more sense than the shoe."

TWELVE

❦

Back to Bite You

No one was willing to inform Madame Stewart that the ice sculptures she had set out for the evening's ball were not, in fact, made of ice. This wasn't normally the case, as the palace had a standing contract with a local craftsman who normally did such work. But when a page had arrived at his shop with the news that they needed their usual batch of thirteen completed in two weeks, he had begun giggling in a highly unstable manner, making pointed gestures with his chisel. Not knowing what else to do, Stewart's assistants had scoured the attic for old glass sculptures, which they then misted with water and threw in the palace freezers. As for Madame Stewart herself, she had recently been struck down by a bout of canapé poisoning and was, as of yet, too ill to notice.

Jon was quite sensibly hiding. Since the maids and secretaries were highly bribable and knew where all the offices were, he'd brought the paperwork he'd been avoiding to a walk-in closet in one of the bedrooms reserved for less important guests. As an extra precaution, he'd left the documents in terrifyingly large stacks between himself and the closet door, an early warning system that had the added bonus of hopefully destroying some of the papers should anyone try to come through.

Of course, that didn't stop people from making the attempt. Jon's head shot up as he heard the sound of the doorknob turning, then the muffled thud of the wood hitting the solid wall of paper-work. It was only when he heard swearing, the source unmistak-able despite being muffled by the door, that he let himself relax. "Don't move," he warned Lawton, pushing to his feet just long enough to move some of the piles out of the way. "My paperwork has been trained to kill all intruders on sight."

Lawton raised an eyebrow at him. "Being in love has clearly done little to improve your sense of humor."

Jon carefully shoved a particularly ornate invitation to the bot-tom of a pile. "Kate would have thought it was funny."

"Which, tragically, shows that love has made her delusional." As Jon laughed, Lawton surveyed the closet with a resigned ex-pression. "You know, Jon, *most* people would have considered a locking door to be an integral part of their chosen hideout." After eyeing and then rejecting a particularly hideous green and purple pinstriped footstool, he gave up and leaned back against the door. "Perhaps even—oh, I don't know—a chair."

Jon smirked a little as he returned to the next document in the stack, a request from a local school of wizardry to run tests on and possibly dissect an heirloom frog skin purse. He immediately signed it—the only reason they still had the purse was because the frog was his Great-Aunt Gertrude's ex-husband. Now that she was dead, it was definitely time to get it out of the house. "The maids don't even look at these rooms unless someone is actually scheduled to be sleeping in them. As an added bonus, most of Madame Stewart's staff seem to be at least mildly allergic to dust."

Lawton's lips quirked upward in amusement. "I take it that you're not about to rush downstairs and start overseeing preparations for the ball?"

Before Jon could respond there was a sudden crashing noise from the general direction of the ballroom, loud enough to be heard even several floors up. Both Lawton and Jon winced. "Someone figured I was the one who wanted the ball thrown together on such short notice, then felt the need to share this insight with Madame Stewart."

"I see." Lawton was trying not to grin at whatever vision was running through his head. "I take it she is less than pleased with you?"

"That's putting it mildly," Jon said dryly. "Thankfully, though, she's too sick to be much of a threat at the moment. Her assistants, on the other hand . . ." Temporarily setting aside the family tree of an enchanted turkey who was requesting sanctuary before he ended up on the King of Nearby's dinner table, Jon made a dramatic slicing motion across his neck. "You'd be surprised how many nails, needles, and scissors those people can pull together on short notice."

"Not to mention the various lengths of measuring tape and ribbon they must have at their disposal." Amused, Lawton gave Jon a carefully appraising look. "Given how pivotal this evening is to join efforts with your darling Katharine, I would have presumed that far more strategizing would occur on your part."

Jon sat back, gaze going distant as he let himself visualize the best part of the evening in front of him. "The Golden Goose has reserved one of their private dining rooms for me the entire night—I don't want us to feel pressured to get there by a specific time, and if she wants to stay until the place closes I'll be an extremely happy man." Careful questioning had left him pretty certain she'd like the food, and if by some off chance she didn't, he'd already made it clear that the restaurant would then locate some food she *did* like. "When we do get there, I've got candlelight, flowers, the whole deal."

Lawton raised an eyebrow. "And then you'll tell her?"

Jon made a frustrated noise. "And then I'll tell her." He exhaled slowly, rubbing a hand along the back of his neck. "She'll forgive me. She'll be annoyed, and she'll have every right to be annoyed, but I'll make her understand why I did it, and she'll forgive me."

Lawton smiled slightly. "And if that doesn't work, there's always jewelry."

Jon was inspired to a smile of his own as he returned his attention to the family tree. "There's always jewelry." He signed off on the sanctuary—with the condition that the turkey accept a job in the kingdom's petting zoo—then hesitated again as a niggling case of nerves made him look back up at Lawton. "Do you think I should have something ready, just in case?"

"I think you'll be fine." A second later, however, he winced. "Rupert, however, may need to have a necklace and matching earrings on hand if he wants to keep this Rellie girl for longer than a few hours."

"Actually, he'd have better luck bringing her fluffy bunnies." Next in the stack was a letter from a Mrs. Peter, who was suing her husband in the royal court for inflicting "years of psychological damage." Apparently, Mr. Peter had a nasty habit of getting drunk and trying to shove his wife's head into a pumpkin shell. "Still, she seems to be pretty easygoing. As long as he doesn't bring up the word 'self-actualization' in front of her, I think they'll be okay."

"Where is Rupert, by the way? From everything you've said about this Rellie girl, I can't imagine even she will be agreeable enough to appreciate the new, even more exasperating Rupert we've all been suffering these last few weeks."

"Hopefully, that's starting to wear off," Jon admitted, surprised at having forgotten about that aspect of things for a moment. But really, someone usually had to be shouting—or be Kate—to make it more than halfway up the list of things Jon worried about. "I checked on Rupert this morning. There wasn't much time to actually talk, but he had that cheerfully unconcerned expression that used to be pretty constant with him."

Lawton grimaced in mild distaste. "As much as it pains me to say this, I'm afraid that I'm relieved by the thought of Rupert returning to his former state of relatively harmless idiocy."

Jon nodded. "If nothing else, he's—"

Another series of crashing noises cut in from the ballroom, followed by a high-pitched scream and the sound of several people running for their lives. If the occasional shriek that followed was any indication of escape, not all of them made it.

After it was quiet again, Lawton glanced over at Jon. "Do you suppose Madame Stewart finally took a closer look at her ice sculptures?"

FINALLY, IT WAS almost time for the best part of Jon's evening. Unfortunately, that was only going to happen after the worst part was finally done.

He timed it as finely as he could, waiting until the absolute last second before heading downstairs to the ever-increasing swarm of newly arrived guests. He took the backstairs to get there, avoiding the area of the palace where his mother had spent the last several hours being sewn, stuffed, and starched into miles of satin and gemstones. After slipping from her grasp during the last ball Rupert would no doubt be pinned down in the next room over, enduring equal trussing in preparation for tonight's hosting duties.

All Jon had to do was make sure everything was ready for Kate, then spirit her away at the first opportunity.

"Prince Jon! Thank the curling papers I've found you!"

Vowing to take sneaking lessons from someone in Lawton's spy network, Jon reluctantly stopped at the frantic cry of his mother's hairdresser. "As long as it's not a fire hazard, I don't care what's happening or what you and my mother consider an appropriate outfit," he said quickly, hoping to stave off the conversation before it started. "Even if it *is* a fire hazard, just have one of the pages follow her around with a blanket and bucket of water."

The hairdresser's panicked expression didn't lessen in the slightest. Without a word, she grabbed Jon's arm and promptly dragged him toward the small room just off the upper balcony in the ballroom. Commonly referred to as the staging area, the balcony was the place the royal family and other nobles gathered for last-minute touches before making a dramatic entrance down the main staircase.

Which, in short, meant he was being dragged right to his mother. "I will pay you not to force me to get involved in whatever problem my mother is causing."

Her grip didn't loosen and her pace didn't slacken as they skirted past rows of pages, all of whom were helping organize the parking of dozens upon dozens of coaches. When Jon dug his heels in and forced the woman to slow down slightly, she made a small sound of distress and yanked even harder on his arm. "Your mother is beside herself with panic and shaking her miniature songbirds loose. I'm doing all the repair work I can, but if you don't calm her down before the cage breaks I can't be held responsible for what happens." When Jon didn't respond, she turned her head back to look at him. "Caged songbirds are *angry* songbirds, Your Highness, particularly with the amount of hairspray we've been using."

Though Jon was desperately trying to convince himself that this was simply a fashion disaster blown out of proportion, he could already feel the tension headache forming behind his eyes. "I know no one seems quite able to process this, but comforting Mother has never been one of my specialties. It's Rupert's presence that always manages to soothe her."

There was a long, terrible silence from the hairdresser before she hauled him forward with more force than should have been possible. Noticing this, Jon's stomach immediately plummeted like a lead weight, and he dug his heels in deeply enough to jerk the hairdresser to a full stop. "Madame Durrell?" he asked, his deathly calm voice completely at odds with what he was feeling. "What's happened to Rupert?"

She opened her mouth, then closed it, eyes somehow growing even wider and more frantic. Jon finally just tore his arm out of her grip, then ran past her and down the hallway toward the staging area.

When he got there, he had to skid to a very quick and awkward stop. The staging room doors burst open only inches in front of him, spitting out three shrieking maids who nearly ran Jon over as they made their exit. Jon ducked at the flash of wings that immediately followed, the songbird barely missing his head as it shot out into the freedom of the hallway.

Inside the staging area, things were only marginally more controlled. Two pages were running in frantic circles around the room, trying and failing miserably to catch the second bird. His mother had, naturally, fainted across the ornamental couch, managing to fall in such a way that the sweep of her skirt still managed to drape itself artfully. She was flanked on one side by Madame Durrell's assistant, who desperately tried to repair the wire cage in the queen's hair that had presumably once been home to the songbirds. On the other side was Jon's father, valiantly trying to pry open Mother's fingers to get at the crumpled paper she somehow still held in a death grip.

Rupert, Jon realized, was nowhere in sight.

Oh, no.

Acutely aware of the immense crowd milling around in the ballroom—and the two very important people who would be joining them any minute now—Jon strode over to a side table and grabbed one of the voluminous floral arrangements. Yanking the flowers out, he carried the vase back to his mother and promptly dumped the water over her face.

The king backed away as his wife shot upright, sputtering and waving her hands in front of her face. "What—? Who dares—?" The assistant, deciding this was beyond the realm of the hazard pay she received, scurried as far away from the queen as the room allowed.

By the time the queen had all the water wiped out of her eyes, all she had left to look at was Jon glaring at her. Almost immediately, she burst into tears again. "I *told* you that your brother needed you." She dissolved into incoherent sobbing, out of which only the occasional sentence fragment could be heard. "Ignore your family for *appointments* . . . might as well have *no* sons . . ."

Jon turned to his father, who had slightly more experience translating his wife's crying jags, but all the man could do was shrug helplessly and gesture at the note still clutched in the queen's hand. "A page came in with it about ten minutes ago. You saw what happened next."

Oh, please no.

Feeling himself go very cold, Jon grabbed his mother's hand before she could move it away. "The note, Mother. Now." Since the sobbing continued unabated, it seemed at first that she hadn't heard, but when he pried her fingers apart they gave in much more easily than they had for his father.

When he had the entire paper safely in his hand, he smoothed it out and angled the words away from everyone so he could read it. In the background, the noise from the ballroom took on a decidedly restless edge.

Dear Family,

I've gone to seek in enlightenment. Unfortunately, I'm not really sure what it looks like, since most of the books I've been reading use really big words I don't quite understand. Not even Jon was able to help me with them, but since he said I should go find someone who could, I think he'd think this is a good idea.

I'm giving the crown to Jon, since he's a lot smarter than me and does most of the kinging stuff anyway. If someone sees him, they should probably tell him he's the heir now, and that I left the crown on the top shelf in the closet in my room next to a box of old hunting trophies.

Cheers,
Rupert

Jon closed his eyes a moment, swearing softly. It was a poor substitute for what he *wanted* to do—scream, beat his head against the wall as a punishment for his sheer stupidity, and kick Rupert so hard he couldn't sit down for a week—but he didn't have time for any of that.

Instead, he crumpled the letter into a ball and turned back to his father, who actually flinched away at whatever he saw in Jon's eyes. "I need the page who brought this," Jon snapped, then pointed at the tallest of the two pages still being thwarted by the bird. "Get me one of the stable boys helping to park carriages downstairs." As the first page raced off, Jon switched his attention to the shorter, still frozen one. "Get me Monsignor Lawton. NOW."

Lawton—he'd decided early on that "Monsignor" conveyed suitable flair while meaning absolutely nothing—could tap his spy network and hopefully start tracking Rupert from the details provided by the page and the stable boy. Also, he was one of a very small number of people who could find Kate and explain the definitely temporary situation that had cropped up. He could fix it, of course—he just needed a little time.

The restlessness outside had gotten infinitely worse in the time it had taken him to read the letter. Only moments after the pages left, it got bad enough the royal announcer abandoned his post and pushed into the room. "Your Majesties, the people are waiting for you!" At the sight of the sobbing queen, he froze and stared at her husband and son in horror. "Her Majesty can't be presented like this? What have you done to upset her so?"

"She's fine," Jon growled, shoving Rupert's letter deep in his pocket. He wanted to leave so he could start seriously working on the situation, but he needed to get everyone here secured first. "And there's not going to be any announcements for this ball—just get the music started. *Now.*"

The steward's eyes widened in horror. "Surely there's *someone* I can announce! At least Prince Rupert—he cuts such a stunning figure in those spotlights."

At this, the queen erupted into a heartbroken wail. "My baby's not even a prince anymmph—" Her husband's hand clamped down over her mouth, but the horror in the steward's eyes made it clear he'd gotten the message anyway.

If the resulting silence had lasted just a few more seconds, it might have given Jon enough time to come up with a suitable cover. Instead, the trumpeter burst in, a desperate look on her face, backed by the sound of a crowd that had started to grow almost angry. "Worthington!" she hissed at the announcer, glancing nervously over at Jon and his parents. "I don't know what's going on in here, but someone needs to get out there immediately."

The steward grabbed Jon's arm and practically threw him through the open doorway and onto the top of the ballroom stairs. The muttering of the gathered nobility turned into a sigh of relief that *someone* had come out to acknowledge their presence, but it faded away as Jon straightened. This was definitely not the member of the royal family they had been expecting.

Jon took a deep breath, already putting together a story about Rupert being called away on a quest at the last minute. Hopefully, everyone could hear him from here.

The trumpet started. "His Highness Prince Jonathan Alistair Crispin Lorimer Charming, heir to the throne of Somewhere!"

There were a few heartbeats of echoing silence, then a lone clapper started somewhere near the front of the ballroom. Soon, others followed, creating a hesitant, scattered round of applause fueled by a mixture of confusion and fear that they might be the only people who hadn't already heard about this. Comforting himself with the thought that he was going to *immediately* fire the announcer as soon as he got clear of the crowd, he smiled in an attempt to assure people this was exactly what was supposed to be happening. He'd mention the quest as soon as the people had finally given up on the clapping, and everyone could start the ball far more relieved than they were at the moment.

Then, he saw Kate, standing by the furthest set of doors. Jon could tell even from this distance she was far too still, but he told himself that could just be some well-deserved shock on her part. He could get past it if she would just give him a few minutes to explain.

His stomach clenched as she backed away from him, almost stumbling in her rush to leave. When she hit the door she turned and ran with enough speed to make it painfully clear that she wasn't planning on coming back.

Without even needing a command from his brain, Jon ran down the stairs after her.

THIRTEEN

Falling Apart

I t wasn't until Kate looked down and saw grass beneath her feet
that she realized she'd run out the wrong door.

Breathing hard, she stared blankly at the manicured gardens that served as the palace's backyard, desperately trying to make her brain work enough to figure out what she was going to do next. Or if there was anything that could be done at all.

Behind her, she heard the sound of running footsteps; Rellie was panting. "Did you mean to come out here?" The question was genuinely curious, and Kate remembered she'd left the girl standing behind one of the doors when she'd stepped into the ballroom. Rellie had no idea what was going on when she saw Kate bolt past again, and it could only be blind luck that the girl had even thought to follow her. "Because I know I'm not an expert on the whole fancy dress ball thing, but I really don't see where this fits in."

Kate squeezed her eyes shut, fighting the sudden and absolutely unhelpful urge to burst into tears. How could she have been so *stupid* as to believe this could work? Sure, the paperwork had *said* there was a Prince Rupert, but the paperwork had been wrong before and she'd *known* that. And Jon—her chest hurt at the thought of him—maybe he'd lied to her because he thought it was the kindest way to get out of having some random girl thrown at him. She didn't know what he'd planned to do when they got to the ball and there was no Rupert for Rellie to dance with, but knowing Jon, he would already have some plan worked out if she hadn't just ruined it by walking in before he was ready.

But the part about pretending to be interested in her . . . There was no need for that, no need at all.

"Kate?" Sounding definitely worried now, Rellie reached out to tentatively touch Kate's shoulder. "What happened? Are you okay?"

Opening her eyes, Kate forcefully shoved everything else aside until she was fairly certain she could trust her voice. "It turns out that Jon is the prince you're supposed to be marrying." Sure, she sounded like someone had been jumping up and down on her throat, but as long as the tears didn't show up she'd take what she could get. "He was announced as the heir to the throne just as I stepped into the ballroom."

There was a long moment of silence before Rellie's hesitant voice said, "But . . . both of you said that the name of the prince I was supposed to be marrying was Rupert. I even danced with his jacket."

"I don't know what happened with Rupert. I don't even know if there was a Rupert." Kate turned around, guilt slicing through her at the rapidly deepening confusion on the girl's face. Just because Kate had been an idiot to trust in the magic she sold, she had no right to drag Rellie into the middle of all this. "I'm sorry, at least part of this is my fault. I lied about Jon being my assistant, and there's a chance that Jon lied about a couple of different things."

Rellie's brow furrowed, as if she knew she must be missing something before it would all start to make sense. "But why? I mean, I get the bit about the assistant—I knew right away that was pretty fishy. But why make up all that stuff about Rupert? And if he was lying, why did he keep coming back? I mean, I'm not very good at lying, but even I know that you're not supposed to hang around afterward."

Kate folded her arms across her chest, a protective gesture that did absolutely nothing to ease the raw ache inside her. The slow burn of anger rising within her only made it worse, lashing her with the memory of each time she hadn't listened to her brain telling her this was never going to work. "He probably had a reason," she said, not wanting to imagine what it might have been. It wouldn't make it any easier to know. "You'll have to ask him the next time you see him."

Rellie stared at Kate, dismay slowly replacing the confusion. "You're not going to be with me? You're my Fairy Godmother! You have to stay with me until we've figured out what to do about all of this!" She blinked as a thought hit her, and her expression cleared for just a moment. "Wait—since there's no Rupert, can't we just sort of cancel this whole thing? I'll keep the dress, you go back and tell your boss that it all fell through, and later we can come back here together and yell at your sweetie for causing all this trouble."

Kate, however, was no longer listening. "My boss," she whispered in horror, eyes tearing at the possibilities that had begun to tumble in her head at Rellie's words. Bubbles wouldn't *care* what had happened, why it had happened, or even what the name of the groom was. If Kate went to her with the news that the entire job had collapsed, she'd just send in another Fairy Godmother to dose everyone with so much True Love they wouldn't come out of it for at least a year. If she never reported back in, Bubbles would've done the same thing.

Jon would end up marrying Rellie anyway, no matter how either of them felt about it now.

She was jolted back into the moment when Rellie shook her shoulders. "Stop looking so freaked out!" the girl insisted, starting to sound more than a little panicked. "You're the one who's supposed to know what's going on!"

A thousand different and equally dreadful emotions swamped her all at once. There was absolutely no way any of them was going to be able to get out of this. "You liked Jon, didn't you?" she heard herself say, the words sounding distant in her head. It didn't mean she didn't hate herself for them. "And I know you'd enjoy being a princess."

Rellie's panic gave way to an even deeper confusion than before. "Kate," she said slowly, hands still on the Fairy Godmother's shoulders. "You're really starting to scare me. I think you should sit down for a while and take a couple of deep breaths or something, because you're making me be the sensible one right now, and I really, really, *really* don't like it."

Kate blinked, saved from having to respond by the sight of a figure emerging from the palace's backdoor. The figure paused, then headed in their direction. Kate cursed herself for not taking five extra minutes to find a spot that wasn't immediately visible to absolutely *everyone* wandering by. Like guards, for example, or people willing to call for them without listening to explanations. One of a thousand mistakes she'd made since first tripping over Jon. "We need to get out of here," she said quickly, grabbing Rellie's arm and heading toward the ornamental maze. A few minutes in a quiet corner was all she'd need to set up a doorway, and which would at least mean prison wouldn't be added to the carriage wreck that had become their lives. "Fairy Godmothers might be okay in the ballroom, but out here without proper authorization, we can be considered trespassers just like everyone else—"

"Kate!"

It took a second for her to recognize Jon's voice shouting her name, and she nearly tripped as her brain missed her body's instant decision to stop moving. Kate whirled around, staring wide-eyed at the figure running toward them. Beside her, relief crossed Rellie's face as she pulled her arm out of Kate's slack grip. "This is perfect," she whispered to Kate. "Now you can yell at him right away, and he can tell you he's sorry that much faster."

Kate couldn't respond, thoughts scattered by the realization that there was no way Jon could have been out there this fast unless he'd run after her the moment she'd fled. But she hadn't thought he'd even seen her show *up*, let alone disappear. And he couldn't just run off when there was an entire ballroom of people staring at him, especially if he were the *crown prince*.

He was close enough now she could see his expression; the desperation on his face was enough to make her heart stumble. Her anger, however, was quick to lash out, grateful to have another and equally deserving target. "Your Highness," she said icily, throwing her internal walls back up as fast as she could. "Taking a quick break from your party?"

Jon stopped a few feet away from her, wincing as if she'd just jabbed him with something. "Come on, Kate, don't look at me like that. Please." His hand lifted briefly, as if he was going to reach out to her, but something in her face made his hand flinch back into place. "I know I was an idiot for not telling you right away, but I swear I was going to fix that tonight at dinner."

She folded her arms across her chest again, fighting off a fresh stab of pain at the reminder of the evening she'd been so looking forward to. "You don't have to pretend we were still going to dinner anymore," she shot back, once again cursing herself for her stupidity and Jon for working so hard to encourage it. "I'm pretty sure I would have figured it out after Rellie made her entrance at the ball and there was no Rupert waiting for her."

Jon's eyes blazed with a rush of anger that was almost surprising. "I swear to you I'll find him," he said darkly. "I'll have to kill him first, but Rellie can have him when I'm done. It may take me a couple of days to drag him back here, but luckily Rupert's an even bigger idiot than I am . . ." He trailed off when he noticed Kate staring at him in confusion, then took a deep breath and started again. "I'll have more of the details after I've talked to a few people, but I only found out that he'd disappeared about five minutes before you did. I haven't really had time to question anybody."

Kate just stared at him, half of her wondering if he was just trying to talk his way out of everything. It was the other half, though, that she needed to be careful of. "So, you're saying that Rupert just . . . ran off before the ball." There was an accusatory edge to her voice, a self-defense that she clung to with both hands. "For no particular reason."

Picking up on everything Kate wasn't saying, Jon's eyes narrowed. "He decided to go find enlightenment. Stupid, yes, but that's Rupert for you." He watched her, a little wary. "Why do you look like you're waiting for me to sell you something?"

Kate opened her mouth, more than ready to start shouting at him, but Rellie had already started answering the question. "She said you were lying about Rupert because you didn't want to be the guy who had to marry me," the girl announced, claiming both Kate and Jon's attention. Rellie glared at Jon, hands fisted on her hips and chin lifted in defiance. "It made her really freak out, which means I'm kind of mad at you right now even though I didn't want to marry you either."

Jon's eyes widened, then his brows snapped back down into a glare as he turned to Kate. "You think I was making the whole—"

But Rellie wasn't quite finished. She turned to Kate, looking just as frustrated with she had at Jon. "But now I'm kind of mad at her, too, because she was just supposed to yell at you and be okay again." She switched her gaze back to Jon, but lifted a hand to jab a finger back in Kate's direction. "But all she's doing is standing here being all frosty, you haven't even said you're sorry *once*, and if you two keep this up we're going to be out here all night!"

Kate had seen the hurt that briefly flared in Jon's eyes before sliding into *anger*, of all things. She was more than happy to do all the yelling Rellie wanted to hear, but the last thing they needed right now was an audience. "Yelling isn't going to fix any of this, but feel free to go back inside the ballroom," she snapped, meeting the girl glare for glare. "I won't be able to give you the entrance we talked about, but Jon should be in to dance with you in just a minute." She shifted her gaze over to Jon, packing as much ice into her voice as it would hold. "I have no idea what it was you were planning, but the least you can do is let her have tonight."

"What I was planning?" His voice sounded strained, like he was barely keeping himself from shouting, his hands curled into fists. "One thing I didn't tell you—*one*—and you're suddenly certain I'm a compulsive liar. A *bad* compulsive liar, which right now might almost be even more insulting."

She gritted her teeth. "Maybe things just got away from you."

"They did! That doesn't mean I made any of it up!" When her only response was silence, his expression hardened. "Believe me, if I'd just been trying to get rid of a pest of a potential bride and her Fairy Godmother, there are plenty of easier ways to go about it."

The words stabbed, as they were meant to, deflating her anger into a knot of grief and heartache that made her lose her stability all over again. "I know. Maybe you were just trying to be gentle." Kate put all her energy into keeping her voice even, resisting the urge to look anywhere but at his slowly widening eyes. She could maybe figure out a way to keep them from getting hit with True Love, but not if she let herself keep pretending she was going to get anything out of it for herself. "If you have any complaints, there's a Fairy Godmothers, Inc. customer service desk."

"*Kate.*" The word had more than a little desperation in it. "I'm begging you not to do this to me. I was sorry I said it as soon as I closed my mouth." Whatever had kept Jon from touching her previously was no longer enough, because he reached out and grabbed her arm before she could think to take a step back. "I don't know what's going on in that head of yours, but I swear the only thing I lied to you about was my job title." His eyes radiated the clearest sincerity she'd ever seen. "Everything else was just my idiot brother and really bad cosmic timing, both of which I will fix the *second* I figure out how."

Kate squeezed her eyes shut for a moment, not quite able to look into those eyes of his anymore. She wanted so much to be mad at him again, since it was worlds easier than having to deal with Jon being sweet. "I shouldn't have accused you of making up your brother." She took a deep, shaky breath, opening her eyes to focus on a point somewhere around Jon's left ear. "I was thrown by the announcement in the ballroom, and I . . . I overreacted."

The tension in his muscles eased slightly, but he still didn't let go of her arm. "Given the circumstances, that is completely understandable," he said gently, taking a step closer. "Next time, though, I'd consider it a favor if you'd just shout at me like Rellie suggested. It would be much easier to take."

Next time . . . Kate heard Rellie's sigh of relief, the small sound only managing to make things worse. "Like I told Rellie, yelling isn't going to fix any of this." Her voice sounded empty and tired even to her own ears, and she could feel Jon's grip on her arm tighten ever so slightly as she spoke. She had to get him to stop, or there was no way she was going to be able to think enough to protect them. "What might help, though, is for you to go back inside and reassure your subjects that you haven't just been kidnapped or run off to join your brother."

She felt fingertips come to rest on the side of her jaw, let her head be turned enough she looked directly into Jon's steady, worried eyes.

"And if I do, you won't be here when I come out," he said. It wasn't a question, but the way his jaw tensed suggested he took her silence as its own answer. "Give me another option, Kate." His voice was rough as he slid his hand up to cup her cheek. "Tell me what I need to do to make sure you don't slip away while I fix all this."

Kate refused to let herself lean into his touch, determined to cling to whatever shreds of control she had left. "You can't fix this, Jon," she said quietly, giving up on any chance of putting her walls back up for the moment. All she could do was keep the tears that thickened her throat from getting anywhere near her eyes, and focus on getting through this so she could keep both of them from drawing Bubbles' attention. "It's not your fault, but too much has gone wrong too fast. The most either of us is going to be able to do is damage control."

"Enough damage control," Jon said softly. "You've usually ended up solving the problem."

"Not this time." She inhaled another shaky breath, closing her eyes when his other hand reached up to cup her cheek. "Don't do that," she breathed, finally making herself pull away from him. "It just makes everything harder than it already is."

"You're trying to leave me." Hurt crept back into his voice.

It was a final rip to her heart, deep enough she realized she had no other choice but to get it over with. Quick and clean, because if she kept trying to do this slowly it would kill her. "If I stay, another Fairy Godmother will just sneak in and dose you with the company love potion." When she felt him freeze, she opened her eyes and tried not to think about what she saw in his. If he knew what was coming, he'd stop trying to make her believe again and start working on the real problem. "It'll convince you that you're so madly in love with Rellie you won't even remember what I look like."

Jon only stared at her, horrified, and she suddenly knew exactly what he'd meant when he said yelling was so much easier to take. Rellie, as always, was much more direct, and gave Kate a half-hearted kick in the leg. "Even *I* know you don't tell guys stuff like *that*, Kate," she said morosely. "You guys are supposed to be *making up*, not making everything worse!"

Kate opened her mouth, but whatever he was about to say vanished forever when she caught the first faint edges of a glow forming behind her. She hadn't even managed to turn around completely before she heard the all-too-familiar sound of tinkling bells and caught the first wisps of purple smoke. She tensed, some ridiculous instinct making her stand between Jon and the doorway as she wished hopelessly that it wasn't Bubbles who was about to arrive.

But it was Ned who stepped through the gate. He held out a wand attachment no one ever used, starting to talk before his feet even touched the grass. "I saw that you forgot this back at the office, and I thought maybe—"

He caught sight of Kate and Jon's faces, processing the fact that Rellie was sitting on the lawn beside them rather than dancing at the ball like she was supposed to. He opened his mouth, then closed it, completely at a loss as to what to say.

"You might as well sit down," Rellie said kindly, gesturing to a spot on the grass beside her. "It looks like we're going to be here for a while."

FOURTEEN

Working the Room

Ned knew he wasn't supposed to be there. He'd been ready with a long explanation about Kate leaving behind what *must* be an incredibly useful attachment (even though he'd never actually seen any Fairy Godmother use one before) and how important it was to bring it to her in the field. Then, if that didn't work, he'd planned to throw himself on her mercy and hope he'd get the chance to at least see Rellie from a distance.

Clearly, no one was having much luck with plans at the moment.

"Uh . . ." Ned stood there like an idiot, trying to make his voice work as he stared at Rellie. No matter how pretty she was, she was the client, and even he knew she was *definitely* not supposed to be out here at this point in the evening.

He turned to Kate, hoping she could somehow help. "Did the ball get cancelled or something?" he asked.

"Ned." Kate hesitated, as if trying to come up with an

explanation of some kind, then clearly gave up and shook her head. She ran a tired hand through her hair, glancing behind him to the spot where he'd just arrived. "Let's just say you really don't want to get involved in any of this."

The one non-panicking part of Ned's brain chimed in its support at Kate's suggestion. Leaving was probably the only way he could actually be of any help in all this. "That's probably a good—" Then Kate turned her head just right, or the light shifted somehow, and he realized she had that look in her eye his mother always had when she was trying not to cry. "Oh, no," he breathed, thoughts of fleeing temporarily forgotten. "Kate, are you okay?"

Kate blinked, startled at the question. "I . . . I'm fine." But she pressed her lips together after she said it, as if she knew just how much the pause had given her away. "Rellie and Jon were just about to go back inside."

Out of the corner of his eye Ned could see Jon take a step forward, hand half raised as he reached out toward her. Ned beat him to it, cutting off Jon's approach as he glared at the other man in a way he wouldn't have normally even considered doing. He turned back to Kate. "Seriously, what happened?"

Kate paused, long enough to come up with a different version of "I'm fine." A relatively gentle kick somewhere in the vicinity of his left calf grabbed his attention. When he turned, Rellie was looking up at him. "It'll just be easier if I fill you in," she said. "How much do you already know?"

Ned was about to tell her when Kate interrupted with a hand on his shoulder. "We've run into some problems, but I'm going to take care of them," she said quickly, shooting Rellie a pointed look that was almost as good as a hand against her mouth. "A few of the job details may end up having to be shifted around a little, but there's no need for you to worry. For my sake, please just go home for the rest of the night and get some sleep. I'll see you back at the office as soon as I can—"

"No, she won't," Jon cut in, suddenly close enough to lay his own hand on Kate's shoulder. He scowled at Ned, a clear warning not to interfere this time, then turned to her with a look that was somewhere between anger and pleading. "Kate, just give me some time so we can talk about this."

Kate's jaw tensed. "What *you* need to do is go back inside the palace and be the prince your subjects are expecting right now. The last thing we need is everyone inside that building knowing what's going on."

Ned's brow furrowed. "Wait, Jon's a *prince*? But that means . . ."

No one else was paying attention. "Everyone had to have seen you running out of that ballroom, and they're probably getting more and more worried that you haven't come back yet." Kate's voice was sharp, frustrated. But at no point did she make a move to shake off Jon's arm. "In fact, someone should be showing up to drag you back inside in a complete panic any minute now."

"No one's going . . ." Jon's denial trailed off, clearly not believable enough to get all the way out of his mouth. "All I'll have to do is threaten to make them my mother's personal assistant. Whoever it is will be back inside so fast they'll leave a flame trail."

"If your job really is anything like you described it, it won't matter what you tell them, because they won't be able to pull themselves back together without you. Both you and they know that." Kate's words were cool, but Ned could feel the anger simmering closer and closer to the surface. Weirdly enough, it was the first comforting thing he'd seen since he'd gotten here. "So you might as well go back inside now. The longer you wait, the worse the mess with your subjects will get and the harder it will be for you to clean up."

Jon's jaw clenched, his own anger flaring like someone had taken a match to it. "What good will cleaning up my own mess do if a Fairy Godmother is just going to show up as soon as I'm done and pump me full of love potion? It's not like you're giving me a choice in any of this!"

Pain flared in Kate's eyes, her face going pale as she fought to get her composure back. "I know," she said, her voice deathly serious. "I promise you I'll figure out some way to keep that from happening."

Helplessly listening, Ned finally started to comprehend the full picture of everything that had gone wrong. Even the *thought* of anyone he knew being forcibly dosed with True Love sent cold chills racing down his spine, and that didn't begin to cover what Bubbles would do to Kate if their boss knew she'd thought about trying to stop the contract. Crushing Ned into an intern-shaped smear wouldn't even slow her down.

The thoughts faded as Ned felt small, cool fingers wrap around his; he turned to meet a pair of violet eyes that sparkled in a way he couldn't have imagined by just looking at the photo. "Could you help me up?" Rellie said. "They're going to be at this for a while, and even when I try to be sensible neither of them listen." She let Ned help her to her feet before brushing some of the grass off her skirt. Then, she grinned at him, bright enough to dazzle, and Ned imagined his brain melting around the edges. "But if you take me inside to dance, maybe they'll be fought out by the time we get back and everybody will be calm again."

Ned stared at her, transfixed. Right at that moment there was nothing he wanted more than to say yes, even as a part of him tried hard to remember the crisis occurring only a few feet away. "I can't. I mean, Kate . . ."

Rellie nodded as if she'd heard some sort of coherent response. "Kate! Can Ned *please* take me dancing?" When Kate turned, still looking frustrated and miserable, Rellie made her eyes go big and puppy-like. "Watching you two argue instead of kiss is really upsetting me, and getting to twirl around the dance floor in my poufy skirt was always going to be my favorite part about tonight. I promise we'll be good and come right back out as soon as you've stopped fighting."

Kate hesitated, clearly wanting to say no, but didn't seem quite able to come up with a good enough reason. Jon didn't say anything, but watched every movement she made with a storm cloud of emotion in his eyes.

Finally, Kate sighed and rubbed her eyes. "This is probably going to be another mistake, but I'll let you go inside for one dance." When Rellie opened her mouth to protest, Kate held up a warning finger. "*One.* And I'm making Ned responsible for knowing when it's time to come back out."

Rellie thought about this for a moment, then nodded in agreement and tugged on Ned's hand. "Come on." She smiled again. "If you want, I can teach you the steps."

IT WILL SERVE Jon right if the guests actually start stampeding.

Lawton felt a quick stab of guilt at the thought, a sure sign that alcohol deprivation was doing terrible things to his brain. Without letting himself think about it he snagged a glass of hideously pink champagne off a passing tray, downing it in a single swallow before grabbing the shirtfront of the violinist who was trying to sneak out the back exit. "Did I say you could stop playing?"

The man crumpled. "We were told we could have breaks!" he wailed, fat fingers trying and failing to free his clothing from Lawton's grip. "I skipped dinner because I knew we'd be coming to this thing and I'm starving! I could hear my stomach growling over the music!"

If Lawton had been free to indulge himself, he would have guided the fool to a heaping tray of Madame Stewart's hors d'oeuvres and watched in amusement as the man sealed his own gastronomic doom. Unfortunately, the distraction provided by the music was currently the only thing keeping the ballroom full of elegantly dressed, nervously muttering sheep from devolving into a total panic. "You should be grateful your stomach at least has the ability to growl in harmony, a skill you yourself apparently lack." He flipped the man around by the shoulders and shoved him back toward his orchestra mates. "Be grateful. I've saved you from a poisoning."

Lawton stayed where he was, glaring, until he heard the music start again. He turned his attention to the other skittish, stupid souls Jon persistently felt was his responsibility to take care of. Of course, Jon was not actually here to take care of them at the moment, having been seen several minutes before on the back lawn in the midst of an intense and apparently unpleasant discussion with the love of his life. Lawton had ordered that both of them be left alone, suspecting there was more at stake than he realized, and had taken it upon himself to keep the crowd contained so no one got spooked enough to counteract his order.

If Jon hadn't calmed his Katharine down in fifteen minutes,

Lawton decided, he was going to go out there and drag the woman back into the palace himself.

He heard whispered discussion from somewhere to his right. Though he hadn't particularly want to, his excessively keen hearing caught the word "prince" at least twice during one of the asides. Accepting the inevitable, Lawton squared his shoulders and prepared to do what he could to hold back the tide of gossip with a few carefully constructed countermeasures.

"What a dedicated royal heir we have—so intent on keeping the country running smoothly he can't even stay for his own party;" "Oh, they've been discussing this for weeks. I heard your approval was the loudest—with how frantic your schedule is, no wonder it's slipped your mind;" "Haven't you heard? It's all the rage for princes to dash madly out of balls. I'd be afraid we were out of fashion if it hadn't happened to us;" "What a delicate, feminine creature our queen is. Of course she's supportive of her son's new position;" "Oh, you know Rupert. Such an independent thinker."

Halfway through his route, Lawton caught sight of one of the pages he often used to keep track of comings and goings in the palace. He threaded his way through enough full skirts to reach the young woman, pulling her into a reasonably soundproof spot behind a life-size, faux-ice sculpture of a unicorn. The girl's face lit with an expression of vehemently-defended innocence. "I swear, sir, the big to-do with the announcers and his Highness's new title was the first *anybody* had heard about it! All of the horses in the stables are still present and accounted for, including Prince Rupert's. And if he'd been seen near any of the departing carriages, there would have been an uproar about it long before now. I can get you a list, just in case, but with the ball tonight most of them have been arriving."

Lawton waited patiently through the guilt-induced burst of information, staying silent for a few moments after it was over to make sure he had truly gotten everything. When he was certain, he gave the page a measuring look. "Now that we've gotten *that* out of your system, it's time to prove that intelligence of yours is useful for something more than crafting excuses. I'll not only need that list of departing carriages, but also the names of everyone who spoke to Rupert this morning. Preferably in chronological order."

The words cut off as he realized someone new had arrived.

As the page scurried off to begin her overtime, Lawton's attention shifted, head turning to follow a newly arrived guest. No horns blew, no announcement was made, and the lack of specialized lighting meant the oohing and aahing was almost completely nonexistent. On top of that, as Lawton discovered when his eyes passed over the staircase Jon had so recently utilized, she hadn't even used the proper entrance.

The girl stepped onto a relatively clear patch of dance floor, her lilac-colored eyes huge and sparkling as she took in the rich decorations and expensive costumes of her fellow partygoers. True, her dress was the same hideous pink as the champagne, but the shade blended surprisingly well with the hideously green, purple, and gold gowns only a few feet away.

She closed her eyes, gracefully stretching her arms out. She spun around once, golden hair floating gently behind her as if she was dancing to fairy music instead of the efforts of the increasingly more off-key orchestra. The surrounding dancers ignored the girl, having long been trained to dismiss anything that didn't follow their well-established societal structure.

Lawton, on the other hand, couldn't help but be fascinated by the sight. Looking at her, it was easier to remember why it was supposedly such a privilege to come to these ridiculous things in the first place.

The girl stopped, as if realizing she'd forgotten something, then resolutely dove back into the crowd. She emerged again, briefly, then disappeared for a second as the hand of her mysterious dance partner began to resist. After considerable physical effort and more than a little sweet-talking, her companion revealed himself to be the young man who had accompanied Kate to her one and only even semi-official date with Jon. Ned, Lawton believed his name was.

Which meant, then, this was Rupert's bride-to-be, though that unfortunate future seemed to be the furthest thing from the girl's mind at the moment. She whispered something to the young man, causing him to blush to the tips of his ears before he began, rather creakily, to follow her into the waltz. She laughed, a sound of pleasure rather than humor at her partner's lack of skill, and even from here Lawton could see a dazed, adoring look in the young man's eyes.

As the song ended, it became clear Lawton was not the only person to have noticed the duo. One of the Baron LeMarche's endless sons took the opportunity to approach the couple, his doublet glittering obnoxiously as he put a proprietary hand on the girl's shoulder. A defensive look flashed across Ned's face, and as the girl turned, Lawton found himself moving forward to assist.

The pink skirt swung out. A second later, the nobleman was bent almost double and clutching his calf as if protecting it from wild beasts. Completely unconcerned, the girl gently guided her partner into the next round of dance.

Grinning, Lawton waited until the next song ended before continuing his approach. These two were definitely worth talking to.

NED KNEW THE stunned expression was probably still on his face, but even a whole song later he hadn't quite wrapped his brain around what had just happened. Sure, the guy hadn't been authorized to dance with her—Ned hadn't really been, either—but Rellie didn't seem the kind of girl to worry about that sort of thing. And the other guy was rich, probably a nobleman of some sort.

Rellie lifted her hand off his shoulder to wave it in front of his eyes. "Hey, you still with me?"

Ned blinked. "I still can't believe you kicked him."

Rellie shrugged, pulling them both into another twirl. "He was rude, and I didn't want to dance with him. I'm having too much fun with you." She smiled, melting him all over again. "Besides, you're really cute when you blush."

Before he could answer, Ned felt a tap on his shoulder, and even as he held on to Rellie more tightly he made himself turn around. It was probably his turn to do the kicking.

As soon as their eyes met, the man—Jon's friend, Ned remembered—held his hands up as he took a quick step back. "I come in peace." His voice was amused, and Ned felt himself relaxing slightly. Lawton turned to Rellie, offering her his hand. "I'm a friend of Jon's. Ned and I met earlier."

When Ned nodded his confirmation, Rellie sighed. "Then could you go outside and make him and Kate stop fighting? They should *totally* be kissing by now, but I can't figure out how to make them do it."

"I would be happy to help, I assure you," Lawton replied solemnly. "I was merely hoping you could offer some insight as to the precise nature of the argument going on outside. I know Jon technically lied about his job title, but as foolish as that decision was, there were mitigating circumstances."

Ned's heart sank as he tried to figure out the gentlest way to deliver the bad news, but Rellie beat him to it. "That part Kate didn't really seem worried about, but she's pretty sure her boss is going to drug Jon until he thinks he wants to marry me." She shook her head, looking over at Ned. "Are you sure you want to keep working for the Fairy Godmother people? They sound even meaner than my stepfamily tries to be."

"You mean there are bosses who aren't mean?" Ned said.

All Lawton could do was stare at the two of them. "Marry you?" Lawton attempted to school his tone back to a more neutral level, knowing its utter incredulity had to be offensive. But sweet angel of the vineyard, this was not the woman Jon had his heart set on. "I thought you and Rupert were supposed to be—"

"Um," Ned interrupted, feeling contractual details were probably his responsibility. "The contract says she has to marry the heir, not a specific person." Rellie had filled him in on some of the details of Rupert's disappearance, but he hadn't had the heart to explain to her just how much trouble they were all in. "And if Rupert's not the heir anymore . . ."

"Ah." Lawton closed his eyes. "Clearly, I'll be needing another drink."

FIFTEEN

Debating Techniques

It was hard to yell at someone who looked like a worried mother, so the argument stayed paused while Kate watched Rellie and Ned walk inside. Jon, who used the time to watch Kate, took slow, calming breaths and tried to figure why exactly he was so mad at her.

Logically, he knew he'd gotten off easy. The entire mess had been nearly as much his fault as it had Rupert's, and except for deciding he'd made his idiot brother up she'd barely gotten mad at him. On top of that, she'd already *apologized* for thinking that, then later did the same about the extremely disturbing corporate-sponsored love potion that wasn't even her fault. If he had any sense, Jon realized, he should probably be grateful at the way things were working out.

As Rellie and Ned disappeared into the ballroom, Kate sighed and rubbed the bridge of her nose. "That was probably a bad idea," she said to herself, the soft words sounding tired and defeated.

Hearing them, Jon was angry at her all over again. "It was the best thing to do," he countered. "We have enough to worry about without having to deal with helpful commentary from an audience."

For a second her eyes narrowed, like she was considering snapping right back at him, but then her jaw tightened and her expression closed down completely again. "You have a point," she agreed. The frustration building in Jon's chest pressed harder. "Though if you want to avoid the True Love, you really need to be the one inside dancing with Rellie. For a couple of days, at least, Bubbles won't check closely enough to tell if you're faking it."

Jon gritted his teeth, reminding himself that shouting at a woman was not the way to make progress with her. "Stop. Trying. To. Make. Me. Leave." When she went still, he forced his jaw to relax and repeated himself for emphasis. "I'm serious, Kate." There was an unfortunate roughness to his voice that he half hoped she couldn't hear. "Short of you saying 'I never want to see you again, you miserable, idiotic excuse for a liar,' I'm not going anywhere."

She stared at him for a long moment, as if trying to look deep enough inside his head to read his mind. Jon, feeling like he was eight years old again and hating it, lifted his chin and stared right back. Without anything to focus on, his anger threatened to crumble underneath the fear that had been hiding just behind it the whole time. If she would give him a chance, he was sure he could figure out a way to deal with evil Fairy Godmothers, love potions, or anything else standing in their way.

But nothing about the last ten minutes seemed to suggest she had any interest in giving him that chance.

Kate swallowed. "Why are you doing this?" she asked, sounding so utterly serious there was no way she could be joking. "Right now the only thing that makes any sense is that taking care of Rupert all these years has somehow made you lose your mind."

At first all Jon could do was stand there, caught off guard by the sudden conversational turn. "Probably," he admitted, brain scrambling to try and find some suitable way to respond. Maybe if he had some idea of what she meant. "But unless that's what the problem is, I'm not entirely sure what that has to do with what we're fighting about."

Frustration flaring in her eyes, she threw her hands up in the air. "I don't know if you've noticed, but I've been trying to *stop* the fight!" She was nearly shouting now, clearly having been pushed over some kind of tipping point Jon hadn't seen coming. "I've apologized! I've forgiven you! I've told you that I'll take care of Bubbles and the True Love, and you're free to go back to the rest of your life!" She stopped, voice losing some of its steam as she took a deep, shaky breath. "I don't know what else it is I'm supposed to say."

Jon stared at her a moment, then swore softly and closed his eyes. "Kate, what exactly do you think it is I've been doing for the last two weeks?"

There was only silence, deep and thick enough to quiet even the noises surrounding them. When Jon opened his eyes he could see Kate's mouth open slightly, like she wasn't entirely sure what to say to him. Her eyes, however, looked trapped, like she knew exactly what she wanted to say and couldn't quite bring herself to do it, and without warning he felt the bottom fall out of his stomach. Not only did she not want to give him a chance, she didn't even want him. She hadn't, apparently, even noticed he'd wanted her.

Or maybe she had, and simply thought it wasn't relevant enough to remember.

Jon sat down hard on the grass, closing his eyes again and hoping the moment would come when the memory of this would make him feel nothing more terrible than impulsive and stupid. That moment, though, was not the one he was in, so right now he was going to stay where he was until the ache in his heart stopped making it quite so hard to breathe.

Then he felt Kate's hands against his cheeks. "You idiot," she said softly, her voice full of the tenderness he'd started to worry he'd only imagined. He opened his eyes to find her kneeling in front of him, voice thick with emotion. "I'm scared to define exactly what it is you've been doing the last two weeks, but I've loved it. You're sweet, you're funny, you make me laugh, you're far more adorable than you have any right to be, and when I'm talking to you I feel just as beautiful, smart, and shining as a kingdom's PR department always makes their princesses out to be."

The words did wonders for healing every injured place in Jon's heart. He put his hands on Kate's arms, holding onto her in case she decided to start being sensible again. "You are that beautiful, smart, and shining," he told her, wanting her to feel the truth of the words as strongly as he did. "A PR department wouldn't know what to do with you."

She smiled, blinking eyes that were suddenly a little damp. "See, just like I said. You've lost your mind." Then she sobered. "But it's going to be hard enough just keeping the True Love away from you and Rellie, especially with Rupert disappeared to who-knows-where. Even with you helping, there's no way we can pull that off and still try to—"

It took only a slight tug for her to be on his lap, only a heartbeat later for her to be in his arms. Her lips were soft and warm enough to drown in, fitting against his as if they were always meant to be there. She fisted her hands in his shirt to pull him closer, and he swore he could hear music start to play.

When they broke apart for air, they separated only a few inches as they tried to return their breathing to normal. "That wasn't fair," she murmured, the tone of her voice suggesting she didn't really mind all that much.

Jon flashed a quick grin as he smoothed a hand up and down her back. "Maybe not, but it was effective." He decided it was time to abandon the safe route, since it was leaving her far too much room for doubt about his eventual intentions. It was probably a good idea, though, to tighten his grip. "I need to keep you around long enough to convince you to marry me."

She didn't respond at all for a moment, as if she hadn't really heard what he'd said. Then she blinked, and he could practically see the words sink in as her eyes went wider than he had ever seen them. "Marry you?" she whispered, stunned.

He nodded. "That's what I've been doing the last few weeks."

"But . . .That's . . ." She sat back a little, mouth working as she tried to come up with a sensible answer. "I can't marry you! You're a prince!"

"You see why I didn't tell you?" He lifted a hand to cup Kate's cheek. "There are no marital restrictions for royalty in Somewhere. It's left the royal family with a couple of unfortunate exes over the years, but right now I couldn't be more grateful."

"That's not what I meant." She reached up to pull his hand off her cheek, still looking at him as if he was insane. Thankfully, she still held on to it afterward. "You're a prince, Jon, and I'm essentially a member of the service industry. There's no way in the world anyone would accept me as a princess for even a second."

"I'm sure Rellie would love to teach you how to twirl around and flutter your eyelashes." When she made an exasperated noise, he pressed a quick kiss against her jaw that made her close her eyes. "You'd be amazing at helping me keep everything in line. All we'd need to do is teach you how to sit through three-hour-long meetings without falling asleep face first in the paperwork."

A grin almost snuck its way onto Kate's face, but then she caught herself and shook her head. "We've only known each other for two weeks! Even if I suddenly were to lose my mind enough to go along with this, there's nothing to say we won't wake up one morning completely unable to stand each other."

A brief vision of his parents flashed across Jon's mind. "Believe me, that's a possibility no matter how long you're engaged." There was a look in Kate's eyes that made it clear she was thinking too hard, and he kissed her again to chase it away. "But I find it hard to believe there's anything about you that I couldn't stand, and I promise you I'll learn to be really good at apology presents."

She made another exasperated noise. "For all you know, I'm rude to waiters and snore like a dragon with a bad head cold." She paused, eyes narrowing. "For all *I* know, you could snore like a dragon with a bad head cold."

Jon laughed. "You could never be rude to a waiter, even if he deserved it, and if we need to I'm certain we could get a deal somewhere on magical earplugs."

This time, the grin made it all the way onto her face, only to slip away a few seconds later. "If only magical earplugs were enough to take care of management." She sounded tired again, but noticeably less defeated than she had only minutes before.

Though it was a subtle enough change she probably hadn't even noticed, it gave him all the hope he needed. "Is there any chance I could just buy out the contract?" he asked, sliding his hand back until his fingers were threaded through the silkiness of her hair. "Make it worth more to leave us in peace than it is to drug me into marrying Rellie?"

Kate, who had winced a little at the mention of the word drug, considered it before shaking her head. "It's a special request from one of the board of directors. I've only met him once, but he seemed rich enough that I doubt money would get him to change his mind." He felt her fingers trailing around the back of his neck, absently playing with his hair as she thought. "Is there any chance of finding Rupert in the next couple of days and getting him to take his position back? Do you have any idea where he might have gone?"

Jon mentally scanned through the last few weeks, trying to locate and put together the pieces he had been too distracted to see the first time. It was the same problem he'd started working on before the steward's unfortunate announcement—he must really remember to fire him—but it was turning out considerably easier to contemplate when Kate was in his arms. "He mentioned wanting to find someone who could help him understand the big words in what he was reading. If he'd tried the university I would have already been called, but there's the Wise Old Woman Training Academy in the woods along our northern border. They're not really big on reporting to local authority figures, particularly this close to tax season."

"Back up a little." Eyebrows raised, Kate held up an interrupting hand. "Rupert ran away and made you the heir because he wanted to find someone to help him understand the big words?"

Jon sighed. "It's a long story, and I don't really want to tell it to you before you're legally related to these people." Kate scoffed but didn't respond further, and he returned his attention to the original topic of conversation. "He's going to start with the closer places first and work out from there, which leaves us with a handful of locations about a day's travel away." His eyes widened a little as a horrible thought hit. "Unless he's trying to be cunning."

"Don't think like that," Kate said sympathetically. "Focus on what we can handle."

Jon nodded. "There are about ten or fifteen inns between the palace and his likely destinations, if not now then in a couple of hours—he usually likes to spend mornings safely protected by bedcovers. If I narrow it down a little with intel from Lawton, I can send riders out to find the inn he stayed at before closing in on him."

The rest of the sentence trailed off as he realized Kate was pulling away from him, out of his arms, standing up. She grabbed his hand and started dragging him upright.

"What you just said is probably the closest thing we have to a plan right now, which means you should definitely be inside talking to Lawton instead of sitting out here with me." When he was on his feet, she looked down at their still-joined hands for a moment before meeting his eyes. "Besides, until we figure out a solution it's still probably safer for you to pretend you're crazy about Rellie, and she's inside, too."

Jon tensed, but when Kate squeezed his hand he made himself exhale slowly and relax. At the same time, it was always a safe bet to hold tighter onto Kate ."Only if you come inside with me."

"What?" Kate looked remarkably close to panic. Then she took a deep breath. "I can't do anything in there, and I really need to get started working on my end of the problem as soon as I can. I should go back to the office, maybe look for something in the old files."

She was right, he knew, but he couldn't shake the certainty that if he let Kate go now it would be the last he saw of her. "The files will undoubtedly be easier for you to access in the morning, and I doubt your boss is interested enough in overtime she'll pick up on our problem before then," he said, moving closer to her. "And don't worry. Even if no one's thought to sedate my mother yet, I give you my word that I'll protect you from her."

"Your mother?" This time, it was definitely panic Jon saw in those silvery green eyes. For one alarming moment, he thought Kate had somehow already met his mother, but then her voice lowered with a kind of muted horror. "You're a prince, which means your mother is . . ." She squeezed her eyes shut, and her voice got a slightly strangled quality to it. "The queen. Who is married to your father, the king."

This was not a good train of thought for her to be on. "Kate."

But before he could say more, her eyes flew open and her voice dropped to a whisper. "The man I met was your father?" When he pulled her close, not knowing what else to do, she stayed stiff for a moment before letting him wrap her in a comforting hug. "I definitely can't marry you now, because I'm going to have to spend the rest of my life avoiding your parents."

"If it helps, I think my father likes you," he murmured against her hair, rubbing her back in what he hoped was a comforting manner. "And believe me, I've spent most of my life trying to avoid my mother. If you marry me, we'd just do it together."

"Tell me that wasn't your attempt at a proper marriage proposal. I'd hate to have to apologize to Katharine for completely failing in your training." At the sound of Lawton's voice, both Jon and Kate looked up to see him walking across the lawn toward them at a properly casual but dignified pace. "Though in your favor, you do seem to have maneuvered yourself into a far more promising position than when I last had one of my people check on you." Before Jon could glare at that last bit, Lawton gave him his driest expression. "I would have myself, naturally, but I found myself otherwise occupied entertaining your guests."

Jon winced, guilty—from the second Kate had vanished out the door he'd completely forgotten the crowd existed.

"I am *so* sorry about that," Kate told Lawton, sounding as apologetic as Jon should have been. "I kept trying to make him go back inside, but there were some things we had to work out."

"Namely, that she was going inside with me," Jon cut in, voice firm enough to make Kate look back to him. Her brow lowered like she was about to argue, but after staring into his eyes for a moment she very carefully closed her mouth again.

Lawton smiled. "Excellent. We have a plan." Ignoring Jon for the moment, he recaptured Kate's attention by lifting her hand off Jon's shoulder and pressing a kiss to her knuckles. "Always a pleasure, Katharine," he said genially, sketching a brief bow in her direction. "Your delightful associates inside filled me in on some of the new complications Rupert's little adventure has left us with. You have my deepest sympathies, though I do have some ideas that may be of assistance."

Kate looked at Lawton, then back over at Jon, before letting out a resigned sigh. "You can tell me all about it once we're inside."

SIXTEEN

❦

Jumping Off

The walk inside, unfortunately, gave them plenty of time to eliminate all the easy options.

"I'm serious, Lawton." Kate shook her head, biting back her rising annoyance. She, Lawton, and Jon stood outside one of the many sets of ballroom doors, doing their best to resolve this particular debate before dealing with the crowd. "I may have looked like I knew what I was talking about during our little spy session, but that was mostly because I'm very good at nodding my head."

Lawton sighed like an adult trying to deal with a stubborn child. "Katharine, it's not as if blackmailing is really that difficult."

"For you, maybe." She heard the stubbornness in her voice, and out of the corner of her eye she saw Jon grin. In a way, it was almost as much his fault— both Lawton and Jon seemed convinced they could alter the course of the universe if they felt like it, and needed reminding that the rest of the world didn't have quite the same skill set. "But if I tried to be threatening, all we'd get out of Director Carlson is hysterical laughter. I'm just not scary enough."

Lawton raised an eyebrow, then turned to Jon. "Is she?"

Kate scowled at them as Jon laughed. "I'm already in enough trouble tonight," Jon said. When the scowl deepened, he grinned and took her face in his hands. "And now, as much as I'd rather stay here and let you explain to Lawton just how wrong he is, I really need to get inside and start making it look like we'd planned this from the beginning." He leaned in to capture her mouth in a quick, toe-curling kiss, frying good sense and nerve endings before pulling away and opening the doors. "Come inside as soon as you can." His voice was warm and soft enough to cuddle. "Seeing you will help give me strength."

It took the sound of the door shutting for Kate to realize she'd started walking after him without any conscious command from her brain. She immediately stopped where she was, waiting until she was sure any more embarrassing impulses had passed. "That wasn't fair, either," she murmured, rubbing her chest as if the motion could settle her heart down at least a little.

Behind her, she heard Lawton chuckle. "I'd rather not repeat that cliché about love and war. It's beneath both of us."

Kate was almost startled into a laugh. "Thank you for that." Then, taking a final deep breath for courage, she opened the door and stepped into the fray.

Admittedly, the position behind the stairs didn't offer the clearest view of the ballroom and its multi-hued swirl of occupants, but the relative privacy made Kate feel secure enough to take a few steps out onto furthest edges of the dance floor. A part of her wondered if she should feel self-conscious about her wings, but in the sea of peacock feathers, miniature jeweled shrubs, and what from here appeared to be genuine gold frosting, she doubted anyone would actually notice.

She hunted for Jon, craning her neck a little to spot his dark head in the midst of the unnaturally tall piles of hair. She found him talking to a couple decked out in abundant, ludicrously tacky jewelry, holding the woman's hand as if he'd just kissed it and smiling confidently like all was right with the world. What was amazing was the way the couple nodded along with whatever Jon was telling them, the slowly relaxing expressions on their faces making it clear they believed every word he was saying.

She folded her arms across her chest, letting herself watch him work for a little while. "It's a little scary how good he is at that," she murmured, feeling absurdly proud of him. It was a lot easier to appreciate that particular talent of his when it wasn't directed at her. "Looking at him, you'd almost think we really did have all this planned from the beginning."

There was a moment of silence before Lawton came forward to stand beside her. "So, why aren't you quite convinced?" The words were light, but Kate recognized the seriousness behind the question. "For a moment, there was a look in your eyes that said you expected all this to disappear right in front of you."

"I want to believe him," she said quietly, feeling like she was admitting something dangerous.

"You sound utterly terrified when you say that."

She took a deep breath, weirdly relieved someone had said it out loud, and worked on relocating her calm so she could hold on to it with both hands. Hoping was one of the hardest things she'd ever been asked to do, and it felt nice for someone in the middle of everything to recognize that. "I'll try to work on that," she said finally. "Could you maybe not mention this to Jon, though? If he starts trying to convince me again, I'm pretty sure I won't survive it."

Lawton stared at her, expressionless, then paused to catch the attention of a young man walking by with a tray full of pink champagne glasses. He snagged two when it got sufficiently close, draining one in a single swallow. Kate had just enough time to hope Ned had the good sense to keep Rellie away from any of those trays before Lawton held the other glass out to her. "It's inferior, but surprisingly fortifying when good brandy isn't within the immediate vicinity."

Kate shook her head, amused. "I don't really like alcohol."

Lawton sighed. "That explains so much." Then, as if he'd somehow gotten an answer that satisfied him, he turned his attention back to the swirling crowd. "Your young charges dance with enthusiasm, I've noticed."

Kate just smiled, climbing the first couple of steps of the immense staircase before scanning the crowd for Ned and Rellie. She found them in almost the exact center of the ballroom, twirling happily around the floor in what from a distance appeared to be some sort of mutant version of the waltz. Occasionally, the duo would bump into nearby guests, who would shift away in annoyance without even turning around to get a good look at the source of their troubles. "Jon spent the last couple of weeks teaching Rellie and me how to dance," she said affectionately, watching them. She wanted to give them as long as she could before getting Rellie for her entrance and staged dance with Jon, both of which were necessary to fuel the information mill Bubbles would make sure she overheard. "I don't think Ned's ever been out on a dance floor before in his life."

Lawton finished off the second glass of champagne before following Kate up the stairs to get a better look at their current topic of conversation. "I can't help but note that, despite their rather erratic path, they seem to be making a concerted effort to avoid any of the ballroom's innumerable entrances. Am I correct in thinking they're trying to avoid us?"

"In a pathetic attempt to keep some control of the situation, I told Ned he would have to bring them back outside after one dance." Truthfully, she hadn't really expected Rellie to listen to the request, and it would be hard for an entire army of dwarves to stop the girl when she was intent on doing something. Ned didn't stand a chance. "They probably think if they stay away from the doors, I won't be able to find them and make them stop."

Kate watched Ned and Rellie pause in the middle of the dance floor, catching their breath in the silence between songs. Rellie leaned close to say something to Ned, who blushed so hard the tips of his ears changed color. Rellie grinned at him, eyes soft and full of affection, and planted a gentle kiss against his cheek. When her lips touched his skin, Ned's eyes closed.

Feeling the weight of the inevitable hit her, Kate sighed. If it had happened at any other time . . .

At her side, Lawton gave his head a quick shake, like he was trying to get rid of a surprising thought. Following his gaze, it was clear to see that he, too, had been watching Ned and Rellie, and it was enough to make Kate give in to what she'd already known. Just because everything else was a mess didn't mean *someone* in the middle of all this didn't deserve a happily-ever-after.

When Lawton noticed her watching him, Kate smiled. "Romance really is infectious, you know. Worse than a cold."

Lawton's eyebrows lifted, smiling wryly. "Is this your professional opinion?"

Kate shook her head, hiking up her skirts and starting down the stairs. "If you're looking for an expert on romance, the last person you want to talk to is a Fairy Godmother."

Returning her attention to the crowd, she took a deep breath and plunged in. After what felt like a mile of plumed headdresses, enormous skirts, and shiny gold buttons—which, apparently, could be blinding if the light hit them just right—Kate finally reached the happy couple. She grabbed Rellie's shoulder, causing the girl to jump like she'd been shouted at. "Rellie, I need to talk to you." Kate tried to keep her voice as low as possible, despite the orchestra blaring in their ears.

Rellie whipped around to face her, somehow managing to keep her hold on Ned in the process. Her expression was panic, while over her shoulder Ned's held an equal mixture of guilt and regret.

"Is it time?" he asked, trying to sound brave.

"That's actually what I needed to talk to you about." Kate wrapped her hand around Rellie's arm, pulling it away from Ned's. "Come with me out into the corridor where we can at least pretend to have some privacy."

Rellie gave Ned one last tragic, worried look, then stepped away from him and followed Kate just outside the nearest exit. Once the heavy wooden doors swung shut behind them, Rellie inhaled shakily and lifted her chin. "Okay, I'm ready." Her voice only wavered a little. "But I'm just going to have to dance with Jon, right? I mean, I don't have to worry about dancing with Rupert until you find him?"

Kate just looked at her, annoyance losing to the sudden rush of sympathy. After all, she knew just how the girl felt. "You don't have to marry Rupert if you don't want to."

Rellie blinked, startled. "I don't?" Her eyes lit for a second, then faded as her brow wrinkled with thought. "But I thought the point of doing all this in the first place was to get me all dressed up and swoony about the prince." Her eyes narrowed. "Don't tell me we're going back to that me-marrying-Jon mess."

"Of course not." The denial was immediate enough a slow grin spread across Rellie's face, and Kate had to follow it up with her best quelling look in order to keep the conversation from digressing. "But I also don't want you to marry someone you've never even met when you're interested in someone else."

Rellie's cheeks flushed nearly as red as Ned's had been. "I . . . it's not . . ." Her eyes met Kate's, and she let all the air out of her lungs in a rush. "Now, I know why you always get so goofy-looking every time you're talking to Jon."

Kate opened her mouth in denial, then closed it when she realized there was absolutely no safe response.

Then a thought hit Rellie. "Wait," she said. "Don't I have to marry Rupert for all of this to work out? I mean, that love potion you mentioned sounded pretty scary, and even if we avoid that stuff, your boss isn't going to be very happy with you."

Kate told herself to think positively. If nothing else, when Fairy Godmothers, Inc. tried to sue her she could at least ask Jon to pay for her lawyer without a twinge of guilt. "I'll try talking to your fa— the man who bought you the contract, convince him that you're safe and happy and . . ." She waved a hand vaguely, having not had much time yet to work out the specific details of her argument. ". . . don't need a Fairy Godmother-style happily-ever-after."

Rellie watched her, an oddly solemn expression on her face. "Do you think it's going to work?"

No, but it would do absolutely no good telling Rellie that. Besides, Kate didn't have a better plan at the moment. "I think we have to at least try." Then, not wanting to answer any more questions, she pushed the door to the ballroom back open. "Now, let's go find the boys before they get themselves into trouble."

IT WAS JON who found them first, intercepting Kate and Rellie before the crowd swallowed them back up. "Is everything all right?" he asked under his breath, not quite able to keep the worry off his face.

He and Kate should at least pretend they wanted to keep his and Rellie's dance together looking believable, but at his obvious concern Kate couldn't stop herself from leaning over and pressing a quick kiss against Jon's cheek. "Everything's fine," she said. Behind her, she could hear Rellie trying to jump high enough to see Ned over everyone else's head. "But we're not going to need Rupert anymore."

Jon tensed, moving closer to her. "I'm afraid more explanation is going to be necessary before I'm comforted."

"It's obvious Rellie and Ned like each other." She drew Jon's attention to the sight of Ned bursting through the crowd, practically skidding to a stop in front of Rellie with a terrified, hopeful look on his face. In response, Rellie threw her arms around his neck. "Okay, so maybe like is too mild a word." She turned back to look into Jon's eyes. "Either way, I can't make her marry Rupert."

Jon was silent for a moment, as if he was trying to decide what his reaction was going to be. Then he took her hand, holding on tight. "Your boss isn't going to be thrilled with this new insight of yours."

Kate took a deep breath, stealing a boost of courage for herself by giving Jon's hand a quick squeeze. It was cheating, maybe, but she needed it. "I'll go to Director Carlson and try to convince him that Rellie can be properly settled without the help of a company contract. As long as he doesn't feel responsible for her anymore, I don't think he'll care enough to argue." She probably wasn't going to mention that Ned was an intern—she'd try not to talk about him at all—and she'd suggest to Ned that a career at Fairy Godmothers, Inc. was probably not the best life plan for him. "If Carlson withdraws, then there's no reason for Bubbles to come after you and Rellie, or even Rupert and Rellie, with True Love."

"I'm starting to feel slightly more comforted," Jon said. Then, catching something in her eyes, his gaze narrowed and he moved her further out of Rellie and Ned's hearing range. "Do you think it's going to work?"

She smiled deliberately, wishing people would stop asking her that question. She wasn't nearly as good at lying as Jon. "I'm pretty sure you're going to need to find me a new job when this is all over. Even if I manage to convince Carlson, Bubbles isn't going to like me going over her head."

Jon lifted her hand to press a gentle kiss to its back. "I've already mentioned the job I think would be perfect for you."

Kate blinked, confused, then realized he was referring to the proposal. She glared at him, even as she felt her heart wobble dangerously. "Let's try surviving this first, okay? Then maybe we'll have the time to talk about this little insanity problem you have."

"I'm going to hold you to that." He squeezed her hand as his gaze shifted to a spot over her shoulder. "Congratulations on not becoming my sister-in-law."

Kate turned around to see a beaming Rellie, standing in the arms of a rather stunned-looking Ned. Kate had made the decision for Rellie's sake more than his, but it was probably a good sign he looked more awed than afraid. "I know! Isn't it great?" Rellie hesitated, wrinkling her nose a little as she mentally reviewed what she had just said. "Not that you would have made a bad brother-in-law, but—"

Jon held up a hand. "I understand."

Rellie settled back, relieved. "I mean, we still need to do the dance and everything so that this Bubbles lady doesn't get tipped off, but I'm not worried about that part. You're a pretty good dancer when we're not worried about marrying each other."

At the word "marry," Ned winced. "Not that I'm not all for making sure Bubbles doesn't come after us with the pointy end of her wand, but haven't we already screwed up the big dance? Rellie's been dancing with me all night, and you and Jon are practically radiating." At Kate's flushed cheeks, he cleared his throat and wisely skipped ahead to the next part of his thought. "Even if Rellie and Jon dance, isn't everyone going to know they're not really together?"

Jon looked over at Kate with the edges of a grin. "We were radiating?"

Kate poked him in the ribs, fighting back her own smile. "Stop being so adorable. It's distracting." She turned to Ned. "Most nobles don't notice individual dancers unless it's someone they know or are specifically trying to outdo. The only reason the big entrance works is that they're genetically pre-disposed to pay attention to spotlights and dramatic music."

Ned lifted an eyebrow. "That's not going to work with you and Jon. He's the prince—everyone's paying attention to him."

Kate heard Jon murmur, "Only recently," before he raised his voice for Ned. "If anyone asks, I'll tell them my mother bought the contract, then expected me to work with the Fairy Godmother to handle all the details." He smiled slightly at Ned, Rellie, and Kate's disbelieving expressions. "Believe me, no one who knows my mother at all will doubt it for a moment."

"Whether or not she could focus long enough to set up all the finer details of the contract, of course, is another matter entirely." Everyone turned as Lawton emerged from the crowd, holding yet another glass of pink champagne aloft as if protecting it from the surrounding ruffians. "Still, since the king and I are likely the only people intelligent enough to bring up that question, I doubt it will be an issue."

Rellie leaned forward, fascinated by the glass in Lawton's hand. "Ooooh, that matches my dress perfectly."

Lawton's brow furrowed as he considered Rellie for a moment, then he very deliberately moved the glass even further out of her reach before turning his attention to Kate and Jon. "I was amusing myself watching your guests eat the hors d'oeuvres when I remembered we hadn't yet finalized a time for the girl's grand entrance. Since it's a mere quarter to midnight, we should likely force ourselves to commit."

Rellie turned to Kate. "Wait, didn't you say that my dress turns back into rags at . . ."

At this, Kate immediately ushered everyone back through the doorway. "I never thought I'd be saying this, but how fast can you two dance?"

SEVENTEEN

❦

Making It Work

The sparkles started first, lit by the glow of a spotlight that was unsurprisingly tinged pink. Out beyond the edge of the lights the orchestra started again, playing fast enough to suggest they were being encouraged from the sidelines.

Jon hoped Lawton had picked a really short number.

Shaking a bit of confetti off his nose—it wasn't dignified to scratch in public—Jon squinted past the edge of the spotlight in the futile hope of catching some sight of Kate. But all he could see were crowds of people who were suddenly focusing on him, which likely meant the scene was far more impressive from the outside than the inside.

Not that he was going to mention that to Kate.

Rellie made her appearance along with the rose petals, and the crowd gave a collective sigh of dramatic appreciation—never mind that several of them had been dancing next to her for over an hour. Despite his and Kate's admonitions, he'd expected Rellie to be running, either thrilled by the all the pink or wanting to get it over with as soon as possible, and his eyes narrowed slightly as he realized she was actually slowing down the further she got into the spotlight. He took a few steps forward, and was ready to pull her closer toward him if he had to, when he caught sight of the suppressed terror in her eyes.

He shot her a sympathetic smile and moved forward to take her hand and lead her into the center of the spotlight. When she grabbed his other hand, holding on tight enough to possibly cut off circulation, he leaned forward to murmur encouragement in her ear. "Just focus on the sparkles and pretend we're practicing in a larger room than usual. Kate and Ned are the only other people here."

"But I need you to remind me what I'm supposed to do with my feet!" Rellie whispered back, panicked. "With Ned I was mostly just swirling around, but now everyone's looking at me and *I don't remember what to do with my feet!*"

"Those aren't glass slippers, are they?"

"No, they're some kind of squishy stuff."

"Then just step up on my feet and I'll take it from there." When she did, relieved, he smiled slightly. "After all, we both have someone we want to get back to."

When she smiled back, he started them into their first turn.

THEY FINISHED WITH four minutes to spare, but they forgot to account for the fact that Rellie had suddenly become interesting to the partygoers. Several people tried to stop Rellie and Jon on their way out the door, all trying to get the pertinent details that would make them invaluable in gossiping circles.

"Darling, your dress is fantastic! You must let me speak to your tailor!"

"You look so much like the Duchess of Flantower. Are the two of you related?"

Jon made a variety of hurried excuses as the clock ticked down, seriously considering whether or not to simply start shoving people out of the way. With two minutes to go, Rellie finally gave in and kicked one man in the shins. After that, people thankfully got the hint and started backing out of their way.

They met Kate and Lawton just outside the ballroom with barely a minute left. Then they sprinted to the nearest empty room.

"We made it," Kate said with relief, a little out of breath as she closed the door to one of the king's old studies behind them. "Remind me to never cut it that close—" She stopped, expression closing down as memory cut through the enthusiasm. "Never mind." She turned away from the door, suddenly sounding tired. Next to her, a swirl of magic transformed Rellie's dress into rags just as the palace clock chimed midnight. "After tonight it's not going to be an issue."

Jon reached out, grabbing Kate's hand and pulling her toward him. "You know, one advantage to switching careers for a man is he tends to want to shower you with presents during the transition," he murmured, pressing a kiss to the back of her hand. The twinge of worry in his chest eased as her expression did, and he smiled as amusement lit her eyes. "Feel free to start asking for yours at any time."

The corners of Kate's mouth curved up. "Are we talking roses here, or a box of diamonds big enough to comfortably secure my early retirement?"

Jon pulled her all the way against his chest. "Since you're going to be retiring with me, I don't think the diamonds are going to be a problem. But since you asked, I was thinking more along the lines of starting our own competing Fairy Godmother company, just to keep you entertained in whatever spare moments you're not busy being a princess."

Kate started to chuckle, then froze at something she saw in his expression. "You can't be serious. There's no way everyone would be okay with us starting up a company like that."

Jon raised an eyebrow. "When I was young my mother had an entire aerie full of miniature dragons built on the back lawn because she decided she wanted one to match each of her ten thousand dresses. My grandfather hired teams of painters to follow him around everywhere and spray everything with gold paint, and my great-great-uncle bought every frog in five thousand miles in case one of them was an enchanted princess."

Kate blinked at that. "Okay, he could have probably used a Fairy Godmother in the family."

"See?" He leaned forward to brush his lips against hers. "No one will even think twice about it."

"Ooh, that sounds like fun," Rellie piped in, safe in a double protective layering of Ned's arms and a curtain from one of the first floor windows. It was a little more dignified than the rags, and they'd been worried her dress would change back in the corridor. Even in the palace, clouds of magic dust tended to attract too much attention. "Because if you guys started a company, that would mean I could join in and be a Fairy Godmother, too. I mean, all that stuff about your boss sounds creepy, but I really like the wings and the wand, and if you were my boss . . ."

Kate pulled away from Jon enough to make an extremely firm cease-and-desist gesture at the girl. "Let's talk about that later, okay? Right now, we have to worry about what we're going to do with you until we have the rest of this worked out." She stepped even further away, but her hand still held on to Jon's as her brow furrowed in thought. "Traditionally, we're supposed to send you back home until the prince or nobleman comes to get you, but the thought of Bubbles somehow tracking you there scares me."

Ned turned to Rellie, clutching her a little tighter. "Kate's right," he said. "You don't ever want to meet Bubbles."

"Plus, we don't want Bubbles meeting her stepfamily." Still, Kate hesitated as she went through every contingency. "What I don't like, though, is the fact that it would also leave the two of you in the same building in case Bubbles decides to try something."

Jon leaned back against the wall, deciding he really did enjoy watching her organize everything. "I also have several dozen guards who would be thrilled to do more with their work days than just stand there."

Kate poked Jon in the shoulder. "I'm serious. If she sends in another Fairy Godmother with True Love, whoever it is can teleport in right past the guards."

"I'll issue the 'No Fairy Godmother' edict before I go to bed tonight." He covered her other hand with his, holding both of them against his chest. "Anyone with a pair of wings or a sparkly skirt caught on palace grounds will be arrested before they can even think about making one of your teleportation doors."

Kate, they had already decided, would come to the front gate and ask for Jon specifically. He touched his ring she had slid over her thumb, the seal on which was enough to get any guard in the palace to send for him.

Kate set her jaw. "Promise me."

Jon nodded, softened by the worry he could see in her eyes. "I promise."

"Um, excuse me?" Over Kate's shoulder, Jon saw Rellie raise a hand. "As sorry as I am to interrupt a moment, you guys still haven't decided what you're going to do with me."

"Is there any way we can hide her out here, at least overnight?" asked Kate. "I'd rather she not meet your family, but maybe we could stash her in one of the dozens of spare bedrooms you seem to have around here."

"I hate to say it, but if I try too hard to hide her then palace gossip will instantly go crazy. Better that we just say she's here waiting for Rupert—" He saw Ned's mouth open, but Kate turned around to shush him. "—and I'm just playing host until he makes it back."

Kate weighed this for a moment, then nodded. "You know how to handle your family better than I—" She stopped when Rellie's impromptu cover shifted, giving everyone a better view of the rags beneath. "Though I do suggest finding her a spare dress as soon as possible."

Jon winced, not sure yet which maid he could trust with the task; he was less than thrilled about hunting for a dress on his own. "Come with me?"

Kate shook her head. "Unfortunately, Ned and I probably should have left already." She took a couple of steps back, as if the only way she could make herself go was if she wasn't in arm's reach of him. Jon felt cold without her, but the reluctance on her face was almost enough to make up for it.

"I need to get into work early this morning so I can get as much of a jump on all this as I can," she said.

Tempted to reach out and touch her again, Jon shoved his hands into his pockets. "A few hours of sleep would probably be a good thing, too, and as much as I hate to say it I can't promise you that here."

"I know." Kate then turned to Ned and Rellie. "You guys have thirty seconds for some last-minute kissing and clutching." The two immediately started making use of their time, and a smile blossomed on Kate's face as she let her eyes meet Jon's. "We, however, better not start," she told him, sounding almost playful. For Jon, it was a brief, hopeful flash of the future he could see in his mind. "I won't be able to enforce the deadline."

Jon grinned, even as he felt his chest ache. She wasn't even gone yet and he already missed her. "We'll have to give you plenty of opportunities to practice."

She laughed, expression tender. "I'll come back, Jon," she said quietly, crossing the distance between them to give him a quick but intense kiss, "no matter what else happens." Before he could touch her, she backed away again.

"Promise me," he said.

For just a moment, her heart shone out of her eyes. "I promise."

IT WASN'T QUITE thirty seconds, but it was still far too soon before Kate and Ned disappeared through the teleportation door. Once they were gone, Jon took Rellie into his mother's spare closet, walking her down nearly five hundred feet before he started hunting through the racks. "She was about forty pounds lighter when she wore these," he told Rellie, shaking his head at a silver dress that was living proof ruffles could breed and multiply. "At least one of them should fit."

Rellie looked doubtful as Jon pulled a green dress off the rack and pushed it at her. "I don't like green," she said, holding the dress up to her. The sleeves drooped so low people walking next to her would probably trip on them. "It makes me look like one of those tree people."

"Fine." He threw an overdress made of small gold coins over his shoulder, mentally earmarking it for the treasury before he found another gown made of white swan feathers and tossed it to Rellie. "There. You can be a bird." She grabbed the dress with delight, but before she could say anything Jon was already moving past her toward the door. "I'll be over by the closet door while you get dressed. Just keep walking back the way you came and you won't get lost."

Before he could make it all the way back, Rellie stopped him with a hand on his arm. "You really think this will work?" she asked softly.

Jon took a deep breath, ignoring the ache in his chest. "We'll make sure it does," he said, willing to believe enough for all four of them if he had to.

She smiled. "You're pretty nice, for a prince."

He smiled back. "Don't spread it around." He caught one of the swan feathers that had come loose and handed it back to Rellie with a flourish. "Now get dressed, and we'll see about finding you a room."

JON EVENTUALLY MANAGED to grab some sleep, nearly a full hour of it before he was summoned down to the main dining room for a breakfast meeting with his mother. Having expected it, he snagged a roll off of one of the serving trays before sitting down several chairs away from the woman in question. "You called?"

She huffed a dramatic breath, setting her fork down with a clatter. "Don't use that tone with me, Jonathan. You know how your brother upset me last night." She sniffed, blinking rapidly and fanning her face on the off chance he was too far away to see her tears. "The thought of my baby going out into the big, harsh world without his crown."

"He was mistaken, Mother," Jon said calmly, taking a bite of roll to cover his urge to yawn. "He and I talked about him doing a little questing before the wedding, and in his eagerness to get started I'm afraid he'd confused some of the details." He lifted an eyebrow at his mother's perplexed expression. "It wasn't his fault. All that writing, you know."

She waved a silencing hand at him. "I'm much too fragile for sarcasm right now, Jonathan." The hand dropped to the table, fingernails clicking rhythmically against the polished surface. "It's just—" She stopped. "I could have sworn I heard you say 'wedding.'"

"I did. Rupert's getting married." He settled against the back of the chair, then leaned forward again as he felt his eyes drifting closed. "His bride-to-be arrived last night."

The queen choked. "His . . . bride?"

"To be," Jon corrected, relieved to see his mother hadn't turned purple yet. As tired and annoyed as he was right now, the guilt he'd feel at giving her a heart attack wouldn't help his day any. "I presumed you were the one who had arranged the entire thing."

"No! I just—" The queen fluttered her hands again, initial shock melting into the lost and helpless look she did so well. "I don't know if he's even ready yet for something as big as marriage. I mean, this is the first time he's even gone questing."

Jon's eyebrows lifted, surprised his mother was actually making things easier for once. "I wouldn't worry about it just yet. When he returns from his first big quest, he may find that he's changed his—"

"Jon!"

Both Jon and his mother started at the sound of Rellie's not-anywhere-near-a-whisper coming from the dining room entryway, but by the time they'd turned around she'd squeaked and vanished back behind the corner. After a couple of seconds, a small, pale hand emerged and waved dramatically up and down. "Jon!"

Jon sighed, then smiled slightly and pushed himself to his feet. "Excuse me, Mother," he said genially. "I must go attend to the girl who may or may not be your future daughter-in-law."

"Jonathan—"

Before she could say anything more, he left the room, rounding the corner to find Rellie in the dress she had gone to sleep in the night before, now sopping wet. She held her equally dripping hands in front of her, as if trying to keep the dress from getting any wetter than it already was.

Jon winced, imagining the other wreckage that had no doubt resulted from whatever had attacked her dress. "Rellie."

Before he could say anything else, Rellie's eyebrows shot up as she threw an angry finger back down the hallway. "This is *not* my fault! You said I could get something to eat from the kitchens, but there was this busboy kind of guy with a big pot of water and he threw it all over me!"

Jon sighed, gesturing with his head for her to follow him toward dry clothes and someplace at least a little further away from his mother. "I doubt he actually threw it on you," he said, making sure to keep her in sight at all times. "It's more likely he just tripped because what he was carrying was too heavy for him."

He stopped when he heard her distant sniffle, realizing he'd lost her at some point during the last few steps. He turned around to find her standing in the middle of the hallway, looking utterly dejected as she made a wet spot on the carpet. "The skirt didn't look this big on the rack," Rellie said sadly, staring down at the straggly feathers. She sniffed again, face wrinkling in teary frustration as she looked back up at him. "I thought I'd be okay like I was with my big pink dress at the ball, but I think Kate must have magicked it because it never caused this much trouble."

"Don't worry about it," he said kindly, reminding himself that this would be good practice for when he eventually had children. "I'm sure we can find another dress that will work. If I remember correctly, she actually went through a pink phase a few years ago."

"And I'll fix this one, I promise," Rellie said tearily, looking far more tragic than Jon was at all comfortable with. "I don't know how hard it is to dry a feather dress, but I figured out a way to do it with the chickens back home and I can't imagine . . ."

"Shhhh," Jon soothed, grabbing her hands in the hopes of calming her down. "I'm sure we'll be able to . . ." The words died as a wave of dizziness hit him, the palms of his hands growing hot like he was holding them too close to an open flame. He immediately yanked his hands away from Rellie's, only to have to grab her again when her legs buckled and she nearly collapsed. Another wave of dizziness hit, worse this time, and he staggered as she clutched at him like a drowning person.

For a heartbeat, everything went completely silent, then he heard Rellie's breath hitch. "Jon?" Her voice was faint, and Jon's grip tightened as he felt an immense rush of protectiveness wash over him for the girl in his arms. He would never let anything hurt such a delicate, lovely creature, with hair like spun gold and eyes like the first violets of spring. He loved her, of course he loved her, and he would write sonnets to her beauty as soon as he reminded himself how the rhyme structure went on a sonnet. He couldn't even imagine ever loving anyone as much as he did Rellie.

No. Oh, please no.

Slowly, he and Rellie looked into each other's eyes. Even through the golden-tinged rush of adoration, he could tell she was just as terrified as he was.

EIGHTEEN

❦

Slippery Slope

Back in the middle of the darkened maze that was the office cubicles, Kate and Ned stood silently as they watched the final trace of magic from the doorway fade into nothingness. Kate could hear the cleaning crew working downstairs. The floor they were on was as utterly empty of people as she'd expected. Even the light behind Bubbles' locked door was off, though Kate had to squash the quiet, paranoid thought that the woman was hiding in the dark waiting for them.

She closed her eyes, letting out a long breath as exhaustion crashed into her all at once. "Can you make it home okay?" she asked Ned. His continued silence was probably a bad sign. "Or do you want me to drop you off?"

"I'm fine." The words had a slightly distant quality that usually meant shell shock, and at the sound of it Kate made herself open her eyes again. It was a perfectly reasonable reaction to have after the evening they'd both been through, but he probably wasn't okay to go home on his own.

She turned, watching him. He was staring off into the distance, eyes a little too wide. If she looked very, very closely, she could see him shaking ever so slightly. "Ned?"

He swallowed, and all the shaking stopped as he turned to look at Kate. "I've changed the whole rest of my life, haven't I?" The distance was gone, and in its place was the tremor of someone who'd realized he not only burned a bridge, but smashed the rubble with sledgehammers and then watched the dwarves blow up any bits that might have been left.

Kate sympathized. "There's still time to back out of this," she told him, voice gentle. She didn't know what she'd say to Rellie, but it would be better for both of them to let Ned go if he wanted. If nothing else, it would be one fewer person to worry about.

He stiffened, flinching like she'd slapped him. "Just because Rellie didn't make me promise doesn't mean I couldn't have," he said tightly, angrier than she'd ever heard him. "Just tell me what I need to do."

Feeling her heart clench at the reminder of the promise she'd made to Jon, Kate rested a hand on Ned's shoulder. "I just wanted you to be sure," she said, knowing she'd never looked nearly as brave as he had just then. "Like you said, we're about to change the whole rest of our lives."

Ned sighed at that, some of his tension dropping as he lifted a hand to rub his eyes. "Sorry." He looked at her again, mouth flickering up. "At least my dad will be happy about all this." Kate lifted her eyebrows and Ned's smile turned wry. "He wanted me to become a shoemaker."

She couldn't quite stop the burst of laughter that emerged.

"If you had, it would have been the elves who'd gotten you into trouble."

THOUGH THEY both made it home, Kate found herself lying awake all night. So, early the next morning they were back in the office conference room going over their plan one more time. It wasn't a particularly good plan, depending mostly on paperwork and Kate miraculously getting better at lying, but at the moment they didn't have much else to work with.

Ned grabbed a blank contract completion approval form out of the supply room, and Kate faked the details of the supposed happily-ever-after well enough to hopefully convince Bubbles that Kate needed to see Director Carlson one more time to get the signature. For Carlson, they'd scoured the archives, looking for the number of clients married to royalty that had ended in either divorce or large therapy bills (records of when and where served as evidence against potential lawsuits). It would then be Kate's job to convince Carlson that marrying Rellie off to a prince would end up giving him more, not less, responsibility for her in the long run, and it would be easier for everyone if he'd just cancel the contract.

If that failed, she would say Rellie was prepared to countersue to get out of it, and the royal family of Somewhere was more than happy to hire her a lawyer to help the process along. Kate felt a little worried she hadn't cleared this particular lie with Jon yet, but if he was crazy enough to want to marry her he'd probably be willing to fake a lawsuit for her.

As they heard their co-workers arriving, Ned looked up at Kate. "Ready?"

"Not really." Despite the words and the hard knot in her

stomach, Kate pushed herself to her feet and headed for the door. She'd promised Jon she'd come back, no matter what, and she couldn't keep that promise until she'd gotten this part of things over with. "If you see bursts of magic coming from Bubbles' office, be smart and go home early today."

"I won't see it," Nate said matter-of-factly as he handed Kate the folder. When she lifted an eyebrow, his mouth curved in a faint smile. "I plan on hiding in here until either you or Bubbles come get me."

Kate stood in the open doorway. "I wish I'd been smart enough to think of that." Stepping into the hallway, she closed the door to give Ned what safety she could before heading into the main office area.

The early morning commotion sounded exactly like it had every day since she'd started working here, the pockets of quiet conversation mixed with rustling files and the clicking of people typing. It was strange to think she'd never hear it again, or wave at the other Fairy Godmothers as they offered her a quick good morning and a sympathetic expression when they realized she was walking toward Bubbles' office. She wondered if she'd miss it once she was gone.

Of course, there was an equally good chance she was just trying to distract herself from thinking about the infinite number of ways this could go wrong.

When she got to Bubbles' office, Kate squared her shoulders, put Jon's face firmly in the front of her mind, and pushed the door open. "You wanted to see me?"

As she'd expected, Bubbles hesitated pointedly over the file she'd been reading before looking up. When she did finally deign to lift her head, she adjusted her glasses and peered at Kate as if the younger Fairy Godmother was an insect that had invaded her personal space. "I certainly didn't call for you."

"Not this morning, but you told me to report back in when the assignment was done." Kate caught her voice turning a little cajoling, and she reminded herself to flatten it out again. If she sounded like having to fill out routine paperwork was important to her, Bubbles would know something was up. "You wanted me to make sure I had finished all the paperwork and gotten a completion signature from Director Carlson before noon."

Bubbles eyes brightened ever so slightly at that. "You completed the job? Without me having to come in and fix it for you?" At Kate's nod, her boss turned to a stack of papers sitting beside her desk and began flipping through them. She hesitated occasionally, making Kate tense each and every time, but eventually she dropped the stack back down and looked at Kate like she would a rodent performing a trick. "Well, this is surprising, particularly with the added wrinkle of the last-minute prince substitution. I was certain you'd screw it up."

Kate felt the knot in her stomach ease, ever so slightly, but she kept her expression blank as she tried to gauge what kind of response Bubbles was expecting. Was that a deliberate dig, or had shock simply compelled her to be more blunt than usual?

Finally, Kate just shrugged. "I know."

Bubbles' eyes narrowed, as if that somehow hadn't been the right answer. "Do you have the wedding date so we can include it in the final report?"

Though they'd talked about it, both she and Jon had decided that particular bit of information would be too dangerous to fake. "I think they were delaying it because the brother was still missing." Realizing what had caused Bubbles' suspicion, Kate made her voice hesitant and a little embarrassed. "I kept trying to find out, but no one would give me anything specific."

As Kate suspected, Bubbles' expression smoothed out again. "You'll have to be the one to tell that to Director Carlson," she said, pulling her wand from her belt to create the transport door that would get Kate into the secretary's office. "I also expect you to continue following the case until you have the date secured—I can't trust any of the rest of you to send the contingency measures, but my time is far too valuable to waste doing your cleanups as well."

Kate nearly relaxed, but her brain snagged on something Bubbles had said. "Wait." The knot inside her squeezed tight. "What contingency measures?"

Bubbles stopped, looking at Kate as if she couldn't believe she was asking such a stupid question. "I started distributing a backup dose of True Love to clients after Thea had her 'accident' and failed."

The world went white as the floor dropped out from under Kate's feet.

"I have no trouble firing you people, but I will get contracts fulfilled in an efficient and satisfactory manner."

Kate stood frozen, afraid to speak for a moment because she was pretty sure the only thing that would come out of her mouth was a scream. Bubbles, considering the question answered, lifted the wand again to open the door, and Kate forced herself to inhale past the icy panic clutching her throat.

"When?" She knew her voice sounded strangled, and she swallowed, reminding herself not to hyperventilate. "When did you give them the dose?" She didn't dare let herself hope they'd somehow managed to escape it.

Oh Jon, I'm so sorry.

"Why do you care?" Bubbles said. "According to you, the contract was completed, which means you had already administered your own dose. I just hurried the process along."

Kate shoved her hands behind her back to hide her fingernails digging dark red furrows into the palm of her hands. "I just want to know for future assignments," she made herself say, taking long, slow breaths through her nose and forcing her brain to stay only in the current moment. If she let herself think about how badly she'd screwed up, or picture Jon and Rellie staring lovingly into each other's eyes completely against their will, she was going to do something completely useless like burst into tears. "It will help me do my job more efficiently."

Bubbles settled back, mollified by the answer. "New policy is to send out magic support first thing in the morning after the culminating event for a particular assignment. You're forbidden from informing the other employees about it, however—if they know I'll be there with a safety net, they'll put even less effort toward proper Fairy Godmothering than they do now."

Anger slammed through the panic for just a second, and Kate clutched at it like a lifeline in a storm. "Fairy Godmothers, Inc. doesn't even have a magic support staff," she snapped, fighting back the urge to yell. For all she knew, that scream might come out.

"Of course, we do," Bubbles scoffed. "They're just not there to support you or the customers."

Panic winning again, Kate grabbed blindly for the door handle. "That makes sense." She opened the door, backing out with the deliberate steps of someone trying very hard not to run. "I'll go find out when that wedding will be held. We really don't need to bother Director Carlson until I have it."

She closed the door on Bubbles' confused expression, knowing if the other woman devoted even five minutes of thought to the conversation they'd just had she'd realize something was horribly wrong (another mistake that was going to come back to hurt them, Kate was sure). Then she turned around and hurried back the way she'd come, barely managing to keep from running. There was another conference room around the corner—the old manager had used it for staff meetings, but Bubbles decided that it had too many exit routes and insisted on using a smaller one down the hall. Kate could create a transport door from there that would get her to the palace in only a couple of minutes.

Knowing she'd be too late no matter when she got there was making it very hard for her to breathe properly.

She turned the corner, nearly slamming into a worried Ned coming the other direction. He caught her shoulders to steady her, but as soon as his eyes met hers his face drained of color. "Kate, what happened?"

She opened her mouth, but there was only a frozen silence as the words stuck in her throat. Ned, however, didn't seem to have any trouble filling in the gap. "Does Bubbles know? What did she say? What did she do?" The panic in his voice climbed with every word. "What is she going to do to Rellie and Jon? What are we going to—"

This time, it was her turn to grab his shoulders. "Ned," she said quietly, knowing there was no way to make this easier. "They were dosed."

Ned's expression crumpled. "Dosed?" he whispered. "Oh, no."

Her own chest so raw it hurt just standing here, Kate gave Ned a small shake. "We will fix this," she said fiercely, hoping she sounded more confident than she felt. They *had* to fix this, though at the moment she didn't have the slightest idea how they were going to do it. "I'm going back to the palace—" His mouth opened, but she shook her head before he could say anything. "No. Trust me, Ned, you don't want to see this in person. I'm going to see how bad it is and tell them everything will be okay."

He took a deep, shaky breath, like he was trying really hard to collect himself. "Do we have any idea how it's going to be okay?"

There was another moment of despairing silence. "No." she said. "But it's our job to figure it out."

REMEMBERING THE "No Fairy Godmother" rule Jon had promised to put in place—which had unfortunately done nothing against Bubbles' super secret army of support staff—Kate had the transport doorway open on the sidewalk across the street from the palace's front gate. She stood there for a moment, watching the posted guards as she pushed her hand into her pocket to grab Jon's ring. Her throat closed up as her fingers wrapped tight around the warm metal, remembering the look on his face as he gave it to her.

This was what hope got you.

Taking a deep breath, she pushed the ring onto her thumb and crossed the street like she knew exactly what she was doing. Walking up to the guard who looked like he was the better fed of the two, she held up her hand with the ring positioned so the seal was clearly displayed. "I need to speak to Monsignor Lawton," she said calmly, not wanting to make the same mistake she had in Bubbles' office. After all, she wasn't one hundred percent certain this would work. Jon had assured her the ring would get him called to the front gates, but there was no guarantee it would have the same effect with Lawton.

The guard peered at the ring, eyes widening slightly when he realized it was inarguably genuine. He gestured to his partner, who came over and took his own look at the ring, then they both moved aside for a whispered discussion while Kate stood there, trying to look like she wasn't about to do anything more stupid than she already had.

Finally, the first guard approached. "Monsignor Lawton wouldn't have given you that ring. Those rings belong strictly to members of the royal family."

Kate's heart clenched. She couldn't ask for Jon. "Monsignor Lawton said Prince Jonathan gave him the ring, which he then gave to me so I could come back here now and ask to speak to him despite the current 'No Fairy Godmother' edict."

The guards' brow furrowed at her unprompted knowledge. Still, the second guard rallied. "Are you sure you didn't get the ring from Prince Rupert?" He didn't actually say the words, but his tone implied what circumstances he thought she and Rupert had been in before the ring was exchanged. "He sometimes gives presents to girls whose company he's enjoyed."

Kate glared, voice sharp. She wanted to strangle them for doing this to her now, of all times, but she had more important things to worry about than getting herself killed. "First, I'd have to drop about fifteen IQ points before I'd even *think* about sleeping with Prince Rupert, and second—"

The rest of the sentence disappeared as a blur of color shot around the corner of the palace, barreling toward the front gate fast enough the figure's golden blond hair—and was that a bathrobe?—flew out behind it. When the figure hit the still-closed front gate, it shook the bars. "Kate! Tell them to let me out!"

Surprise had Kate frozen for a split second, but as soon as she came back to herself she pushed past the guards and moved close enough to wrap her hands around Rellie's. "It's okay, sweetie," she lied, stomach twisting at the tear tracks both old and new still visible on the girl's cheeks. "Tell me what happened."

"I don't know!" The words were practically a shout, but Rellie leaned in closer to the bars as if she wished that Kate could hug her. "I was in the kitchen and some stupid guy dumped this big pot full of water at me, and I felt really guilty about ruining the feather dress so I went to find Jon to say I was sorry. He grabbed my hands to make me feel better—" Rellie's eyes widened and she yanked her hands free of Kate's fast enough she threw herself back a little. The guards, who at this point were seriously confused, gave up and decided neither woman was enough of a threat to pay attention to. "I'm sorry!"

"You cleaned the love potion off already," she reassured her, reaching through the bars to grab her hands again. "It must have been in the water that was . . ." Her voice caught for a moment, brain helplessly calculating how much True Love might have been in that pot. ". . . dumped on you. I'm so sorry."

Rellie's eyes widened even further. "*That* was the love potion you were talking about?" she whispered, horrified.

Kate nodded, the knot in her stomach tightening even further. "I will fix this, Rellie. I promise. Tell—"

"Not Jon." Rellie shook her head violently. "Even when the inside of my head is screaming 'No, no, no,' all I have to do is just look at him and—"

"It's okay," Kate said, heart curling up into a tight, painful little ball at the picture she wasn't quite able to fight off in time. She leaned forward, lowering her voice. "Tell Lawton what happened, and that I'm working on finding a way to fix this. I just need a little time."

Rellie nodded, then dropped her forehead against the gate. "If this is happily-ever-after, I hate it," she whispered.

Kate touched her own forehead to the bars. "Me, too."

NINETEEN

True Love

He was going to bury Fairy Godmothers, Inc. so deep in lawsuits it would take twenty years to claw their way back up to simple bankruptcy. While the royal family's battalion of expensive, shark-like lawyers got started on the paperwork for that, he would personally do everything in his power to ruin the company's reputation and destroy their client base. If he had time, he'd also bankrupt each and every member of the management team and get them cursed by the best evil sorceresses money could buy.

Unfortunately, none of that would be any use against his mother.

"You're mistaken," Jon repeated flatly, voice like ice as he stalked down the hallway toward the kitchens. After he and Rellie had ripped themselves away from each other—his mind clamped down on the dreamy sigh he wanted to add to her name—he had immediately ordered her to the far corner of the palace grounds. His mother, however, had already seen the entire show, and for some unholy reason decided it provided an excellent distraction. "I told you—she's Rupert's fiancée."

"It's not as if I didn't hear you," the queen huffed, picking up her skirts as she once again had to hurry to catch up to her youngest son. "But that has very little to do with the fact that you're clearly in love with her."

"I'm *not* in—" The word stuck in his throat, the nightmarish love potion rebelling enough to stop his voice, and Jon cut the rest of the sentence off in a growl as he fought the urge to slam his hand against the wall in frustration. His mother, he knew, would only take it as further evidence she was right. "She had an accident in the kitchen, and came to me upset and worried that her dress was ruined." He made sure not to trip over any more verbal landmines the potion might have left in his brain. "I was helping her. That. Is. All."

For a moment, the only response was blessed silence. Jon kept walking, allowing himself a brief, wild moment of hope that his mother had decided harassing him was no longer worth the trouble. He should promise her a new dress and send a seamstress by her room later to keep her sufficiently occupied.

Then he heard her voice again, coming from further down the corridor. "Then why won't you look me in the eye?"

It was an unexpected moment of insight from a woman who had always devoted the bulk of her thought processes to figuring out what style of crown would be most in fashion next season, and Jon was thrown enough by the response to hesitate mid-step. He turned just enough to see his mother standing there with her hands bunched up in fists at her sides, chin lifted, and a gleam in her eye that could only be described as triumphant. It was clear she had some goal in mind, though the precise nature of what she felt she was getting out of this particular line of questioning was not something Jon had the mental capacity to fathom at the moment.

Instead, he lifted an eyebrow and aimed for what he knew would be a sure target. "I'm surprised at you, Mother. Attempting to rip Rupert's bride-to-be out of his arms while he's off trying to uphold the family honor." He couldn't stop the rush of fierce satisfaction at the thought of stealing Rellie away from Rupert, but he immediately slammed it back down by focusing on the absurdity of stealing something a person never actually had. "What would your 'baby' say if he came back and found his darling mother had taken away his true love?"

Rellie, his one and only true love, with a voice like songbirds and skin like the freshly fallen snow . . . Jon tightened his jaw, forcibly dragging his thoughts back into line. He had to get off this topic of conversation—he was giving the love potion exactly what it wanted.

His mother was too distraught to take any advantage of the opening. Her eyes widened at the mention of her "baby," tearing up enough to pick up the shimmer of the nearby lights. She murmured something that might have been Rupert's name, looking lost for a moment, but then her expression slid into anger. "You always do that!" she shouted, skirt moving as if she was stamping her foot. "I am your mother, and you talk to me like I'm some ridiculous child! I've spent the last week trying to tell you serious, important things, and yet all you've done is ignore me!"

Jon blinked, thrown for a moment. "What does that have to do with any of this?" If this was the first sign of the same sort of breakdown that had hit Rupert, he was going to put enough locks on that miserable library door to keep out the entire Somewhere army. "It's not as if my getting married will suddenly help you win arguments."

The triumphant look returned, and the queen threw her arm forward, pointing a finger. "I saw the way you looked at the girl! Before you got all high and mighty and ordered her outside, you looked as lost and flustered as I've ever seen you. If she keeps you smitten you won't be so busy and in charge all the time, and you'll finally have time to listen to important things like the details of my social calendar!"

Anger surged even hotter than it had been. "If I didn't walk around here all 'busy and in charge,' the kingdom would collapse around your ears and leave you without either the money or the time to buy shoes." He remembered Rellie's flexible clear shoes, an elegant variant on the traditionally expected glass slippers. "And if you think *Rellie* has me flustered, I'm sure you'd adore—"

Kate.

Everything froze as the memory of her face burst into Jon's mind. Kate, who hadn't entered into his thoughts once since he'd taken Rellie's hand. Kate, who deserved all the words the potion was making him use on someone else.

He didn't have time for this.

Jon took a deep breath, feeling the fog of the love potion creep back in. Still, it had been enough. "If you'll excuse me." He gave his mother a small, stiff bow, not waiting for her response before turning around and stalking down the hallway toward his original destination.

Unfortunately, the kitchen staff proved as useless as Jon would have expected if he'd been thinking clearly. They remembered the giant pot of water in far more detail than the young man who had been carrying it, mostly because they'd been grateful they weren't the ones who'd needed to haul it around. Further questioning might have yielded a scrap or two of mildly useful information, but after a while Jon started to notice the younger and more easily frightened kitchen staff had vanished utterly. Even the more experienced ones were all pressed against the edge of their counters, watching him with the looks of people desperately trying to disappear into the walls behind them.

Jon, recognizing he would still need these people after his life had regained some semblance of order, restrained himself from firing them all. Instead, he retreated to one of the spare offices upstairs, hoping the quiet and lack of a certain blond young woman who he would *not* name—though he'd keep her in his heart, loved, and . . . no, no, NO—would help him find the mental clarity he needed to figure out what he was going to do next.

Leaving the lights off, he sat down on the floor with his back against the door and closed his eyes, exhausted. There had to be some sort of cure for this, didn't there? A corporation the size of Fairy Godmothers, Inc. would have to be aware enough of potential lawsuits to have some sort of way out. Not that it would save them this time, of course, but he seriously doubted he was the only person in the company's history to not sit back and say "Yes, please" as they slipped everyone drugs.

Jon braced himself when he heard the knob turn. He felt someone try to push the door against his back, but it was the surprisingly polite knock that followed which caused his head to jerk in attention. He was pretty sure his mother had never knocked politely in her entire life, but there was always a chance that Rellie— darling, fragile Rellie—had wandered back inside and was trying to find her own place to hide.

"While I applaud the idea of sitting with your back to the door as a sort of rudimentary locking system, Jon, the fact that you are momentarily reminding me of your father is far too alarming to allow this state of affairs to continue." Lawton's voice always took on that extra-dry edge it got when he was forced into crisis-management mode, and even from the other side of the door Jon found it surprisingly soothing. "Also, a brief conversation with our young friend downstairs has made it clear the two of you have had an excessively exciting morning."

In the process of standing up and letting Lawton in, Jon froze with a death grip on the handle. "She's not with you, is she?" he asked, horrified at the yearning that ran beneath the panic in his voice.

There was a too-careful pause on the other side of the door. "She is not," Lawton said, in the tone one might use on someone who was about to fling himself out of a rather tall window. "Open the door, Jon. I haven't even smelled a proper glass of alcohol all morning, which means now is not the time to frighten me."

SOME TIME LATER, after the events of the last few hours had been related to him, Lawton said, "Obviously, we're going to have to destroy them."

Jon stopped his pacing and pointed at his friend. "Thank you! That is *exactly* what I've been saying." Then he sighed, running his hands through his hair. "Unfortunately, destroying them will have to be put on hold for a moment. There are few more pressing matters that need to be dealt with first."

"Such as the fact that Miss Rellie has the alarming tendency to get dewy-eyed at the mention of your name, and then scream and flee as if she were being chased by demons of some sort?" It was a straightforward recitation of the basic facts of the situation, which by depressing coincidence sounded remarkably like Lawton's usual bracing sarcasm. "Or the fact that she has you so terrified and tongue-tied you've been rendered completely incapable of finishing a sentence?"

Jon glared at him, shoving any thoughts of comforting sweet Rellie deep enough into submission they hopefully wouldn't have a chance of escaping again. "Unfortunately, I've been perfectly capable of completing each and every sentence I've started since I woke up this morning. If I haven't said something, I assure you it was only because I was busy dragging the thought to the back of my head and destroying it."

"Fair enough," Lawton said, his brow furrowed in thought. "I can have some of my people keep an eye on our girl, though you'll probably want to assign one of your men to help her navigate the palace and get her anything she needs. The slightly less naturalistic choice may draw some unfortunate attention, but it also eliminates the chance that whoever it is will feel any obligation to listen to your mother."

"I'll ask Dobbs to do it." Very close to retirement, the man's finest quality was a complete lack of interest in asking questions of any kind. "Do you think the original cover story is going to work? That R— that she's Rupert's fiancée and is staying at the palace until he comes home from questing?"

"As long as neither of you go anywhere near each other and we both manage to outtalk anyone who thinks to question it." He hesitated longer than was comforting. "Maybe."

Jon sighed. "Unfortunately, I think that's the best we can manage right now." Rubbing a hand along the back of his neck, he resumed pacing at a somewhat slower speed. "What I'm really worried about, though, is how we're going to get our hands on the antidote before I do something stupid like propose marriage to the wrong girl." He grimaced at the all-too-detailed picture forming in his head. "I doubt the company has told the Fairy Godmothers about it, or Kate would have mentioned it to me as a possible contingency plan during our initial bout of worry."

He looked up to find Lawton watching him with an extremely careful expression on his face, and his eyes narrowed again. "What?" Jon asked.

Lawton lifted his shoulder in a move too subtle to be called a shrug. "You mentioned Katharine," he said quietly. "I had been wondering how far-reaching the effects were."

Jon's jaw tightened, feeling the guilt of temporarily forgetting Kate hit him all over again. Then came the guilt for thinking of Kate instead of Rellie, which made him even more miserable and annoyed at the universe as a whole. "Scientific curiosity?"

"An attempt at guarding my tongue so as not to trip on any particularly sensitive spots in your psyche, an effort I am quite relieved to note was clearly wasted." Lawton relaxed back on his heels, as if satisfied the matter was settled. "Now for the far more pressing question—if not even Katharine was aware of there being an antidote, what makes you so confident there's one to be found? If I remember the stories correctly, Fairy Godmothers have never been particularly interested in offering return policies."

Astonishingly, Jon felt the corner of his mouth flick up. Lawton might consider participating in a hug only under the threat of enforced sobriety, but he excelled at shaking people out of black moods when they needed it. "Lawsuits. There have to have been at least a few of them over Fairy Godmothers, Inc.'s long and *rich* history, and I have no doubt the powers that be would have created a way to get out of them without having to pay all that unfortunate settlement money."

"As shocking as it is to believe, not everyone thinks like we do."

"Your other option is to shoot me and put me out of my misery."

Lawton paused. "All right, mild optimism it is." This time, it was Lawton's turn to pace, lost in thought. "Even if an antidote does exist, it seems logical that the company as a whole will not be pre-disposed to sharing their little secret. I presume the legal option you discussed would take far more time than we're willing to devote to this particular matter."

"I'd say that's putting it mildly." Jon scrubbed his face with his hands, trying to chase away the fresh wave of exhaustion that had hit him.

"I have some excellent thieves on the payroll, but even a genius at larceny will run into difficulty when he has no idea what he's been sent to retrieve." Lawton stopped and tapped his fingertips against his chin. "If I remember correctly, young Rellie said something about Katharine working to somehow repair this from her end. Though I understand entirely why you might not to wish to be the one to contact her—"

Jon shuddered at the possibility of facing Kate while having these incredibly inappropriate thoughts about the sweet, lov—anyone but her. "No!"

"—but I suspect she would appreciate whatever assistance I might provide. Though it would undoubtedly only make things worse if I presented myself at the Fairy Godmothers, Inc. front desk and demanded to see her. I assume you've acquired some private way to contact Katharine during your whirlwind romance?"

Jon opened his mouth, ready to answer, then closed it as realization slowly sank in. "I don't have anything."

"You can't be serious."

Jon threw his hands up in the air, profoundly frustrated with both himself and the universe as a whole. "If you remember, I spent most of our relationship trying to make sure she didn't figure out I was a prince. That sort of situation tends to put a damper on exchanging personal information."

Lawton just stared at him for what felt like a full minute, then closed his eyes and sighed in a long-suffering manner. "It strikes me as horribly ironic that you apparently need a Fairy Godmother to properly manage your courtship of a Fairy Godmother."

The sound of someone knocking politely at the door interrupted any further insight into Jon's lack of dating skills. Jon tensed, hating how jumpy he'd become, but Lawton waved a reassuring hand in his direction before opening the door. A young woman in page's clothing was standing on the other side, managing to look both alert and deeply nervous at the same time. "You asked to have anything unusual reported to you, Monsignor, particularly if it's related to the queen." She kept her eyes only on Lawton, either not seeing, or pretending not to see, the prince standing in the shadows.

When Lawton nodded, she handed him two folded sheets of stationery and scurried away. He began reading the first even as he shut the door and turned back around. As he got closer Jon could see the royal seal faintly through the other side of the paper. He didn't need to see the handwriting on the other side to know what it looked like, full of spidery loops that suggested the woman was trying to make ruffles out of ink and paper. "Intercepted letters from my mother's desk?"

"Sadly, only two of what appear to be several." Lawton handed the letters to Jon, an unpleasantly solemn expression on his face. "As surprising as it is to believe, it seems your mother has been an extremely busy woman."

Jon scanned the first sheet of paper, feeling the headache develop before he'd gotten even halfway through the first paragraph. The queen had written the Dowager Queen Marietta of Over There, asking whether she knew any details about a princess or noblewoman in disguise who just happened to match Rellie's description (an inaccurate one, of course—her hair was golden, not blonde). The queen was hunting for Rellie's family, which meant her stepmother and sisters could show up any time now.

"Not unless I drop dead first," Jon muttered to himself.

That bravado vanished as he scanned the second letter. He knew he shouldn't be shocked, but it did nothing to ease the fury as he read it one more time to make absolutely sure the situation was as bad as he thought it was.

He looked up at Lawton, who nodded gravely before confirming the unspoken question. "Unfortunately, your mother seems quite determined you're getting married."

TWENTY

A Fate Worse than Paperwork

"It has come to our attention that several clients of Fairy Godmothers, Inc. have reported seeing an insufficient number of swans and trained doves during the use of the Official Fairy Godmother's Incorporated Grand Entrance Accessories Package . . ."

Kate closed her eyes against Bubbles' voice, absolutely certain that coming back to the office was a sign her mind had actually snapped at some point during her nightmare of a morning. Deep down, though, she knew any chance of fixing the mess she'd made was going to be here at work, and if she didn't want to make Bubbles suspicious she had to sit through this stupid meeting without screaming.

After all, it wasn't as if it was making it any *harder* to come up with the miraculous save-the-day plan she'd promised.

". . . use of at least one of the bird types included in the Royal

Class B model is mandatory for all client packages—I'm not going to bother reading the last few paragraphs, which are mostly about copyright laws followed by a few carefully veiled threats about monitoring." Bubbles looked up, eyes taking in the assembled Fairy Godmothers. "Rest assured, if management follows through it will be my threats you have to worry about. Are we clear?"

Kate wasn't paying enough attention to nod. The truth was, she had no idea what to do next—all the company files that even mentioned the love potion were encrypted, and both she and Ned had taken turns trying to guess Bubbles' password until the security system tripped and locked them both out. Her next step—her last one, unless she had some completely unprecedented moment of genius—was going back to the secretary she'd bribed and hoped her ethics hadn't improved much.

One of the Fairy Godmothers was foolish enough to try and say something, but only got a few words out before Bubbles silenced him with a glare. Then she sighed, shaking her head as if she couldn't imagine how she'd ended up working with such incompetents. "It's this kind of ridiculousness that leads to such an inappropriately long turnaround time on cases. When I was out in the field, I completed several of my assignments in less than twenty-four hours."

Kate couldn't be sure how much time they had. Rellie and Jon were clearly fighting the True Love as hard as they could, but the odds were stacked against them. The potion had to be terrifying if no one was willing to even gossip about it, and Kate's stomach twisted at the thought of what would happen if a victim was practically soaked in an entire cooking pot full of the stuff. Even if Jon and Rellie hated each other, there might come a point where it wouldn't matter.

Kate's eyes found Ned, hunched down in the furthest corner of the conference room. Bubbles had finally stopped beeping him for errands about a half-hour before the meeting started, and though he hadn't dared to skip the meeting any more than Kate, he was currently doing his best to make sure his boss entirely forgot he was there. Only his leg, bouncing so much it was practically vibrating, showed the fear Kate could feel clawing at her own chest. They were the last people in the world anyone should be depending on to save the day.

What if they weren't able to do it?

Up at the front of the room, Bubbles had built up enough steam in her list of grievances that standing up was the only way to make her disapproval sufficiently clear. ". . . You are the representatives of more than one hundred years of tradition, and you *will* fulfill your duties in a manner benefitting that tradition and the name of Fairy Godmothers, Inc." She leaned forward, slapping her hand against the top of the table for emphasis. "We are supposed to be in *control* of each and every situation we come across, and if you cannot, I assure you that you'll be pruned from the company even more rapidly than Thea was."

Thea. Kate's mentally kicked herself. The answer had been right in front of her the whole time, and she hadn't seen it.

The patches.

How could she have been so stupid as to forget the patches?

Kate's hands gripped the tabletop as a wave of exultation hit, her brain already calculating how impossible the idea would be to actually pull off. The lifeline they needed was still guarded by the local equivalent of a fire-breathing dragon—Bubbles. All she and Ned knew about the patches was that they were somewhere in her locked office, either in one of the (also locked) desk drawers, or a safe of some kind she could have hidden anywhere. And despite any minor breaking-and-entering skills Kate had picked up during her years as a Fairy Godmother, she was fully aware she didn't know the first thing about committing an actual robbery.

Not to mention Bubbles wasn't about to let anyone leave the room. Unless she wanted to kill any chance they had now, the best thing Kate could do was finish out the meeting.

". . . these tulle skirts are an honor . . ."

Once that had been taken care of, she'd figure out how to become a thief.

UNFORTUNATELY, BUBBLES MUST have been feeling particularly annoyed at their most recent performance reviews—Thea's name came up a few more times—and it was almost an hour later before the meeting finally ended. Kate, who by the end had clung to patience with both hands, only barely managed to restrain herself from knocking everyone else over as she sprinted out of the conference room. Moving nearly as fast as Kate wanted to be, Ned grabbed her arm as they headed out the door. "Kate, we need to—"

They both froze at the sight of a woman clearly waiting for them in the hallway. It was the same secretary Kate had been hoping to bribe again, looking nearly as annoyed as Bubbles.

"Seriously," the secretary said, "if all of you Fairy Godmothers made me leave my desk like this I'd never get any work done." She strode toward them with one of the spare managerial wands stuck in the loose topknot of her hair. "I've beeped you three separate times, Ms. Harris, but apparently you felt the need to hide your beeper attachment in some deep dark hole this morning."

"I was in a staff meeting," Kate said flatly, not caring about office politics. She still might have to bribe the woman, but right now she simply needed to get her out of the way. "Hold on for a minute while I hang my head in shame at having inconvenienced you."

Ned leaned close to her ear. "Is that really a good idea?" he whispered.

The secretary just raised an eyebrow. After a couple of seconds, the corner of her mouth quirked and she nodded. "Fair enough." Relaxed now, she pulled the wand out of her hair and turned to sketch the transport door. "It's not me. Carlson needs to talk to you in his office."

Kate tensed, and Ned's grip on her arm tightened enough to cut off blood flow. "Is it about the paperwork?" she guessed, trying to figure out whether Carlson could possibly know before Bubbles did. She knew Bubbles still didn't know, because if she did there was no way Kate would have left the meeting alive. "Because I have a few more forms I didn't want to rush through. I promise I'll get everything to him first thing in the morning."

The secretary snorted. "You seriously think that the board of directors cares about paperwork? They stack it around the edges of their desks to make themselves little impenetrable paper fortresses where they think no one else can see them." She finished the door, turning back to Kate. "No, he has some people in his office he needs you to talk to in relation to your last case. A woman and her two *extremely* annoying daughters." For a moment, she actually looked sympathetic. "If he tries to get you to give them freebies, just say no. It would take the entire company's supply of True Love to get anyone to give either of those two a second glance."

Ned leaned close enough to whisper in Kate's ear, ignoring

the lifted eyebrow the secretary was shooting him. "What should I do?"

Kate just shook her head. Ned gave her arm a quick squeeze before letting go and heading back to the cubicles. Ignoring the secretary's smirk, she pushed past her and stepped through the gate. Once she was on the other side, she hurried on to Director Carlson's office before the other woman had the chance to get both her feet on the ground again.

When she arrived at the actual door, she stopped and took a deep breath before opening it. While she only had to keep her job long enough to steal the patches from Bubbles—at which point she'd be fired and face criminal prosecution—being fired early would make things much harder than they already were.

She opened the door, pausing a moment to get her first and hopefully last look at Rellie's stepfamily. Director Carlson leaned against the front of his desk, blond hair slightly mussed as he shifted enough to nearly knock over one of the stacks of paperwork. The three women sitting on the chairs in front of him, oddly enough, looked exactly like they'd sounded during that one overheard conversation at Rellie's house—Belzie had angry little eyes to go with her rolls of fat, Lucinda's mouth was stuck in a perpetual pout, and Maleeva was eyeing her as if she was a servant who hadn't polished the silver as thoroughly as she should have. All together, they were the closest thing Rellie had to family, a thought that only managed to make Kate that much angrier at the universe.

Wanting to get this over with as quickly as possible, she stepped inside and closed the door behind her. "You wanted to see me?"

Carlson turned to her, eyes lighting with something that looked suspiciously close to relief. "Ah, yes. Just the Fairy Godmother we needed to speak with." He gestured toward Maleeva. "These women are here to ask about . . ." The words trailed off a moment as his brow furrowed.

"Cinderella," Kate and Maleeva said at the same time, with almost the exact same snap in their voice.

"Cinderella. Yes, of course." His expression promptly smoothed out again. "These women are her stepfamily, and they have a few questions they were hoping to have answered about the follow-up to her Fairy Godmothers, Inc. package."

After shooting Carlson a glare, Maleeva turned her attention to Kate. "Given the fact that the palace held a formal ball last night and Cinderella was absent this morning during the time we normally insist on breakfast, I came to the conclusion that this oaf had finally decided to secure some long-term plans for the girl's future. I will say, however, that his choice of her intended spouse was absolutely ridiculous—either one of my daughters would have made a far better wife for a prince—"

"I would have made the best wife. Belzie's so fat she wouldn't even fit on the throne."

"They can always make me a bigger throne. Too bad they can't make you a bigger *brain*."

"Children!" Once her daughters settled back into their earlier mulish silence, Maleeva turned back to Kate. "As I was saying, it's become clear that Cinderella did not return to my home after the ball as would normally be expected, which means I am owed some information as to future proceedings. Given that on our way here we passed one of the city's finest dressmakers hurrying to the palace with a carriage full of supplies, can I reasonably presume the prince has decided to eliminate the traditional kingdom-wide shoe-fitting, and move straight to the wedding?"

The idea caused a fresh surge of panic to kick against Kate's ribs, but after so many times in the same day it had lost the ability to rattle her. "I'm sure high quality dressmakers are regularly called to the palace," she said, trying not to imagine the added level of mess this might mean for Jon. He had Lawton there to help deal with it, and she'd be there the second she figured out how to get the patches. "Though if it is preparation for a wedding dress, I'm not sure what your concern is. The reason Fairy Godmothers, Inc. phased the shoe-fitting out of their standard package in the first place is because of all the 'emotional stress' we were hearing from the stepfamilies."

"Oh, come now." Maleeva huffed. "I'm certain that—"

"'Emotional stress' is a polite way of saying they were cutting parts of their feet off to make the shoes fit," Kate said.

Director Carlson's eyes widened again in surprise—Kate had thought he, at least, would have gotten the memo—and Maleeva and her daughters turned different shades of green at the thought. Lucinda's lip even trembled. "Mother, you know I faint at the sight of blood! I can't—"

"Don't be ridiculous, Lucinda," Maleeva snapped, the edge in her voice betraying her own reaction. "You know I can't have you getting blood on my carpets." Further comment seemed to escape her as the stepmother collected herself, using a single well-manicured finger to smooth an invisible hair back into place before returning her attention to Kate and the original conversation. "While some of us who have chosen this particular lifestyle are far more rational than others your company has apparently worked with, far be it from me to question your abandonment of such a long and rich tradition." She sniffed, glaring sidelong at Carlson as if he was personally responsible for denying her the opportunity of being the first stepmother in history to pull a switch on the prince and

get her favorite standing next to him at the altar. "With preparations for Cinderella's wedding occurring even as we speak, I have
a second, more immediate concern." She leaned forward. "I am
aware that her future husband's family will be making the entirety
of the arrangements, as is proper for royalty, and that would lead
to the accommodations for the bride's family. I'm sure they're reasonable, educated people, but those of us who have dedicated our
lives to being a proper wicked stepfamily hear . . . rumors."

It wasn't until the expectant silence that Kate realized there
had apparently been a question in the middle of all that. "I'm sorry,
but I'm not entirely sure what you're asking."

Maleeva pursed her lips in annoyance, but Belzie was more than
happy to chime in. "She wants to know if they're going to make
her dance in red-hot iron shoes." Her mother whipped around to
shoot a furious glare at her daughter, but Belzie only snickered.
"We still hear stories about when it happened to Grandma."

Kate opened her mouth, then closed it again. Her first instinct
had been to lie and tell them Jon's family was definitely a red-hot
iron shoes kind of people, because the last thing they needed to
throw into this mess was Rellie's idiotic stepfamily.

But there was a dressmaker running to the palace with a speed
that suggested he or she was about to get a nice large paycheck.
There was no information anywhere about whether or not True
Love could eventually shut off all your decision-making ability or
how fast that might happen, and Kate still hadn't figured out how
to commit the stupid robbery. More mess might not make things
better, but it would certainly slow things down.

She pasted on her warmest, sweetest client smile. "I can assure you Jon's family would welcome you with open arms, and
would be horrified to hear iron shoes were even brought up." As

their expressions relaxed somewhat, she took a step closer. "In fact, the decision not to include the shoe hunt was made by Fairy Godmothers, Inc., not the royal family. If you went over there right now, it's entirely possible they would be willing to arrange one right there at the palace. I'm sure the prince would be more than happy to accommodate his future in-laws."

Maleeva's eyes actually lit, and Kate mentally added it to the list of things, for which she'd have to beg Jon's forgiveness when this was all over.

Hopefully, he'd give her the chance.

TWENTY-ONE

Fields of Battle

Jon stared down at the chaos on the ground floor, more than a little disturbed by how close to self-torture this was. The True Love kept making him think ridiculously swoony thoughts about carrying Rellie up to the altar; and watching his mother and the dressmaker attempt to get her fitted for a wedding dress left him feeling both depressed that she was so clearly not interested, and nauseated at himself for feeling that way. He also couldn't help but be embarrassed that he was hiding on the upper walkway rather than trying to stop her from being assaulted with seed pearls, despite that by doing so he was sparing her from feeling the same mopey self-disgust he suffered from.

Of course, she was clearly doing a pretty good job of taking care of herself. The sheer entertainment value was more than enough to keep his feet rooted to the spot.

"I told you!" she shouted again, swinging the bolt of silk wildly enough one of the assistants actually fell backward in an attempt to get away from it. The dressmaker himself had long ago backed out of range of any easily accessible weaponry. "I don't want a wedding dress, I don't want people sticking pins in me, I don't want you for my mother-in-law, and I don't want to get married! Why won't you people listen?"

"Don't be ridiculous," the queen snapped, attempting a step closer. In a ludicrously self-sacrificial move that should probably earn her a raise when this was all over, one of the maids grabbed the queen's arm to pull her away from a swipe that would have gotten her crown knocked off. "You're *clearly* one of those poor tragic creatures who knew nothing about her noble heritage before falling in love with a prince. Those kind of girls all dream about getting married in dresses that cost more than what small kingdoms make in a year! It's practically law!"

Standing next to Jon, Lawton nodded dryly at the scene below them. "Clearly, your mother managed to absorb something from all those years technically helping to run the kingdom."

"Technically nothing," Jon said. "Before she left, Grandmother set up a special edict that stated Mother wasn't allowed within fifty feet of any decision that had any actual effect on the country. Before I finished school and took over most of his responsibilities, Father managed things by focusing on the paperwork and having Grandmother threaten people remotely."

"I believe you mentioned that to me at some point, though I never remember it. I have difficulties picturing your father spending even that much time interacting with the rest of humanity." Lawton smiled at Rellie's next swipe, which hit the queen's upsweep directly enough to knock out a few persimmons. "I do feel a certain sympathy for the man that he's not here to witness his wife's inevitable defeat, however. He would undoubtedly find it even more of a heartwarming sight than I do."

Jon ruthlessly crushed a burst of pride in Rellie at Lawton's words, which although much deserved, kept generating thoughts that started with "my darling." He actually closed his eyes briefly when she blew a lock of golden hair away from her face, keeping her vision clear while the assistant who wasn't unconscious circled just out of reach. "The mature, responsible thing to do would be to go down there and end this before someone draws blood."

"Since I suspect the blood would either be your mother's or one of the dressmakers, I would hate for you to spoil the fun early." Lawton shook his head sadly as Jon's mother called for the guards, who had left after the queen's first frustrated shriek and were likely out of earshot by this point. "Besides, I suspect your guilt over not rushing down there to settle matters comes not so much from any sense of maturity or responsibility, but from the uncomfortable reminder of your current difficulties in controlling every ebb and flow of the universe."

Jon's eyes narrowed. "I run an entire kingdom and try to keep the rest of my family from killing themselves or each other. I'm just doing my job."

"You've been dosed with a remarkably strong love potion, you have no idea what's happening with the woman you *actually* love, your brother is missing, and your mother seems to have finally gone mental completely. And I am certain that, deep down, you are convinced the entire list is nothing more than a temporary hitch in your plans."

Jon glared at Lawton, more than willing to lie but not sure he was in any shape to pull it off convincingly, when out of the corner of his eye he saw the assistant lunge. Naturally, his sweet

Rellie responded with a solid forward jab and hit her opponent in the target favored by women throughout the ages—the young man undoubtedly regretted removing his heavy leather work belt—but as he doubled over, Jon noticed the dressmaker move. A larger man easily three times Rellie's size, he picked up his own bolt of cloth and inched toward her blind spot.

Jon swore softly. "Doing this is not going to make me more willing to pay them."

Lawton watched the clumsily executed strategy through narrowed eyes. "He's moving more slowly than he should be to set up the proper rhythm with his assistant. Rellie might intercept him before he's moved into position."

"She'd still be left holding off two men with a bolt of fabric." Jon sighed, already able to feel the headache sharpening again. It didn't help that the love potion kept pushing him to rush down and bravely defend his angel from the brigands who threatened her. "I don't suppose you could possibly—"

Lawton shook his head. "I could provide our young friend with physical assistance. However, the only reason the dressmakers didn't allow a burst of good sense to send them home twenty minutes ago is that your mother promised them a ludicrous amount of money to complete the dress. I, magnificent though I am, don't have the necessary authority to contradict that promise."

Knowing he was right, Jon turned and headed for the stairs. "Could you . . . ?"

"Shout a friendly warning should the need arise?" Lawton nodded, following him. "I will also endeavor to get Rellie out of your immediate visual range as quickly as possible."

"We both thank you." Jon kept moving, ignoring the brief sense of loss Lawton's statement inspired. "I haven't had time to inform Dobbs of his new role as Rellie's temporary manservant, but the man hasn't protested an assignment in ten years. I doubt he'll give you any trouble."

When they hit the bottom of the stairs, Lawton headed toward Rellie while Jon aimed for the dressmaker. Getting his arms far enough around the man for a suitable restraining hold would have been a challenge, so Jon grabbed the bolt of fabric sticking out over the back of the dressmaker's shoulder and jerked it downward. The move was sudden enough to rip the bolt out of the other man's hand, and when the dressmaker turned around, Jon used it to whack him in the head. "We need to have another talk about not taking commissions from my mother without consulting with me first."

The dressmaker's face turned white. "Your Highness!" Business owners who dealt with the palace recognized Jon far more quickly than anyone else in the kingdom, since he held the final say on all major expenditures. "I . . . I presumed your mother wanted it to be a surprise . . ."

The queen scowled, jabbing a finger in the dressmaker's direction. "You traitor! See if I send for you the next time I want to commission a gown for the Fall Spectacular!"

Behind her, Jon could see Lawton ushering Rellie out the door with his hands over her eyes. Rellie's hand was on top of his, as if making sure it didn't come off—and Jon kicked himself for the pang of jealousy he felt seeing it. She let go long enough to feel ahead of her for the edge of the door. Just before they passed through it, she lifted her hand in a wave clearly meant for someone behind her.

Jon felt himself melt, immediately hated himself for it, and scrubbed a hand across his face before his mother could see the besotted expression he knew struck him a few seconds ago. Then, even more annoyed than he'd been before, he turned back to the dressmaker. "If you leave now, you have about a fifty percent chance of receiving a consultation fee for being completely embarrassed by an untrained girl at least half your age. In a perfect world you'd probably be arrested for the combined charges of incompetence and assault, but watching her hold the three of you off with a roll of fabric has unfortunately been the sole high point of my day."

When the older man flushed, mouth opening to formulate some sort of defense, Jon narrowed his eyes at him. "If you don't leave now, I assure you royal inspectors will become a significant part of your future. The more miserable they make your life, the more money I plan to pay them."

The queen, distracted from the affront of the dressmaker's betrayal, turned to Jon. "How dare you! You have no right to send someone away I called for, even if he is a sniveling little trai—"

She fell silent at whatever she saw in his face as he glared, the calculating expression on her face making it clear she'd postponed her side of the argument rather than ended it.

No one else felt quite that brave. The assistant whom Rellie had taken out with a direct hit was still curled in a protective ball on the ground, not caring what else was happening in the room. The one who'd fallen earlier had stood at some point and was carefully trying to inch her way out of Jon's field of vision. The dressmaker, who had gone pale at the mention of royal inspectors, wisely dropped his eyes when he realized he was the center of attention once again. "Why, precisely, haven't you left yet?" Jon snapped.

The dressmaker became even paler, actually backing up a step.

"Perhaps one of my assistants could repair that loose thread on your sleeve before we go?"

Jon pointed a finger in the direction of the doorway. The dressmaker finally accepted his absolute lack of ground to stand on, and hurriedly collected his things. The standing assistant poked the one on the ground with her foot to nudge him upright, and within a few moments the three of them had gathered their scattered equipment and wisely fled the room. Once the door shut behind them, Jon turned to his mother. "Out of curiosity, what exactly was your plan there?" he asked. "Did you expect that, somehow, the sight of her in a wedding dress would magically make me—" He could feel the love potion waiting eagerly in the back of his mind for any mention of its favorite triggers, so he shifted mid-sentence. "—forget everything I've said to you all morning?"

The love potion, deeply annoyed by the denial, threw back a mental image of his beautiful, golden Rellie running to him in a wedding dress. Gritting his teeth, Jon shoved it aside with a vision of a dragon eating the entire management team at Fairy Godmothers, Inc. When he felt he could safely refocus on the argument he'd started, he found his mother glaring at him in frustrated confusion. "If you're going to accuse me of something, Jonathan, the least you could do is make sure you're paying attention!"

Since revealing anything to do with the love potion would be bordering on suicidal—his mother, he had no doubt, would simply consider it a part of the normal courtship process—Jon threw his hands up in the air and swung the argument in a different direction. "If you're going to suddenly take an interest in my life at the worst possible moment, the least you could do is tell me why! Up till this point we've both been very comfortable with the fact that

you barely acknowledge my existence, and if this sudden attention is a side effect of Rupert not being around, then I will end
his quest right now just to make him come back and distract you!"

The queen blinked at that, though whether it was from the
question itself or merely her son's vehemence Jon couldn't say for
certain. Either way, the surprise didn't last long—she was quick
to frown at him. "*Most* sons would be grateful their mother was
making an effort to show more of an interest in their lives." At
his incredulous expression, she made a frustrated noise. "Fine. So
perhaps I was a bit overly dramatic this morning when you refused
to tell me anything about the fact that you had clearly fallen in love,
which is the first thing you've ever done that any reasonable person
can expect me to have an interest in. Then when I try to encourage
you by dressing up the girl so you can be struck by a music-swelling
burst of romantic feeling and immediately propose to her as you
should, you kick everyone out and have the gall to yell at me!"

Jon just stared at her for a minute, mentally sorting through
what she'd said in an attempt to connect it to some kind of logic
his love potion-battered head could understand. Giving up, he
closed his eyes. "If I get Rupert off his quest and drag him back
here, is there any chance at all you can start planning a wedding for
him and forget about me again?"

"Don't be ridiculous. My darling Rupert is clearly much too
fragile to get married. His job is to perform the traditional naughty
escapades, which I may then coo and tut over as a mother should.
He also lets me tell him about my projects, and though my poor
dear does usually fall asleep halfway through, at least he has the
decency not to interrupt me with sarcasm." She said the word like
it was something evil, right up there with things like "chores" and
"sensible shoes." "You, on the other hand, ignore me, and insist

on spending all your time with numbers and meetings and all those ridiculously boring things that my father used to pay so much attention to!"

Jon, surprised enough at the slightly hysterical edge that had crept into his mother's voice, opened his eyes to stare at her with the slowly sinking realization that the conversation was heading toward some kind of psychological insight. As that was the last thing he wanted just then, he changed to the soothing tone he used on skittish ambassadors who were afraid to commit to anything. "You're right, Mother. I shouldn't have dismissed the dressmaker without allowing you to express your fully justified displeasure with him." Noting the surprise on the queen's face, he bowed and flourished his hand toward the door. "If we hurry, I believe we can catch them before they leave the palace grounds."

Thankfully, his mother was mollified enough to sweep out of the room, heading for the palace entryway in the hopes of making an appropriately large scene. Jon, exhausted but oddly relieved, followed behind at a much slower pace.

But when he arrived at the main doors, his relief vanished at the sight of three women arguing with Lawton and his mother in the entryway. Rellie—delicate, beautiful Rellie—was luckily safely out of sight, but her ball-crashing stepfamily was quite busy expressing their displeasure at Lawton through a mixture of shouting and overly dramatic hand gestures. Even his mother seemed to be somewhat put off by idea of facing people who could rant as loudly as she, and was doing quite a bit of gesturing of her own as she refocused her frustration with the dressmaker on the more convenient target.

For a moment, all Jon could do was stare at the burgeoning chaos, already able to picture the inevitable moment when someone started throwing things. Then, sighing, he headed forward to take over for Lawton. "Can I help you?"

The stepmother—Maleeva, he thought he recalled his darling Rellie calling her—snapped her attention to Jon. "I need to speak this instant to the prince who's planning to marry my stepdaughter. I was assured we would be welcomed with open arms by his family, but this insolent servant refuses to let us be properly received!"

Hearing the word "servant," Jon glanced over at Lawton. Normally, the other man would have already dispatched the three with some cutting witticisms and a few strong guards, which was his general policy for those foolish enough to waste either of their time. Though sweet Rellie's presence had complicated matters, Lawton knew better than anyone that family rarely improved the situation.

Lawton, catching the question in Jon's eyes, twisted his mouth into a rueful expression. "Apparently, it was the Fairy Godmother overseeing young Miss Rellie's case who'd personally assured these women of our welcome."

Jon's eyes widened, heart kicking against his ribs even as his brain tried to make him feel guilty for all the wrong reasons. He repeated her name to himself like a mantra in retaliation, forcing it through the fog as he turned back to their unwelcome guests. "You spoke to Kate?"

The queen cut off whatever she was about to say to stare at Jon with a newly confused expression. Maleeva was still furious. "Why would I bother asking what the woman's name was?" she scowled. "She was an employee." When Jon didn't respond, she sniffed and lifted her chin. "All I know is that she suggested asking the royal family to initiate a proper shoe quest for our dear Cinderella, a fine and upstanding tradition that the Fairy Godmothers themselves failed to provide for her."

Jon tried to analyze this newest development through the haze of the love potion. There was no reason management would bother with a shoe hunt after doping them both up with enough love potion to fell a giant, but as far as he could tell Kate didn't have any more—

A light clicked on in his head.

More time.

Stepping forward, Jon gave Maleeva and her daughters his best salesman's smile. The piece he'd just been handed may have been ridiculously tiny, but it was a relief to have a chance to get back in the game at all. "Let me assure you, Madam. I have always firmly believed in the importance of upholding tradition."

TWENTY-TWO

Breaking and Entering

After everything else that had gone wrong over the last few days, Kate and Ned decided a simple plan was the least likely to get them carted away in handcuffs. They waited to put it into action until after everyone had gone home for the day, so that when they *did* screw up they would hopefully have a few hours head start before Bubbles found out.

"I'm so, so sorry to be bothering you like this," Kate repeated for the fifth time, clutching a very full folder to her chest as she hurried after the Fairy Godmothers, Inc. night janitor. The man's legs were a good six inches shorter than hers, and it was taking a bit of work to not actually pass him. "But my boss said I needed to have this on her desk by tomorrow morning at dawn or I could kiss my job goodbye."

"Okay, okay." The man waved an exasperated hand, which was Kate's cue to quit the nervous rambling. Ned swore he'd done exactly the same thing a month ago, though in his case the folder had contained an actual case file rather than the random paperwork she'd shoved into this one. "Just make sure you're quick about it."

When they made it to Bubbles' office, the janitor sorted through his keys as Kate shifted from foot to foot. "I really am sorry about this," she said one more time. "I knew I should have gotten it to her earlier today, but she sent me back out into the field at the last minute to take care of something for another client, and by the time I got back everything was locked up." She forced herself to take a breath after that, making sure the real I'm-going-to-get-arrested panic didn't overcome the fake I'm-going-to-get-fired panic. Not that the man would even notice—people tended not to pay much attention to annoyances, she'd discovered over the years.

Finding the right key, the janitor unlocked the door. Kate glanced back the way they'd come, but the area was worryingly quiet except for the man's occasional muttered grumblings and the small click of Bubbles' lock giving way. When she turned again, a nervous smile plastered back on her face, he straightened and pushed open the door. "Hurry and drop it on her desk," he said gruffly. "I need to lock everything up behind you."

"Oh, of course," Kate said seriously, not moving an inch. The Fairy Godmothers, Inc. janitorial staff made sure the only way to get a hold of them was in person—management tended to bother them less that way—and if Ned didn't come running down the corridor in the next thirty seconds she didn't have the slightest idea what to do next. Pretending to drop something would give her maybe fifteen extra seconds in the office, tops, but with the janitor standing there the delay wouldn't be nearly en—

Both Kate and the janitor's heads jerked up at the immense, multi-part crash that suddenly rolled down from the ceiling. The sound was loud enough it echoed through the empty offices for a minute. After it finally faded into silence the janitor swore creatively and looked at Kate. "Listen, I need—"

"It's okay," she said quickly, shaking off her own surprised reaction as she waved him toward the stairs. She resisted the urge to look up again and tried not to picture what had happened to turn the simple cracked pipe they'd planned on into whatever caused that noise upstairs. "You go do whatever you need to do, and I'll make sure to shut everything up so you can come back and lock it when you're done."

The janitor didn't even hesitate before hurrying off. Trying not to think about whether or not Ned had gotten away in time, Kate slipped into the office and shut the door behind her. Tucking the folder into the waistband of her skirt, she took a quick survey of everything she'd have to deal with. She knew she was going to get caught, but there was no sense in making it easier for them. There were several rows of filing cabinets, all of which seemed to be full of rigidly organized folders. Different editions of the company manual lined the shelves, and Bubbles' performance awards from when she'd been out in the field covered the walls. Knowing the woman, there were probably at least a few secret panels stashed around the room, but if Kate started thinking like that without checking all the logical places first she was going to be here all night.

She had almost finished examining the desk drawers when a hesitant knock came at the door. Kate froze, knowing there wasn't a hiding place big enough for both her and her Fairy Godmothers uniform.

Then there was a second knock. "Kate, it's *me*."

Her shoulders sagged in relief at Ned's attempt at a stage

whisper. "It's not locked," she said, bending back down to the drawers as he came in. She re-closed the center one—it was unsettling to see paperclips laid out that precisely—and realized Ned's footsteps had a distinct sloshing edge to them. Brow furrowed, she looked up as he came around the other side. "Do you want to talk about it?"

Solemnly, Ned shook his head. A single forlorn drop of water slid off the tip of his nose. "Have you found anything?"

Kate straightened, pointing to the bottom right-hand drawer. "That one has a lock, even though it's hard to see it." Pulling the folder out of her waistband and handing it to Ned, she retrieved her wand and took a few steps back. "If we're lucky, this is where the patches will be."

Ned raised both eyebrows. "Since when have we ever been lucky?"

She sighed. "You're right. Start looking for secret panels." Then, taking a deep breath, she pointed the wand at the drawer. Neither she nor Ned had ever picked a lock in his or her life, and all Fairy Godmothers, Inc. wands were only useful for a limited set of spells that unfortunately had nothing to do with breaking and entering. As for destroying the lock, Ned's misadventure upstairs made it clear even magic didn't make it easy to destroy something only a little bit.

There were some things, however, the wands had no trouble doing.

She concentrated on keeping the spell as tightly focused as possible, carefully moving the wand as she closely watched the swirl of fairy dust form. After a few seconds the front of the drawer burst outward, stretching and swelling into a full skirt made out of thin strips of wood paneling. The newly formed skirt pushed out a little further as an inch or so of bodice became visible beyond the edge of the desk. As she wrapped up the last flourish, the brass handle was transforming into a rosette.

She dropped to her knees, the knot in her stomach finally relaxing a little as she lifted up the edge of the wood skirt and rooted around inside. Ned crouched next to her, finger tracing the curve of the half-formed flower with something close to awe. "Wow," he whispered, looking nearly as excited as when he'd walked in the door the first day of his internship. "I didn't say anything, but I didn't really believe you when you said you could do this. The edge of the desk didn't even ruffle."

"That's okay. I didn't really believe me, either." Pulling out the first thing her fingers touched, Kate grimaced when she realized she was holding a huge, half-full bottle of True Love. "Luckily, the spell wasn't smart enough to know it wasn't working with fabric." Shoving the bottle back inside—hopefully, it would still be there when the dress turned back into a locked drawer at midnight—she tried not to think about anything else she might be touching until her fingers brushed against something box-shaped. Pulling it out and yanking off the plain brown lid, she let out a breath of relief at the row of tightly packed, star-shaped patches lined up inside. "This is it."

Ned leaned over to get a better look at their find. "How many do you think we should take? I know that one was enough to fix Thea, but if we lose one or something else goes wrong it's not like we can come back for more."

"Which is why we're taking all of them," she said, standing up and sliding the box into her pocket. "Bubbles probably knows the exact count of how many patches she has left, and we'll get in the same amount of trouble no matter how many are missing."

She didn't add that Bubbles was capable of trying to dose Jon and Rellie again even after they fixed things. They needed all the ammunition they could get. "Now, we need to find a quiet corner for me to set up the—"

Something loud rumbled upstairs, followed by an ominous rushing noise. They jerked, then looked at each other, and without another word ran for the exit.

THE TRANSPORT DOOR, which Kate had needed to set up more quickly than she'd originally planned, took them to the spot on the palace grounds where Jon had found her after she'd ran out of the ball. She still remembered the coordinates for the room inside the palace where they'd held the dance lesson, but with their luck they'd either land right on top of a guard or get completely lost. This way, at least, they could ask for Lawton at one of the doors and convince him to let them in.

Ned looked down at his still wet uniform. "I know this is serious, but are you sure we shouldn't have taken the time to stop somewhere and change? I'm kind of obvious wandering around like this."

Kate shook her head. "My wings are enough to give us away, and if we can get Lawton to say it's okay we're here, it won't matter what we look like." She stared at the palace, which was still mostly lit despite how late it was. Jon was in there somewhere, either constantly fighting the inside of his own head or composing love sonnets to the majesty of Rellie's eyes.

She pressed her lips together, the knot that had spent the day in the pit of her stomach tightening into a hard little ball. They had one chance.

"Not that I'm one to talk, but I really don't think you're supposed to be back here."

Kate's breath hitched as she whirled around at the unexpected voice, grabbing Ned's arm in case they needed to make a run for it.

When the blonde, square-jawed man popped up from behind one of the ornamental hedges, she stopped and squinted at him. Palace guards didn't walk around in gold shirts that would probably shimmer in better lighting. And something about his face told her brain she should recognize him. "And how do we know you're not the one who isn't supposed to be back here?" she asked. "Hiding behind a bush in the dark doesn't say much for your sense of belonging."

She felt Ned tense beneath her grasp, and she turned to see him glaring at the other man. "It's the prince," he said darkly, pulling his arm from Kate's grasp. "The first one, who was supposed to marry Rellie."

The man—Rupert, her brain confirmed with a resigned groan—lifted his eyebrows in surprise. "No one told me I was supposed to get married. It's kind of hard to go out and seek self-act . . . actu . . . that philosopher thing, when you've got a wife who doesn't like to travel because it gets her hair dirty. Though if she really is that much like Mother, maybe being away all the time would be a good idea. We'd start running out of offices to hide in if both Father and I used them."

Ned stepped forward. "You are not going to have to worry about any of that, because—"

Kate stuck an arm in front of Ned to block his way. "You no longer have to worry about getting married, Your Highness," she said, resisting her own urge to throttle the man. If nothing else,

Jon deserved to be the one to do it. "We've decided to go a different direction."

"A very different direction," Ned seconded.

She looked at Ned, voice firm. "You're not helping." When he finally stopped pushing against her arm, she lowered it. "And how, by the way, did you know what Prince Rupert looked like? I haven't even opened that file since I finished Rellie's dress and shoes!"

He shrugged, looking a little sheepish. "I was doing a little light reading?"

Rupert, who had shrugged off his earlier concern the moment Kate told him not to worry, became mournful. "I tried that reading thing—it's not nearly as easy as Jon always made it look. Even the wise old lady waiting at the crossroads, whom Father always said I should listen to if I was traveling anyplace, didn't have any idea how to help me understand what I was talking about. Not even after I gave her some of my bread, because she was complaining about being hungry."

Kate had thought Jon was exaggerating when he said Rupert had been looking for help understanding big words. Not that she hadn't met other royals who were clearly a few dwarves short of a mine, but most of them didn't seem to be bothered by it. "As tragic as that undoubtedly is, I still don't know how you ended up hiding in your own backyard. After taking all that trouble to run off, you certainly didn't stay away very long."

Rupert lifted his chin with an air of arrogance that made him look royal for the first time since they met him. "I didn't just run off, I was trying to find out how to actualize myself and be a happier person like the book said I should." Then he deflated, shoulders dropping with a sigh as he looked back at the palace.

"Only I rode all day yesterday and asked everyone I came across, and no one knew how to explain the stuff in the book in a way that meant I could actually do something about it. So, I spent all day today riding back to ask Jon if he could give me some advice about where I could find someone to talk to. He wasn't that specific the first time."

Kate rubbed her hand across her eyes, feeling guilty for getting angry at Jon the night before. "Okay, but why don't you just go inside and ask him?" she said finally, waving a shushing hand at Ned when she saw him mouth the word *crazy*. If Rupert could be persuaded to let them in to find out where Jon and Rellie were, they wouldn't have to worry about whether or not Lawton was mad enough to torture them a little. "From the way he was talking last night, he'll be more than happy to have you come back and take over your old spot."

Rupert shook his head. "I don't think so. Jon always did all the stuff the heir's really supposed to do anyway—he mostly just needed me for the parties. It's a lot easier if he just keeps the job, and after I've got this whole inner child business taken care of I can smile and shake people's hands when he needs me to." He scratched his nose thoughtfully. "The problem is, Mother really doesn't like it when people do things she doesn't want them to, and I don't think she wanted me to go off and do the whole cosmic search thing." He glanced back at the palace. "She's probably going to cry when she sees me again. A lot."

Kate fought for her last shred of patience. "If it would help, you could probably get someone to sedate her for you."

Rupert smiled a little. "That's what Jon always says." He narrowed his eyes at her in enlightened speculation. "You sure sound pretty friendly with him for someone I've never seen before. Plus, you made me talk about what I was doing out here, but you never said what you were doing."

Kate grasped for a relatively simple explanation, then realized one didn't actually exist for this particular situation. "He's under a really evil spell," she said finally, wincing, when she saw Rupert's eyes widen in alarm. Still, if it was enough to get him to risk facing his mother and let them both in . . . "I've brought something that will help get him out of it."

Rupert started toward the palace, quickly enough that Kate and Ned had to run to catch up with him. Before they'd made it past the ornamental fountain, however, he slammed to a halt and turned back around. "How did Jon get put under an evil spell? He doesn't do stupid things like kissing witches' daughters or chopping down enchanted trees. He keeps me from doing stuff like that. People who like using evil spells don't usually bother with princes who act sensibly and spend most of their time doing paperwork."

"That part, actually, is my fault," she admitted, the knot in her stomach tight as ever. "I dragged him into it without meaning to, and I'm trying really hard to set things right again."

Ned moved forward, then took a fairly sizeable step sideways away from her. "They're dating," he explained—Kate realized he'd meant to move himself out of arm's reach. "The evil spell came because our boss doesn't think they should be, and we've come to save both Jon and Rellie so they can end up with us instead of each other." When Kate glared at him, he held his hands up helplessly. "That's what happened! Did you really want to keep standing here while he dragged the entire story out of you?"

"Are you embarrassed to be dating my brother?" Rupert asked, an edge of anger in his voice.

Kate's cheeks reddened. "No! Of course not! It's just . . . I . . ."

She sighed, giving up. "I'm crazy about him, but I'm not sure he's even going to be willing to speak to me after all this is over."

Rupert smiled. "Of course he will. The hero always gets to marry the person they save." He turned, gesturing over his shoulder for Kate and Ned to follow him.

TWENTY-THREE

If the Shoe Fits

Sometimes, a plan required holding secret meetings with top advisors and issuing half-veiled, precisely calculated threats. Other times, it required digging through your great-grandmother's shoe closet.

Jon was in her collection of "Late Summer/Early Fall" shoes at the moment, a sizeable mound of rejects in a haphazard pile around his feet. He knew the pair he was looking for was still back here—if they'd been moved at any point during the last decade, he would have been the one to approve it. Of course, he hadn't thought he'd end up needing them for anything.

He heard the closet door open behind him and the sound of someone crossing several yards of closet. "I knew you could work fast, Lawton," Jon said lightly, coasting just ahead of his exhaustion. "But this is extraordinary even for you."

"What is he working on, precisely?" His father's voice was

quiet, but there was an edge to it that Jon had never heard before. "Or, more importantly, what are you working on?"

Jon still didn't look up as he dropped the empty box on the ground and reached for the next one. He'd already gone through at least half of his great-grandmother's collection, and if he didn't find the pair he was looking for soon, he'd have to rework that part of the plan. "If you're trying to avoid Mother, she's in the Powder Blue Sitting Room drinking tea and exchanging barbed comments with Rellie's stepfamily." He reached for the next box, yanking his mind away from the vision of the golden-haired little girl and the words "Rellie" and "family" created together.

He really needed to work in another few hours of sleep at some point.

The king paused. "Should I be expecting screams?"

"Maybe, but only worry if they're Mother's—she can do whatever she wants to the other women." Jon found himself grinning at the thought as he lifted the lids on the next entire row of boxes. None of them held the shoes he was looking for, and he dismissively swept them off the shelf. "I'm just grateful she was willing to keep them out of my hair for a few hours."

The king flinched when the boxes crashed to the floor, but didn't step back as his son moved his attention to the next set of shelves. He watched Jon for a few minutes, silently, before speaking again. "Why is your mother convinced you're in love with the wrong woman?"

That question made Jon jerk his head up, staring at his father with a surprise he no longer had the mental resources to hide. When their eyes met, the king shrugged. "I don't get involved much, but that doesn't mean I don't pay attention."

Jon shook his head, fighting a brief stab of guilt and the

sudden urge to write Rellie that love poem he kept avoiding. "Let's just say that I'm deeply grateful you and Mother never decided to hire Fairy Godmothers, Inc. for either of your children." He took a deep breath, bracing himself to dive back in to the task at hand. "Do you remember where your grandmother stored those shoes you told me about? The ones her brother wore to his birthday gala?"

The king's brow furrowed. "The glass slippers? They're big enough you could wear them. Why would you . . . ah." His eyebrows lifted as he mulled over the new information. "I noticed the pages dusting off the thrones and moving them into the ballroom."

"The throne room isn't big enough for all the people I'm going to need." Jon turned back to the next row of boxes, lifting the lids on each to confirm that the slippers weren't there either. "Plus, I wasn't comfortable with the fact that it only had one entry and exit. I'm not sure I'm going to need more, but it seemed like a good idea to have them available just in case."

"Should there be some extra guards ready?"

Jon swept the row of boxes off the shelves, ignoring them as they crashed against his legs. "I hadn't decided yet. I'm aiming for something closer to a public relations disaster than a panic-and-run disaster, but I haven't had a lot of luck with things going like I expected them these last few days." He winced as his brain reviewed the past eighteen hours. "You should probably have the guards ready."

The king nodded. "Of course." He was quiet as Jon started opening the next row of boxes, but now the worry was evident in his eyes. "You haven't mentioned Kate."

Jon stopped, staring at the shelves even though his eyes refused to focus on anything. The love potion, not quite sure what do to with the rush of emotion crashing against it from the opposite direction, tried a desperate grab for guilt before it threw its metaphorical hands in the air. "She's trying to take care of things on her end," he said finally, voice a little rough. "She'll get here when she can."

The expression on the king's face made it clear he didn't find the answer sufficiently comforting, but he knew there was nothing he could say that would improve the situation. It was almost a relief when the door opened again, breaking the silence.

"I presume I'm not interrupting anything?" Lawton asked dryly. When Jon started to say something, Lawton pointed at him. "Before you ask, I have yet to collect the crowd of women I promised you. I was distracted by an unexpected guest." He tilted his head toward the hallway. "He'd like an audience, if you have a few moments."

Jon studied Lawton's pleasantly bland expression for some sign of what he wasn't saying. The man had a sense of humor that left most people feeling like they'd brought a pen to a sword fight, but he could be almost ruthlessly protective when he had to be. If the "unexpected guest" was trouble, Lawton would have kept him far enough away they could get a plan of attack ready. As for someone good . . . the fact that he hadn't said "she" essentially eliminated that possibility.

The only option left, unfortunately, was more complication.

"Fine. He gets sixty seconds." Jon went to the door, the king following behind at a more leisurely pace. When Lawton stepped aside to let them pass, Jon glared at him. "If this 'guest' annoys me," he muttered, "you're the one responsible for his death."

Lawton nodded. "Naturally, though you may want to consult

with your father before doing anything rash." He pushed the door open wide enough to show who was standing behind it.

Jon's eyes widened for a moment, then closed. He knew he should be yelling at his brother, but he didn't even have the energy to be angry anymore. "Hello, Rupert," he said. "Want your crown back?"

"Of course, not. Why do people keep asking me that?"

Jon saw his brother peering worriedly at him. "But I heard you were under an evil spell, and that I was going to maybe get married at one point but now I'm not," Rupert added. "So, the question I was going to ask you can probably wait a little while."

The love potion sent out an almost painfully strong burst of jealousy at the thought of Rupert marrying Rellie, undoubtedly in revenge for that earlier reminder of Kate. Jon no longer had the energy to fight it, or even care. The fine edge of exhaustion-fueled energy that had kept him going this long had disappeared, and all he wanted to do was go back into the closet and keep looking for the stupid shoes until he fell asleep standing up. "Right now, I couldn't care less what your question is," he said flatly. "And you are definitely not getting married, but what you are doing is staying right here where I can have guards on you at all times. If you even think about wandering off again and leaving me here in the middle of a ball, which you know how much I hate—"

He felt cool, slender fingers brush against the side of his neck. Then they disappeared, and he could see a faint pink mist out of the corner of his eye as some kind of stiff fabric slapped against that same patch of skin. As soon as it made contact, a sensation like icy cold water rushed through his brain.

When it was done, he felt clean. Jon tested it by picturing the curves of Rellie's face, concentrating on the sound of her name, and all that followed was the vague affection he imagined he'd feel for a little sister if he ever had one. The relief of it was so profound it nearly staggered him, and he felt those same slender fingers touch his shoulder as if intending to steady him. An instant later, they disappeared again.

So he turned around, grabbed the mysterious hand, and dragged its owner into his arms.

Kate made a small sound of surprise as he pulled her against him, but Jon just wrapped his arms around her and held on as tightly as he could. A second later he heard the sound of a wand dropping to the floor and felt her arms slide around his back. Her fingers curled in the fabric of his shirt as she held on to him just as hard.

He pressed his face against the softness of her hair, finally feeling like he could breathe again. "You'll tell me if I start cutting off your air supply, right?"

She huffed out a laugh that ended on a slightly damp note. "Not if it means you'd let go of me."

He grinned, tempted to pick her up and start spinning around like some sort of love-struck idiot. As that would mean he'd have to give her a little breathing room, he settled instead for squeezing her tighter. "That's not something you're going to need to worry about."

Beside them, he heard Lawton's chuckle. "I told you he'd be happy to see you, Katharine. One of these days you'll learn not to doubt me."

That was enough to make Jon pull back to look at her. "You thought I wouldn't want to see you?" he asked. When he saw the telltale spark of guilt in Kate's eyes, he took her face in his hands.

"Kate, I begged you not to leave after that whole mess at the ball. I made you promise me you'd come back, and somewhere in the middle of all that I'm sure I proposed to you at least twice. Were you not paying attention to anything I said?"

"I also got you doused with True Love, because I didn't think about how paranoid Bubbles would be after Thea's accident." Kate pressed her lips together for a moment, but it wasn't enough to keep her voice from breaking. "I left you, and you got hurt while I wasn't there. You had every right to be mad at me."

The words were a gift Jon hadn't known he needed, and he felt his throat tighten as he wrapped her back in his arms. "But you also came back," he murmured. "Just like you promised you would."

She buried her face in his neck. "I'd love to promise you I won't leave again, but I'm pretty sure I'm going to be dragged away by law enforcement at some point."

He almost laughed. Not that someone trying to arrest Kate wasn't a possibility—now that he knew there was a cure, he had no trouble believing Fairy Godmothers, Inc. hadn't wanted to let it go. But they'd have to get through him first, and that wasn't about to happen. "Don't worry, sweetheart. Law enforcement doesn't stand a chance against me."

She laughed a little, tightening her arms around him. "You know, we really have to talk about this whole 'controlling the universe' thing."

"Believe me, he and I have had that particular discussion on more than one occasion," Lawton said.

Beside him, Jon's father spoke for the first time. "I have to ask—law enforcement?"

"Oh, they're not so bad," Rupert chimed in, completing the

helpful commentary. "Not that I do that sort of thing anymore, but they were always really good about getting me home when I woke up and didn't know where I was. And when that ogre started chasing me with a club after I accidentally thought he was a girl, they were nice enough to keep him from beating me up."

"I don't think that's what Kate's worried about," the king said gently.

Kate lifted her head to look at the king. "My boss dosed Jon and Rellie with a love potion as part of a contract agreement. Ned and I had to steal the antidote." She gave everyone a brief explanation of what had happened, starting at her discovery of her boss's definition of an insurance policy and ending with Rupert bringing her and Ned to Lawton.

"And when this Bubbles of yours finds out the patches are missing, you expect her to unleash the fury of whatever retribution she has at her disposal?" Lawton asked. When Kate nodded, his brow lowered in thought. "So, we should have at least until morning before there's a chance of her discovering the absence. Depending how often she opens that particular drawer and whether or not you thought to leave the empty box in the drawer as camouflage, it could be as long as a week or more."

Kate winced. "The next time I find myself doing a little breaking and entering, remind me to bring you along."

Lawton's smile held only the faintest trace of his usual smirk. "I look forward to it."

Jon gave the corridor a quick scan. "Should I be worried that Ned isn't here?"

"I haven't met a Ned yet." The king held up a hand. "How does he fit into all this?"

"He fell in love with the girl I was going to marry for a little while," Rupert said. "Which means it's probably good I was off trying to find out how to get inner peace when she came by. That would have been awkward,"

Kate shot Rupert an odd look, then shook her head and turned back to Jon. "Lawton told him where to find Rellie. He wanted to be the one to give her the antidote himself." She grinned. "Which makes sense, given the perks that come afterward."

Jon leaned forward for a kiss, his heart racing fast enough he probably couldn't fall asleep now even if someone enchanted him. At some point he was probably going to end up collapsing whether he wanted to or not, but with Kate here, he doubted it would be anytime soon.

They broke apart to a light smattering of applause, and Jon grimaced. "You know," he murmured, "I actually forgot about them for a second."

Kate smiled softly and pressed a quick kiss against his cheek. "I consider it a compliment."

Threading his fingers through Kate's, Jon faced the rest of the group. "I know the three of you have already technically met, but now that we're finally all in the same place again, it's time to be a little more formal about this. Father, Rupert, this is Kate Harris—Fairy Godmother extraordinaire, and your future daughter- and sister-in-law. Be nice, and try not to frighten her any more than she already has been until I get her to the altar."

Embarrassment lit Kate's eyes. "*Jon . . .*"

"You promised you wouldn't leave me again," he reminded her, pressing a gentle kiss to her cheek. "That certainly sounds like you said yes to me."

"Normally, we're not quite this overwhelming." The king gave Kate a small, kind smile. "Not that you haven't done wonderfully."

"Besides, you saved Jon," Rupert added confidently. "Unless he wants to get himself into trouble again, which would be really hard because he doesn't usually do this sort of thing at all, you've pretty much got to marry him."

Jon smiled. "My brother's right, you know." He brushed an errant lock of hair away from her forehead. "You're the only one I'd trust to save me again."

Kate stared at him for a heartbeat, then leaned forward to give him a quick, fierce kiss. When they broke apart, she narrowed her eyes. "Stop being adorable for five minutes so we can talk about this seriously." Her expression softened as she lifted her hands to cradle the sides of his face. "I'm crazy about you, and right now I'm pretty sure I'd follow you anywhere you wanted me to, but we need to take a little time and see if we'll end up killing each other without a crisis to distract us."

Jon raised an eyebrow. "Which we can do just as easily engaged, particularly if I promise to hold off the wedding for a year."

Beside them, Lawton sighed and shook his head. "Clearly, Katharine, the two of you are meant to be together. I've never met another woman who, upon being given heartfelt, yet appropriately poetic declarations of a man's affection, urges him to 'stop being so adorable' and begins the emotional version of trade negotiations."

"She's doing fine," Jon snapped, shooting his friend a quelling glare. He turned to Kate, gesturing with his head back toward the closet door. "I know I should have suggested this a while ago, but how about we retire to some place a little more private?"

They ducked into the closet, and Jon shut the door behind them and leaned against it. Kate, the corners of her mouth tugging into a smile, tapped her finger against the wood. "You know, they can still hear us if they try hard enough."

"Maybe, but it'll be harder for them to contribute." He traced his fingers along the edge of her jaw, expression solemn. "Take a chance, Kate. We're good for each other."

"Are you sure you've been paying attention at any point during the last twenty-four hours?"

"Which proves my point. I would have had a much better day if you'd been here instead of Rellie."

Before she could respond, someone knocked on the door behind him. Jon squeezed his eyes shut, tempted to ignore it, but there was still too much potential for trouble. "Tell me we can just let Lawton take care of it."

Kate sighed and kissed his cheek. "If we could, he wouldn't have let whoever it was knock in the first place."

When they opened the door, the king was standing in the corridor alone. "Lawton thought you should both know Rellie isn't where he left her." He pointed down the hallway. "Apparently the young man with the wings is already looking for her, and Lawton and Rupert followed to help him search."

Kate and Jon looked at each other, then hurried out of the room after them.

TWENTY-FOUR

❧

All the Little Things

K ate couldn't stop herself from imagining worst-case scenarios as they went to find Rellie. The miracles of the last hour had undoubtedly used up every shred of good fortune she was ever going to have—and probably a few other people's allotments, to be honest—which meant it was about time for something else terrible to happen.

"Another left turn, down one more corridor and we'll be there," said Jon, pointing to the corner ahead of them. They had decided to start at the room where they knew Rellie had last been to give themselves a starting point for the search. "Of course, with our less-than-stellar luck, they decided to start looking on the other side of the palace and we'll still have no idea where to find them."

When he caught sight of her face, he stopped in his tracks and focused on her. "You know she's fine, right?" he said, assurance in every word. "After everything else we've had to deal with, this is nothing more than an overly complicated game of hide and seek."

She took a deep breath, trying to believe him. She hadn't had enough practice yet to be any good at it, and as wonderful as it was it didn't provide nearly as steady a ground as planning for the worst. "I'm never going to be very good at hoping for the best," she warned softly, meeting his eyes in a silent plea for understanding. "If this has any chance of working, you're going to have to be okay with that."

He watched her for a long, careful moment, then flashed a grin that was almost enough to make her fall in love with him all over again right there. "I've always thought I could use a little more hard-headed realism in my life."

She was stunned to find a laugh bubbling up. "No, you didn't."

He was unrepentant as they started moving again. "True, but only because I didn't know you would be the one providing the realism."

Luckily, they didn't have much further to go; Ned was at the far end of the corridor, quietly checking each room and clearly trying very hard not to panic. Concerned, Kate let go of Jon's hand to hurry over to him. "Are you okay?"

"No." Ned closed his eyes, leaning his forehead against the door he'd been about to open. "I don't know where Rellie is, I can't go very far to look for her because it'd be too easy for me to get lost and be completely useless, and I can't even make any noise trying to find her because the queen and Rellie's entire stepfamily are all in the same room at the other end of the hall."

At a loss, Kate decided to at least try and get at little more information. "Why is Rellie's stepfamily still here?" she asked Jon.

Jon shrugged. "I'm not sure yet if I'll need them for the plan I'm pulling together. I was trying to keep them contained until I'd made a decision, and then you distracted me." His gaze shifted to Ned as he caught a change in the younger man's expression. "You've thought of something."

Kate turned back to see Ned's eyes unfocused, staring at whatever idea was unfolding in his mind. After a second, he blinked and shook his head. "Never mind. It's probably stupid."

Kate prodded him in the shoulder. "Tell us."

"It's just . . . if there was a chance Rellie heard her stepfamily coming, she's not exactly the kind of person who would try to run away."

Understanding hit Kate and Jon at almost the same time. They turned to look at each other, then Jon gave her a rueful smile. "Sadly, I believe my greatest contribution to the proceedings from this point would be to stay safely out of the way and let you handle this."

Sympathetic, Kate gently patted his shoulder. "I'm sure you'll get to save the day again before the night's out." She turned to Ned. "Right now, however, it's your turn."

The two hurried down the corridor, slowing as they got closer to their target. Ned had already gotten out one of the patches and was attaching it to his wand as Kate eyed the doors to the rooms on each side of the room with the queen and Rellie's stepfamily. "Rellie would have been coming from the same direction we did, so this one would have been the closest." She reached for the doorknob, then stopped. Really, this was Ned's moment. "Do you want to go first?"

Ned hesitated, no doubt wrestling with the potential risks and advantages. One of the things they'd always had in common was the tendency to overthink things. "I'll be right behind you," he said, finally.

Gingerly, Kate opened the door, chest loosening in relief as the light from the hallway fell on the edge of a pink skirt. Rellie was standing close to the wall adjoining the room where her step-family was, eyes closed and ear flat against the wallpaper as if trying to listen to whatever conversation was happening on the other side. "There you are," Kate said quietly, not bothering to hide the relief on her face.

Rellie's eyes flew open as she leapt away from the wall. "Kate! You're—" She froze, every ounce of her attention focused over Kate's shoulder. Her eyes were huge, full of fear and hope and a little guilt. "Ned?"

Kate stepped out of the way so Ned could move forward. "It's me." He peeled the paper backing off the patch. "You kind of scared me for a minute there, Rellie."

"I heard Belzie yelling at someone, and I wanted to know what they were doing in the palace," she whispered, taking a hesitant step forward. "Ned, you know it was just the love potion, right? I don't really want to get all fluttery when I—"

"I know," he cut her off gently, shaking his wand until a fine pink mist formed. "We'll fix it." He moved close to her, brushing her hair away from the side of her neck. "This won't hurt, but it's probably going to feel weird."

She squeezed her eyes shut. "Just do it, please."

Ned swallowed as he pressed the patch against the side of Rellie's neck, holding it there. When the girl swayed he wrapped his other arm around her, and a few seconds later she opened her eyes again. His arm tightened and she grinned up at him. "You are so much cuter than Jon," she whispered and threw her arms around his neck, holding on for all she was worth. Ned, having a firm grasp of priorities, dropped his wand so he could return the favor. "So. Much. Cuter."

Kate gave in to her own grin as she picked up Ned's abandoned wand before retreating into the corridor. At the other end she could see Jon talking to Lawton, who had apparently given up his own search for Rellie sometime in the last few minutes. When she moved closer, Jon shifted his attention back to her. "So, everyone's back to normal now?"

"Relatively speaking." She kissed his cheek, happily moving into the circle of his arms for some snuggling of her own. Everyone she cared about was safe and accounted for, and she was going to let herself savor that state of affairs for as long as it lasted. "They need a few minutes alone, but after that we should all find someplace slightly less out in the open. I'm all for collapsing in relief for a little while, but not this close to your mother and Rellie's stepfamily."

"There are a few rooms in the east wing we keep ready for diplomats, which means they've been recently dusted." Jon smoothed a hand down Kate's hair. "Once everyone's settled in, I can double-check that everything's moving ahead on the little show I'm getting ready."

Lawton raised an eyebrow at his friend. "Don't be ridiculous, Jon. You've had what, fifteen minutes of sleep in the last forty-eight hours?"

Kate pulled back, alarmed. "Really?"

"He's exaggerating," Jon protested, then sighed when Kate narrowed her eyes at him. "It was about an hour, but I'm fine. Really."

"Oh, that makes *such* a difference." Lawton looked at Kate.

"Katharine, I beg you to make him sensible for me. I need to go retrieve Rupert from whatever trouble he's undoubtedly wandered into in the last few minutes, and hopefully force him to assist me in rounding up assurances from the women Jon insists he'll need for his master plan."

After he'd left, Kate stepped back and gave Jon her most resolute look. "He's right, you know. Bubbles isn't going to know enough to come after me until at least late tomorrow morning, and hopefully we'll have even longer than that. If you get some sleep now, we'll still have plenty of time to finish putting together that plan you mentioned."

"I'm fine," Jon repeated stubbornly, the effect ruined when the last word broke off in a yawn. This time, it was his turn to narrow his eyes. "I blame that on Lawton."

She kept the smile from showing, knowing he was fully capable of charming her out of making him go to sleep. Luckily, she wasn't completely defenseless against him. "If we're going to make this work, then I've got to be able to take care of you, too. Equal partners," she said gently, brushing her knuckles against his cheek. "Which means that right now, it's my job to make sure you get some rest before you fall over."

His expression softened as he lifted a hand to capture hers. "I like the sound of that."

The conversation would have likely dissolved into sheer romantic nonsense at that point, but Rellie and Ned's arrival interrupted them. Kate couldn't help but notice they held hands so tightly it would have taken an army to pry them apart. "Feeling better?" Jon asked, clearly pleased by the sight.

Rellie grinned at Ned, who blushed. "I definitely want to kiss the right person again, if that's what you mean."

"That's exactly what I mean," Jon said. Reluctantly, he moved away from the wall, taking Kate's hand in compensation. "Ned, Rellie, it's probably a good idea for neither of you to go home tonight. We'll get you settled into some rooms and see about anything else you might need." He caught Kate's eyes. "Then, all four of us are going to get some rest, and I'll get your help with the shoe-fitting in the morning."

Ned's brow furrowed. "I'm not sure how a shoe-fitting is going to help keep Bubbles from killing Kate and me."

"Image, mostly." Jon's eyes lit with anticipation. "And lawyers."

AS IT TURNED out, they didn't make it all the way over to the east wing—pages kept flocking to Jon like enchanted minions, and Kate finally dragged him and the rest of their little group into the nearest bedroom and locked the door behind them. Rellie insisted she wasn't tired, but after they'd taken care of the dust clouds, and Ned had cuddled up close on the couch, she was asleep within moments. Kate and Jon stretched out on the still-made bed, arms wrapped around each other, and immediately drifted off into a long-awaited slumber.

The next morning, it was Kate's turn to spend some quality time in one of the palace's many closets.

"I thought, 'How hard can it be? Even royalty has to have something better to wear than a Fairy Godmothers outfit,'" she muttered, peeling off a brocade gown stiff enough to potentially injure innocent bystanders. "They have to wear something normal occasionally."

"Normal's boring, and you're just being picky." Rellie, who had invited herself into the dress-up session after complaining of

Kate's slowness, held up a silver dress seemingly covered in three-inch-long fringe. "How about this one? It even sort of matches the shoes."

Kate sighed. "With my luck, someone will mistake me for a duster." She did like the shoes, though—she'd made them earlier, a set of "glass" slippers almost identical to Rellie's, but a little too large even for Lawton's feet. Then she'd given Ned her wand and shown him how to change their size, a set of moves he was currently out in the bedroom practicing so he'd be ready when she put the shoes on.

If she could, she would have taken over his part of the plan in a second. But that wasn't how fairy tales went.

Grabbing a dress off the floor and holding it in front of her, Kate opened the closet door a crack and poked her head out to look at Jon. "Next time we get ourselves into this kind of trouble, all I ask is that you come up with a plan where I get to wear something sensible."

Jon shook his head regretfully. "Not with those wings, sweetheart. Everyone's fine with fairy princesses, but no one's ever heard of a fairy serving girl."

"This is so much easier when I get to be the one holding the wand."

Lawton, settled back against the couch, looked amused as he took a sip from his glass of brandy. "It continues to fascinate me how much you remind me of Jon sometimes." He turned to Jon. "In answer to your previous question, eighteen of the twenty-five women are downstairs getting dressed and waiting for further instruction. The rest should be arriving within the hour."

"I'll be babysitting any kids they had to bring along," Rupert chimed in, stretched out along a bare spot of floor. "It'll let some of the women hide the fact that they're not really single, and I'll get to hide from Mother until all of this is over."

"Good. I've already prepped the lawyers." Jon nodded as he mentally reviewed the plan. "Their other clients are exactly the kind of people who use Fairy Godmothers, Inc., and they've already assured me they'll be more than happy to spread the word that the company no longer offers the reliable service it once appeared to."

"And gets in the way of other socially-appropriate love stories, such as the handsome prince falling in love with the fairy princess who magically fits the glass slipper." Lawton's smirk broadened as he lifted his glass in an imaginary toast.

"People, you have to stop calling Kate a fairy princess. It will make her even crabbier than she is now." Rellie stuck her arm out underneath Kate's, a mass of velvety deep blue fabric bunched up in her hand. "Try this on. It's the absolute most boring thing I could find in here." When Kate took it, the girl used the same route to duck out of the closet completely. "Jon, you probably need to kiss her again."

"I'm not crabby, I'm frustrated," Kate said. "There's a difference."

Jon lifted an eyebrow. "Does that mean I can't kiss you?"

Kate's cheeks went red, but she felt a smile itching at her mouth. "Wait until I've gotten changed."

She shut the door again, holding up the dress Rellie had found for her. It was extremely basic, with long straight sleeves and a skirt that didn't pouf out at all—it was probably meant to be an underdress originally for some of the more ridiculously complicated seethrough things they'd found in here already. Even better, the back clasps looked like they would work with her wings.

Kate opened the door again, fastening the top clasp by feel as she stepped out of the closet. "Okay, now I'm ready to actually do something useful."

Jon grinned at her, coming over for a quick kiss. "As much as I'd like to say being glued to my side is where you're most vitally needed at the moment, it's the perfect time for you to give the other women some acting cues for the shoe-fitting. I'm going to go see if I can—"

He stopped as someone knocked at the door. Everyone turned; even Rupert lifted his head. "Is there any chance that's Father coming to see how we're all doing?" he asked.

"If it is, he won't mind that we're being a little cautious." Jon gestured for them to stay where they were as he approached the door. "Still, there's no reason to worry. At worst, it's probably one of Madame Stewart's assistants annoyed that they're not in charge of whatever's being set up in the ballroom."

But the visitor turned out to be a short, neatly dressed man with a touch of gray in his hair and a stack of paperwork in one hand. "Your Highness, I'm aware you're busy with a personal project, but I've been needing to speak to you about one of our suppliers for several days." Whatever else he'd been about to say trailed off at the crowd gathered in the room. "Ah." The man's eyes widened as Rupert slowly got to his feet, and he cleared his throat, before meeting Jon's eyes again. "Perhaps another time."

"If you wouldn't mind, Graham." There was more than a trace of guilt in Jon's voice. "I'm sorry I haven't been as available as I should be, but I'm hoping to have this project wrapped up sometime in the next day or two. We'll talk then."

"Of course." Graham nodded, gaze sliding back to the still-silent group as if he couldn't quite help himself. "Forgive me for asking, Your Highness, but speculation over the details of your personal project have run rampant this last week or so. You've been responsible for some of the most solid management the kingdom has seen in years, and your recent distraction has been the cause of some concern."

Jon winced. "Like I said, I'm truly sorry. I promise you things should return to normal within a few days at most." He paused a moment, considering something, then turned to look at Kate. She grimaced as she realized what he was about to do, but he was speaking again before she could try to signal him. "As to what my personal project is, let me refer you to someone far more qualified to answer that question than I."

Kate glared at Jon, but he just tried to look supportive as he tilted his head toward Graham. Not knowing what else to do, she joined him at the door. "Hi, I'm Kate." She held out a hand to the other man, who was looking almost as startled as she felt. "I guess you could call me the personal project."

"Well, that would make sense." Graham's expression slowly eased, and he gave Kate a bow instead of taking her hand. "It's a pleasure to meet you, ma'am." He straightened, smiling. "The staff will be comforted by the news. There has been some speculation in this direction, but the young blond girl who has been staying with us the last day or so seemed to be the most likely candidate for our future queen. Naturally, that has been the cause of further concern." He nodded at them both, ignoring Rellie's indignant "Hey!" in the background. "Good day to you all."

Once he left, Jon shut the door and put an encouraging arm around Kate's shoulders. "See? They like you."

Not having a sufficiently witty answer to that, she groaned.

TWENTY-FIVE

Romantic Destiny

Evening was rapidly approaching and there was still no sign of Bubbles. Jon had sandwiches brought in to feed the gathering crowd he needed for his plan. Unfortunately, the queen arrived a few minutes later. She stood next to Jon outside the ballroom doors, glowering at the crowd of women sitting on the ballroom floor, their borrowed skirts spread around them as they laughed and chatted with each other. "Princes do not find their true love in the middle of some fancy dress picnic, Jonathan. You said this entire display of yours would show me the woman capable of finally making you act properly besotted."

Jon patted her on the shoulder. "Our villainess hasn't arrived yet. Trust me, it'll look much more impressive once we get started." He resisted the temptation to walk her inside and introduce her to Kate, who had gone to hide behind the stairs the moment Lawton had come in to warn them the queen's arrival. "Out of curiosity, why aren't you still upstairs playing dominance games with Rellie's stepmother?"

The queen huffed. "That ridiculous woman. It completely escapes her that I am the one ruling a country." She glanced over at her son. "It's probably for the best that you aren't madly in love with that blond child. It's been years since royalty received carte blanche to execute the in-laws."

Jon made sure his mother had turned away again before he let the amused smile escape. "True, but it seems like a bad idea to let them wander around the palace un-chaperoned."

"Oh, they're fine. Your father offered to show them the armory." His mother's brow furrowed. "It was rather sweet of him, actually."

Jon's response was cut off when one of the palace guards hurried toward them. Jon hoped the man's determined look was a good sign. "Any news?" Jon asked.

The guard bowed as the queen turned to look at him. "A woman matching the description you gave has been seen in town, Your Highness, along with four men wearing what appear to be private security uniforms. It seems she's been asking questions about a Fairy Godmother who works for her."

"Excellent. Have your men collect the entire group and escort them to the palace. Tell them this is not an arrest, but that their presence has caused a disruption among the citizenry and the royal family has some questions they need answered." The guard bowed again and left, and Jon turned back to his mother. "The show's about to start. Do you want to be the one to collect Father and our guests, or should I have a page do it?"

The queen appeared to have other things on her mind. "This

'true love' of yours had better not be that Fairy Godmother," she warned her son, eyeing him suspiciously. "I can't have one of my daughters-in-law employed by people she'll outrank. I could never show my face at a ball again."

Jon just smiled. "I'll let you know in a few hours." He turned and headed into the ballroom. "Places, everyone! We're about to have company!"

A HALF-HOUR LATER, the guards walked a gray-haired woman in a pink Fairy Godmothers uniform and four men who looked like security personnel through the main ballroom doors. The men, who kept glancing over at the palace guards, looked increasingly confused and uncomfortable with every step. The gray-haired woman—Bubbles, undoubtedly—was glaring as if she were a giantess being ordered around by pixies.

Jon ignored her for the moment, slipping the gigantic glass shoe over the foot of a very happily married woman who ran a leather goods shop in town. With one hand braced on Lawton's shoulder, she lifted her foot to show the gathered crowd that the shoe was much too large for her foot. Both she and Jon shook their head solemnly as the rest of the room made a disappointed sound in almost perfect unison. The woman gave a single, delicate sniffle before heading back down the steps, allowing the next in line to approach the throne and test her foot in the shoe.

It was only then that he looked up at Bubbles, as if he had just noticed her presence. He gestured to Lawton to take his place, then stood and approached her with a carefully surprised expression on his face. "A senior staff member of Fairy Godmothers, Inc.? If I had known I would have sent for you immediately." His voice was welcoming as he gestured to the crowd behind him. "Clearly, this was where you wanted to be all along."

Bubbles' eyes widened as she stared at the women, then narrowed again as she snapped her gaze back to Jon. "You shouldn't be holding a shoe-fitting," she accused. "Your contract was fini—" She drew in a low breath, her expression closing down. "I see Kate lied about that as well." Her voice was full of repressed fury. "Your Highness, my people and I need to leave immediately and resume our search. The company has an internal matter that needs to be taken care of."

"Clearly," Maleeva interjected. She'd been relegated to a corner with her daughters after both of them were denied a place in line. As such, all three women found comfort in sarcasm. "If you'd been at all competent in handling Cinderella's case, the royal family wouldn't have needed to make up for your deficiencies."

Ignoring them, Jon made a dramatically confused face. "I fail to see what your internal matter has to do with the scene you were making in town, and I assure you I will require a far more complete explanation before I allow it to continue." He granted her his most brilliant smile. "Until then, you can oversee the shoe-fitting. I know the practice has fallen somewhat out of use these days, but my family has always been a firm believer in tradition. It's unthinkable that the royal heir would take a bride without it."

He looked over at his parents, who were overseeing the proceedings from their respective thrones. They looked remarkably dignified and royal for the moment, and the queen lifted her eyebrows at her son's cue. "Of course. It is the way I gained the crown, and I would expect nothing less from my future daughter-in-law." The king, grateful not to have been given a line, merely offered a noble smile.

Bubbles blinked once, lips pressing together for a moment as she rallied. "Normally, the prince is supposed to go out among his subjects for a shoe-fitting," she said tightly. "If you'd like, my men and I can take you to the home of the girl I'm certain will fit your glass slipper."

"No need. Bringing them here is far more efficient." He turned, heading back to Lawton and the next young woman in line to have proven not to fit the shoe. "We kept careful records of every woman who attended the ball that night. One of them will undoubtedly fit the glass slipper that my mysterious beauty left behind, and I'll find the woman whom I'm destined to spend the rest of my life with."

When Lawton stood to hand over the shoe, he leaned in close to Jon's ear. "Careful not to let the drama of the moment run away with you," he murmured.

"You're just annoyed you're not getting all the best lines."

Lawton's flashed a grin. "True."

Then it was back to the plan, and Jon knelt before the next woman to go through the same routine with the glass slipper. This one was an aspiring actress, and sobbed dramatically enough one of the guards was inspired to give her a consoling pat on the shoulder as she went by. The next woman stepped up to take her place, and Rellie moved ahead to the waiting area at the base of the stairs. She was hiding behind a large fan so her identity wouldn't be given away too early, but now that she was close enough, Rellie gave Jon a quick wave when no one else was watching.

The woman ahead of her hurried through the fitting so fast she barely touched her toes to the inside of the shoe before yanking her foot out and hurrying to the opposite side of the ballroom. Rellie walked up to Jon much more slowly, snapping the fan closed and exposing her identity only when she was standing right in front of him.

The second everyone saw Rellie's face, Bubbles made a face and started toward her with such obvious intent the guards had to move in to block her way. Jon raised his head to look at Bubbles, lifting an eyebrow. "You wished to say something?" he asked mildly.

Bubbles opened her mouth, then seemed to rethink whatever she was about to say and closed it again. "No, you may continue." One of her hands lifted slightly, as if reaching for her wand, but before she could get to it the nearest guard clamped her wrist in a firm grip. Outraged, Bubbles tried to yank her hand away. "Unhand me, you cretin," she demanded.

The guard glanced at Jon, who nodded. "You may release her, Corporal." As Bubbles pulled her hand away with a triumphant expression, he added, "And now you may confiscate her wand."

Her glare snapped back around to Jon. The guard wisely took advantage of her distracting anger and lifted the wand out of her belt. "You have no right! If I am here in a professional capacity, I have every right to utilize the registered tools of my trade."

"Unless," Jon corrected, "they're used to intimidate the citizenry." He turned to Rellie. "Did you feel threatened? I certainly did."

Rellie shivered dramatically. "She's creepy."

"Oh, for—" As if appalled at her near outburst, Bubbles forced down her anger, her jaw tightened as she took a step back. "She'll fit the shoe, Your Highness. Though I can't release the details of her particular case due to the internal issue I mentioned earlier, you have the word of Fairy Godmothers, Inc. that she is the young woman who danced with you at the ball."

Over in the corner, Lucinda stood and flung a trembling finger in Rellie's direction. "You have no right to fit that shoe, Cinderella! I'm the one who should be marrying the prince!"

Jon raised his eyebrows in mock surprise. "Clearly, there's some question as to whether or not you're correct." He bent forward as Rellie lifted her foot, slipping the shoe on so slowly Lawton had to cough back a chuckle. When the shoe was technically fitted in Rellie's foot, he pulled his hand away so Rellie could lift her foot higher.

The glass slipper dangled off the end of Rellie's toes, swinging gently in midair.

Bubbles went pale with horror, and Jon grinned inwardly as Rellie curled her toes downward and dropped the shoe off her foot entirely. He caught it before it hit the ground. Rellie shrugged and looked over at Bubbles. "Sorry," she said brightly, bounding down the stairs to go stand by the other women.

All Bubbles could do was stare, moving back and forth between the shoe and the completely unrepentant Rellie before settling a glare at Jon again. "That's not possible," she said flatly. "I received several reports of the prince dancing with a young blond woman matching her description the night of the ball. I suspect Katharine Harris has something to do with this. If you've seen her, I insist you let me know immediately."

The queen rose to her feet, her face full of majestic fury. "The shoe-fitting is about romantic destiny, not reports," she said scornfully. "As a Fairy Godmother, you should know that better than anyone!"

Maleeva, shushing both her daughters, stood up. "I agree completely, Your Majesty. This is obviously a sign that Fairy Godmothers, Inc. isn't to be trusted, and that both my daughters should immediately take their place in line."

Jon, ignoring Rellie's family again, shook his head sadly at Bubbles. "It's not going to be good for business for people to hear that Fairy Godmothers, Inc. is arguing against romantic tradition." When the horror flashed across Bubbles' visage again, he smiled. "And I assure you, I know a good number of people who would be happy to tell."

Jon kept part of his attention on the line of women and saw a cloaked figure move from behind a column to slip into a spot near the front of the line.

Bubbles, who gave no sign of noticing, was busy attempting to marshal together an argument of some kind. "Fairy Godmothers, Inc. has a copyright on glass slippers, and since the girl was the only client of ours at your ball, that means she was the only one who could have been wearing them," she maintained. "Which means you danced with the girl, or whoever you *did* dance with couldn't have left a shoe behind. I *insist* that you try it on her again."

The queen raised an eyebrow, clearly enjoying herself. "You have no authority to insist that we do *anything*, peasant."

Jon listened in fascination, surprised Bubbles hadn't yet tried to claim there was a binding contract at stake. Perhaps the company lawyers had prepped her—though any noble who hired the company was legally bound to whatever agreement had been reached; the fact that the intended's family was never even informed as to what was happening left Fairy Godmothers, Inc. on far shakier ground. Their strength, apparently, had been in making certain that things moved along so traditionally the other family never even questioned it.

Rellie wasn't nearly so interested. "Romantic destiny isn't supposed to have all this arguing," she called out, causing a few of the women still waiting in line to giggle. "Get back to the good part."

Belzie scowled. "Shut up, you little idiot."

Jon bowed in Rellie's direction. "Actually, I agree with the young woman's suggestion." He turned to his mother, willing to extend her moment in the sunlight. "If I may?"

She lifted her chin haughtily. "Of course." Beside her, the king nodded.

Jon knelt back down, continuing the pretense of fitting each woman in line with the shoe. The ladies went through the routine beautifully, each adding their own little flourish as they showed it didn't fit and went down the stairs to join the other women. As the last woman left, Jon shifted so the shoe was briefly hidden by his body. When he moved it into view again a moment later, the brief swirl of magic from Ned's spell had faded almost entirely.

Then, finally, the woman wearing the cloak stood in front of him.

Back in the corner, Belzie threw her hands up. "Of course, it's going to be the mysterious woman in the cloak! It always is!" She turned to her mother. "Can we finally go get some dinner now?"

Maleeva slapped her. "Shut up," she hissed.

Bubbles, still ringed by the palace guards, continued to glower at both Jon and the cloaked woman as if the heat of her anger could somehow physically hurt them.

Jon looked into Kate's eyes, safely hidden beneath the edge of her hood. He imagined her wings were stiff after being squashed even this long, but she gave him a smile that made his chest warm with pleasure. He kept his voice blandly pleasant as he held up the shoe. "Your foot, ma'am?"

Resting a hand on Lawton's shoulder for support, Kate lifted her foot into position. Just as slowly as it had with everyone else, Jon slid the shoe onto Kate's foot.

It fit perfectly.

Finally able to show off his grin, Jon let Kate lower her foot to the floor before clasping her hand in his. "My love," he whispered, able to see the emotion shimmering in her eyes as he placed a gentle kiss against her knuckles.

The crowd cheered.

Maleeva stood, yanking her daughters upright with her. "What a ludicrous waste of time," she announced, voice barely heard above everyone else's enthusiasm. The three swept toward the exit, and after a discreet nod from Lawton the guards stepped aside to let them pass.

The queen watched Kate with a speculative expression. "You do already have him looking slightly dazed, which is a promising sign." She gave an impatient wave. "Take that hood off and let me have a proper look at you. I need to know what my future grandchildren will look like."

Kate glanced at Jon, a final flash of worry in her eyes. Jon squeezed her hand, offering support, and she slowly lifted her other hand and pushed the cloak off completely.

Bubbles' eyes lit in triumph as she jabbed an accusing finger at Kate. "I demand that you arrest her immediately!"

TWENTY-SIX

❦

Heroes and Fairy Godmothers

Even though she knew it was coming, Kate couldn't help but tense at the word "arrest." No matter how much she trusted Jon, she hadn't left him a lot to work with.

The queen, however, was having none of it. She shot up from her throne, face blazing with royal fury. "How dare you speak that way of a princess-to-be? You're the one who should be arrested!"

Bubbles swung a sharp look at the queen, dipping into a low bow as her instincts for dealing with upper management finally started to take over. "You don't want this woman as a daughter-in-law, Your Majesty. She's an employee of Fairy Godmothers, Inc. who has stolen valuable company property." She glanced at Kate, rage flickering in the depths of her eyes. "She's nothing more than a common thief."

"A thief?" The queen's brow lowered as she looked at her son. "Worse, a common one? I know that ridiculous Lady Marian ran off with some sort of highwayman, but a prince certainly can't indulge in such nonsense."

"I certainly can." Jon's voice was easy, but pitched to catch the crowd's attention. When they turned to him, he stepped forward and gently tugged Kate with him. "Her true love was being tormented by the effects of a wicked spell, and she stole the item needed to set me free. It's a nearly textbook definition of a quest, and as such, everything Kate did in the last forty-eight hours is covered by questing law. She's a hero, not a thief." He smiled, absolutely certain, and Kate tried valiantly to look as relaxed and confident as he was. "The fact that the shoe fit merely confirms that she is, indeed, my true love."

Bubbles' expression remained triumphant. "That's a lovely story, Your Highness, but Fairy Godmothers are exempt from questing law. Since she was legally employed by the company during the commission of her crime, that particular argument is useless."

Jon's eyes narrowed as he gripped Kate's hand tighter. "You're lying."

"I'm not. It's stated quite plainly on page three hundred and eighty-seven of the Fairy Godmothers, Inc. employee contract." Bubbles' smile was evil. "You were told to read the entire document before you signed it, Kate. Apparently, your unwillingness to follow simple instruction is finally coming back to haunt you."

Both the king and queen were now staring at Jon with lowered brows. "Why didn't you tell me you were under a wicked spell?" the queen asked, warning in her voice. She turned to her husband. "Did he tell you he was under a wicked spell?"

"There. Was. No. Wicked. Spell," Bubbles insisted, glaring at

Jon's parents as if she could make them agree with her by sheer force of will. "It was merely a misunder—"

The queen's righteous indignation swelled as she glared right back at Bubbles. "I should think my son can be trusted to know whether or not he was under a wicked spell!"

"Thankfully, that's not the issue we're dealing with at present." Bubbles gritted her teeth, a muscle visibly working in her jaw by the time she turned back to Jon. "I'm tired of playing games. Even if you stop my security force from taking her away, I can call the city police to arrest her. I have mirror video of her committing the crime, which is sufficient evidence to convince them. You have no legal right to stop me."

Lawton moved forward to stand next to Kate. "My dear," he murmured low enough for Bubbles not to overhear, "we really do have to teach you how to be a better thief."

She could tell he was trying to be comforting, but it wouldn't work this time. Jon's jaw was tense with fury, but Kate recognized that terrible lost look in his eyes from the night of the ball. She was leaving him again, and for once, he couldn't rewrite reality fast enough to stop it.

"I can have my lawyer file a motion of delay," Jon said, glaring at Bubbles. "That way, you can't arrest her until they've had time to review the case."

"And how long will that buy her? Hours? Maybe a day at most? If you start the legal game, Your Highness, rest assured that Fairy Godmothers, Inc. will finish it." Bubbles turned to Kate. "You've lost. Let him go now, or I'll drag his name through the mud right along with yours."

Kate's heart clenched. No matter how much she hated it,

Bubbles was right. Grandstanding now would only ending up hurting the people she wanted to protect. "It's okay, Jon," she said quietly, deliberately turning away from the other woman. "Let her call the police. I've never been arrested before, but it will probably be easier if I go quietly."

"*No.*" Jon's attention snapped to Kate, anger and desperation in his eyes. "I don't care what they do. I'm not letting you go."

"Sadly, I agree with Katharine." Lawton's voice was low. "You know we'll get her out, Jon, even if we have to plan a brilliantly complicated jailbreak to do it."

"No jailbreaks." Kate gave Lawton a firm look, then focused on Jon. It wasn't exactly a happy ending, but saving him had been enough. She could take whatever else came.

At least she didn't have to deal with it all on her own. "Just take care of everyone for me, and please get me a good lawyer." Kate didn't mention Ned's name, knowing that Bubbles had enough evidence to get him arrested, too. Hopefully, he had the good sense to stay out of sight. "I'll be fine. I promise."

"I won't be." Jon's grip was tight enough now to cut off circulation. "Let me do this, Kate."

"I stole those patches so Fairy Godmothers, Inc. would stop hurting you. I'm not about to start doing things differently now." Throat tightening, Kate touched his face. A love potion couldn't even begin to duplicate everything she was feeling right now. "I'm not leaving you, Jon. I'm just going to be busy for a little while."

"We'll get you out," Jon vowed, kissing her hand. The desperation hadn't left his eyes, and Kate suspected her "no jailbreaks" edict was going to be overruled.

"They can try," Bubbles cut in, sounding so pleased with herself Kate was surprised she wasn't cackling. "While you were having your little moment, I used my mirror to call the police. And once they have you, rest assured Fairy Godmothers, Inc. will bury you so deeply you'll never see sunlight again."

The words snapped something inside Kate. Bubbles had dictated her life for so long, but Kate refused to let the woman think she had the power to touch what really mattered. "You know what? I don't care." She turned back to Bubbles, letting go of Jon's hand and stalking toward the other woman. "I spent my whole career keeping my head down while I tried to do the best I could in a bad situation. Even when the rules weren't right, I pretended to follow them because what else was I supposed to do? That stupid job was all I had."

The guards, who had a decent sense of the dramatic, moved aside so Kate could stand almost nose-to-nose with Bubbles. "But people are more important than rules, and I would steal a dragon's hoard if it would keep these people safe. I would certainly go to jail to keep them safe. If I had to, I would bring the entire company down around your ears to keep them safe."

Resentment flashed in Bubbles' eyes. "They'll forget about you in a second."

"We really won't." Jon's voice was steel as he moved to stand beside Kate. "Rest assured, Fairy Godmothers, Inc. has made a lifelong enemy."

"It doesn't matter." Bubbles glared at them both, refusing to back down. "The justice system will be on my side, not yours. Fairy Godmothers, Inc. hasn't broken any laws."

"What about ethics violations?" Everyone turned at the highly unexpected sound of the king's voice. He cringed a little under the sheer weight of all the attention suddenly focused on him, but he pushed ahead. "I know the Council of High Sorcery gets really upset when magic is used outside of the rules. If Fairy Godmothers, Inc. is using evil spells, won't the council have something to say about it?" When everyone just kept staring at him, he shrugged. "What? Like I said, I pay attention."

"That's nonsense," Bubbles snapped. "I keep trying to tell you, we don't use evil spells!"

"But you do use compulsion spells, which is close enough that a sufficiently clever lawyer should be able to persuade a jury," Lawton said, moving to stand on Kate's other side. "And one thing we do have in surplus here is clever lawyers."

"Curses aren't illegal." The frustration in Bubbles' voice was soothing. Kate knew she was still going to get arrested, but at least Bubbles wouldn't get to enjoy it.

"Unauthorized curses are." Now that he had a new angle to work, Jon's voice sounded more controlled. "My guess is that none of you are licensed evil sorceresses, who are the only people legally allowed to use curses or compulsion magic. Given how many years you've been operating, I can only imagine how many times the company has broken that particular law."

Bubbles looked horrified. "We're not evil sorceresses!"

"Which is the exact reason the council will be so annoyed with you." Lawton almost sounded cheerful. "We won't even need to bother with destroying you in court. The council will do that for us."

"And even if you did get licensed, where would that leave the company?" Kate's smile had absolutely no humor in it. "No one wants their children or grandchildren in a marriage arranged by an evil sorceress. What would the neighbors think?"

Before Bubbles could answer, the ballroom doors opened to reveal several very confused members of the local police force being guided inside. They paled a little when faced with most of the royal family, but their leader was resolute. "I'm Captain Green, and I've been told there's a thief on the premises."

Kate sighed, holding out her wrists. "That's me."

Next to her, Jon tensed. "Did she show you any evidence?"

The Captain actually looked apologetic. "Ms. Bubbles here mirrored us the video she had of the theft. I'm not sure what's happening here, but the case looks pretty open and shut."

"It is," Bubbles said, the distraction having given her time to collect herself. Hate shone out of her eyes as she glared at Kate. "It doesn't matter what nonsense story about curses and evil spells you tell these people. You can't prove any of it, and no one will listen to a useless little nobody like you."

Kate lifted her chin as one of the officers put the cuffs on her. "It doesn't matter. I still have no regrets about what I did."

Bubbles looked disgusted. "Does that idiocy actually comfort you?"

Next to Kate, Jon was talking to the Captain. "Let me come with her to the station. I'll have her lawyer meet us there."

Behind her, Kate heard the queen's voice. "Jon, you'll do no such thing. You can't be seen at a police station!"

"Why not?" Lawton asked the queen. "Your elder son is quite a familiar guest there."

The sound of running footsteps immediately distracted Kate away from the rest of the argument. She looked over Bubbles' shoulder to see Ned and Rellie running into the room, with Ned frantically waving his fist in the air.

Kate was confused for a second—she had thought both of them were still behind her—then, panic hit and she tried to catch one of their gazes. She couldn't gesture at them to run because

Bubbles would see it, but maybe she could glare them both back out of the room. Ned might think he was trying to help, but the last thing Kate wanted was for him to go to jail with her.

Sadly, Ned didn't seem to be in agreement with this plan. "I have it!" he shouted.

Everyone's attention immediately turned to him. At the sight of the wayward intern, fresh indignation lit Bubbles' eyes. "Arrest him, too! He's her co-conspirator!"

The police moved toward Ned, and Rellie stepped in front of him as if she could shield her sweetheart. "Not yet. He's got something to say."

Ned, not looking nearly as worried as Kate thought he should be, turned to Captain Green. "Could you arrest Bubbles for illegal sorcery if you had proof she was using a compulsion spell on people?"

The police captain turned to Bubbles. "Are you a licensed evil sorceress?" Bubbles looked insulted. "Don't be absurd. I'm a Fairy Godmother."

"Then, yes, I could arrest her." He turned back to Ned. "But I'd need clear evidence, young man. Without an open case, we can't arrest someone just on witness testimony alone."

Ned grinned, opening his hand just enough to reveal Kate's bottle of True Love. She'd taken it off when she'd changed out of her uniform, and had completely forgotten about it. "Here it is. Bubbles hands these out to all the Fairy Godmothers who work under her." Ned showed the captain the bottom of the bottle, where the company logo was clearly embossed.

"It's a company-issued love potion," Jon explained, giving Bubbles a single withering glance. "I was recently dosed with it against my will, and I would be happy to testify about the way it held my mind hostage and made me betray the people I care about most. Kate's 'theft' was to steal the cure so that Rellie and I would be free of its effects."

"It's true," Rellie added. "It made me feel all kinds of creepy things I didn't want to."

Captain Green looked graver and graver as they spoke. "I still need proof that this is a compulsion spell, but I can't test it on anyone in case you're right."

"They're all lying." Bubbles seized on the opportunity. "They knew you wouldn't feel comfortable about testing it, so they're trying to pass off a mere bottle of perfume as magic."

Kate smiled. "If it's just perfume, you won't mind getting spritzed with some." She held her cuffed hands out for the bottle, and when Ned gave it to her she pointed the spray nozzle at Bubbles. "Come closer. Let's see what this perfume of yours smells like."

Bubbles froze. "No. I refuse."

The captain watched Bubbles with growing suspicion. "If it's just perfume, you shouldn't mind getting some on you. Let her spray you with it."

"No." Pure fear filled Bubbles' face now. She took a step back. "You can't make me."

"Why not?" Kate let all her anger out into her voice. "You made Jon and Rellie."

For a second, no one moved. Then the captain nodded. "Fair enough. If you could put that thing away?" When Kate handed the bottle to one of the other officers, Captain Green stepped forward and unlocked her cuffs. "Even if she is a licensed evil sorceress and is just lying about it, that's definitely enough to get a case started. I take it you'd be willing to testify for the prosecution?"

"Absolutely," Kate said, rubbing her wrists. "Ned will as well."

"Then I think we can overlook the theft charges." Captain Green looked at both her and Jon. "I hate to say this, but you'll need to stay where we can contact you."

"She'll be right here," Jon said, taking Kate's hand again. "We'll cooperate with anything you need."

"We'll even offer some assistance with interrogations, if you wish," Lawton added. "I know a few gentlemen who can be quite persuasive."

"Thank you, but I think we'll be fine," the captain said wryly. Then he turned to Bubbles. "You're under arrest for the unlicensed casting of curses and other related spells."

As he continued reading her rights, Bubbles looked at him in horror. "You can't do this!" Her glare shot to Kate. "I'll get you for this!"

Lawton cocked an ear. "Surely there should be some dramatic music any moment now." After a moment, he shook his head. "Such a missed opportunity."

Captain Green gestured to his men. "Take her away." Jon nodded at the palace guards to follow them out. The security guards Bubbles had brought with her took the opportunity to make their own escape.

Once they were gone, Jon walked over and pulled Ned into a bear hug. "I could kiss you."

Rellie grinned. "Sorry, that's my job."

Kate just stood there, still reeling from the sudden turn of events. "You mean everything worked out?"

"Well, you'll probably have to suffer through several terribly dull days of court cases, but I do believe they at least allow the witnesses refreshments." When she didn't laugh, Lawton's expression turned sympathetic. "Cheer up, Katharine. We won."

"And you were magnificent," Jon added, pulling her into his arms. He held on tight, burying his face in her hair. "My hero."

She hugged him back just as hard, feeling tears prick. "I finally had something worth fighting for."

Rellie threw her arms around both of them. "That was so cool!" She laughed, squeezing them tight. "You and Jon totally have to start that company so I can be a Fairy Godmother just like you are."

Ned came up to add himself to the hug. "You did good, Boss," he told Kate.

She moved her arm so it was around him as well. "So did you. You got over your fear of True Love."

"No, I didn't." Ned pulled away at the same time Rellie did, and a second later the two of them were holding onto each other. "But like you said, some things are more important."

"I am vastly impressed with all of us, which means this is a perfect opportunity for us all to celebrate our mutual magnificence," Lawton said, turning to look for a convenient page. "I'm sure they have some sherry tucked away somewhere."

"Jon, don't be absurd." The queen swept forward, looking upset. "You can't get us involved in a court case! Fairy Godmothers and evil sorceresses are both part of the service industry!"

"I can, and I will," Jon said firmly. "And she's going to be your future daughter-in-law, so you might as well get used to the idea."

"We're going to open a fairy godmothering company together," Rellie chimed in. "If Kate still has her wand, she can make you all kinds of neat dresses."

The queen looked as appalled, and Kate made a mental note to figure out some way to distract Rellie from that particular idea.

Then Ned spoke up. "Can I get a job there, too? I don't think I'm ready to be out in the field just yet, but I could do office work until I am."

"I'm sure we'll have a place for everyone once the details get worked out," Jon said. When Kate smacked him on the arm, he grinned at her. "Face it. Marrying me and starting a company is your destiny."

She sighed. "You're all going to make me crazy."

Lawton chuckled. "And you'll enjoy every minute of it."

The queen's skirt moved in a way that suggested she'd stomped her foot. "I refuse to let my son marry a member of the service industry. I'm sorry, my dear, but a princess can't be a Fairy Godmother."

"Even when that would also make her a fairy princess?" Jon said, gesturing to Kate's wings.

The frustration melted out of the queen's expression. "We've never had a fairy princess in the family . . ."

Before the queen could get too many ideas, a little girl suddenly appeared from between two people and dove beneath the edge of her skirt. The queen jumped, frantically trying to lift the layers of fabric hiding the child from view. "Jonathan, I'm certain I didn't approve my gown being used as play equipment!"

Kate and Jon grinned at each other, then she pulled out of his arms to crouch down in front of the queen. "If I may, Your Majesty?" She lifted several layers of skirt just far enough to reveal the curly-haired child, who giggled at being discovered.

Jon leaned forward. "Hide and seek, I presume?"

Just as the girl nodded, a much taller figure burst through the crowd. "Lucy, I told you you're not supposed to go . . ." The voice trailed off, and the little girl dashed off again as everyone else looked up at the suddenly frozen Rupert.

He stared at his mother. "Um . . . hi?"

The queen's eyes widened with delight. "You're back from questing! Oh, darling, this is wonderful! I have so much to talk to you about . . ."

Panicked, Rupert glanced over at Jon, then sketched a quick bow to his mother before turning and disappearing back into the crowd.

The queen's eyes narrowed again as she whirled on her youngest son. "Jonathan, *explain*."

Jon sighed, and Kate smothered a laugh as she put a consoling arm around his shoulders. "It's a long story."

ACKNOWLEDGEMENTS

There's no one waiting to cut to commercial, but I'd still better keep this short. Jolly Fish Press, thank you so much for giving me this chance. Mom, thank you for reading all eighteen versions of this story and having intelligent things to say about every one of them. I know you would have read eighteen more.

My fellow authors, thank you for the much-needed advice and camaraderie. Rachel, thank you for co-plotting and doing all the ridiculous things I asked when I needed someone to help me block scenes. And to my online readers (you know who you are), thank you for helping me grow the seed of this into something more. Your interest kept me going.

About the Author

Jenniffer Wardell is the arts, entertainment, and lifestyle reporter for *The Davis Clipper*. She's the winner of several awards from the Utah Press Association and the Utah Headliners Chapter of the Society of Professional Journalists.

Wardell currently lives in Salt Lake City, Utah.

CPSIA information can be obtained at www.ICGtesting.com
Printed in the USA
BVOW071908250613

324277BV00002B/173/P